The
TIN NOSE
SHOP

Don J Snyder

Legend Press Ltd, 51 Gower Street, London, WC1E 6HJ
info@legendpress.co.uk | www.legendpress.co.uk

Contents © Don J Snyder 2022
The right of the above author to be identified as the author of this work has
been asserted in accordance with the Copyright, Designs and Patents Act
1988. British Library Cataloguing in Publication Data available.

Print ISBN 9781915054609
Ebook ISBN 9781915054616
Set in Times. Printing managed by Jellyfish Solutions Ltd
Cover design by Clare Stacey | www.headdesign.co.uk

Don J. Snyder was born and raised in America. He is the author of ten novels and non-fiction books and wrote the movie *Fallen Angel* that starred Gary Sinise and Joely Richardson. He now lives in Scotland where he established the world's only caddie training school for soldiers, to try to help restore servicemen from around the world who are suffering from PTSD.

Visit Don
www.donjsnyder.com

author note

During the Great War, more than 60,000 British soldiers had their faces mutilated by machine-gun fire and exploding shells in the world's first truly mechanised warfare. Being left so horribly disfigured meant that after surviving the horrors of war, they now faced the most difficult journey of all... the journey home to their loved ones.

Frances Derwent Wood, born in the Lake District in 1871, had trained as an artist and sculptor. He enlisted at the age of forty-four – too old to be sent to the battlefields – and became a private in the Royal Army Medical Corps based at a hospital in London. It was there that he realised that his artistic skills might be used to create new 'faces' for those most disfigured by war. Using photographs of the men in their prime, he created and painted thin, lightweight masks that gave them back their identity at a time when surgery was rudimentary and could never have restored them to their former selves, allowing them to return to their loved ones with some measure of dignity.

By 1917, his activities had been reported on in *The Lancet* ("My work begins where the work of the surgeon is completed. When the surgeon has done all he can to restore functions... I endeavour by means of the skill I happen to possess as a sculptor to make a man's face as near as possible to what it looked like before he was wounded.") And so the Masks for Facial Disfigurement Department – quickly dubbed the Tin Nose (or Noses) Shop – was created. It inspired similar work in Paris.

The Tin Nose Shop in this novel is set in Northern Ireland, at a time when the British government was just beginning to explore this idea and to test its viability. It is an imagined world, but the techniques used – and the injuries suffered and treated – are representative of what transpired soon after at the hospital in London.

In the summer of 1997, my wife Colleen and I travelled around Ireland with our four small children aged seven and under. We went to the farm in Sligo that Colleen's grandmother, Sarah Burke, had fled for America and Ellis Island in 1918. We also visited Omagh, and when I heard about the bombing the following year, it tore my heart out.

I returned there twice to research a novel. On the second visit, in 1999, I got talking to a barman in a local pub. He pointed out three people who were wearing government-issued masks to conceal their faces, which had been mutilated in the blast; they had chosen masks rather than undergo many months of plastic surgery. The barman casually mentioned that the British government had made similar masks for soldiers whose faces had been destroyed in the First World War and raised this question: did the government make masks so the soldiers could hide behind them? Or to prevent the rest of society from witnessing the horrors of war? That question and our conversation stayed with me, inspiring me to find out more. That is the point of origin for this novel, which is dedicated to a small army of wee grandchildren – Cooper, Daisy, Ezra, Owen, Leo, Gray, Liam, Bo, Emma and Sonny – who, I pray, will never know anything of war.

prologue

For most of us, it takes a while to realise that we cross lines in our lives. Silent, unmarked borders of time that we pass, as if in our dreams, without ever realising what we are leaving behind. We do not see that the matchless nights of being cherished and held close are vanishing even as we live them, and that we are all refugees from one war-torn country or another, or from one war-torn love story or another. Time moves so deceptively that we never say, "This is the last walk I will take with you along the shore." Or, "This afternoon I carried a child in my arms for the final time." Perhaps early this morning while we dressed and put the kettle on, our destiny advanced, unwatched.

BOOK I

summer

Of course, the three of them are still far too young this summer
to know any of this. This summer of 1912, two years before
the Great War begins. Katie has just turned twenty. Both boys,
Sam and Ned, are a year behind her. This disparity of a single
year has given her a certain authority over them since they
were small children, following her up and down the street they
all live on in Brighton, just a short walk from the Palace Pier.
Because she could easily outrun them, both boys remember
their childhood as a time spent chasing after her. A time
when their daily adventures were defined by the dimensions
of her imagination and her ambition. Her mother had died
soon after she was born, leaving her to be raised by her father
and her three older brothers, the result of which meant there
was practically nothing that could shock her, and suitably she
drove a hard bargain. Quitting was intolerable. Crying and
whining, along with any form of complaining, were strictly
forbidden. So now, while most of England just before the
war is nodding off in their teacups to the symphonies of Sir
Edward Elgar or Ralph Vaughan Williams, Katie prefers
climbing onto the pale green table in the conservatory and
regaling the boys with the Broadway hit from America, 'By
the Light of the Silvery Moon', while they try to pretend they
are not looking up her dress.

Maybe this is something her mother would scold her for,

if she had a mother. Actually, it is thrilling for her in a way she can't quite comprehend, though she wishes that just once she would see in Sam's eyes the same kind of physical hunger that pours out of Ned and that she knows she is responsible for inspiring in him. Because there is no doubt in anyone's mind that Sam possesses a brilliant talent. He will attend the Royal Academy of Arts in London in the autumn and on these summer nights when Katie lies in her bed, waiting for sleep to come, she tries to picture what it would be like to be Sam's muse. What would it be like for her to strike a certain pose quite unwittingly that inspires him to suddenly say, "Wait! Don't move!"? And then to paint her. *To paint her*. What could ever be more thrilling? But Sam is always slightly beyond her reach. And the physical hunger that animates Ned so thoroughly and predictably is matched in Sam by a quiet longing. *Longing for what?* Katie wonders. Something neither of them would be able to name, she suspects. Or even begin to speak about. Something you only sense in the piercing light of the stars or in the waves thundering along the shore, and may finally understand when you have grown old and all life is transformed into memory.

It is completely different with Ned. He knows what he wants and he has a look in his eyes like he is going to go after it in the next five minutes. Why long for something when you can just take it? "He is such a boy," his mother has always said of him with pride and delight. Moving with great velocity. From the day he learned to run, he seldom walked anywhere again. Most people go their whole lives without ever getting in a fist fight. Ned washes the blood off his knuckles to prepare for the next confrontation. He seeks out the bullies in order to test himself. What is life without a trial of some sort?

The Crouch cars appear this summer from a factory in Coventry. These long rectangles of steel and wood can do thirty-five miles per hour along the high street. *Built By Enthusiasts For Enthusiasts*, their advertisements say. But they are not nearly fast enough to escape Ned, who charges full speed at them from out of the shadows and does his running handsprings off their long engine bonnets. Before the drivers know what's happened, he has disappeared down the other side of the street. It's mad. And this madness is becoming increasingly difficult for Katie to remain indifferent to. It seems to her that youth is wasted without a certain measure of madness to overpower your fears so that you won't end up regretting what you were too frightened or timid to try. Ned's madness is just one more thing about him that makes Katie shake her head and smile. He is one of those boys who will still be a boy long after he becomes a man. And this gives him certain qualities that she finds irresistible. He's restless. He throws himself at life. He holds nothing back. Unlike Sam, who keeps everything inside until the instant his charcoal pencil or his paintbrush with the bronze ferrule touches the canvas and it all comes rushing out of him, all the emotion that he has stored away and guarded the way we protect our deepest secrets. She has wondered for years where these lovely paintings come from. Especially the portraits that Sam renders with just a few simple strokes. "How do you know what to put in?" she used to ask him again and again until he finally told her.

"It's not what I put in, Katie. It's what I decide to leave out."

The walls of her bedroom are covered with his paintings and drawings. She has fallen asleep in that room every night of her life, surrounded now by what Sam decided to leave out.

Many of the paintings are of her with Ned. His face, close to hers. "My two favourite people in the world," Sam has told her. And he seems quite resigned never to be in the paintings with her, and to remain in the margin of her life. Her life with Ned. A life he has made holy by the way he renders it in colour, light and shadow.

This summer she is acutely aware of his gift and of the gift he will bestow on the subjects of his paintings. The gift that only an artist can grant. The gift of immortality.

cliffs

On a brightly lit morning in June of 1913, the three of them travel by train to Katie's grandparents' farm in Dorset. Sam cannot look out across the English Channel from the pale green rolling hills without recalling conversations he has overheard and been part of in London, where the wars taking part in the Balkans seemed to hold the possibility of a wider war. A war that could sweep him away from England before he can finish his training at the Royal Academy of Arts and then set up shop in a studio near Kensington, where he will try to make his way into the world somehow as a painter. There are two galleries run by an eccentric opium dealer who is interested in his work. One of these is exhibiting the cubist-style paintings of the French artist Jean Metzinger that intrigued Sam from the time he first saw them. Even as a small boy making deliveries with his father in the old man's milk wagon, Sam felt in some chamber of his heart that he had been set on this earth to paint, but now at the age of twenty, he is beginning to doubt this. Something with the power of a tide seems to be pulling him away from what he was always so certain of.

At the farmhouse, as Sam shaves in the yellow bathroom at the top of the stairs, he wishes once again that he had at least a trace of whiskers on his face so that he didn't look so much like a school boy. All he has is peach fuzz. And there beside him is Ned, who can grow a beard in his sleep.

Ned throws his arm around Sam's shoulder. "We're in Thomas Hardy country," he exclaims. "Do you remember your Hardy? Or were you busy drawing when old Mr Fowler was annihilating him for a whole new generation with his gasbag lectures, and the line of drool running down his chin?"

"Some of it," Sam answers. "I remember some of it."

"Poor Thomas Hardy."

This makes Sam laugh and ask, "Why should we feel sorry for Thomas Hardy?"

"He's too fucking old for the war that's coming, that's why. Poor bastard is going to have to miss all the fun."

"You're that sure of it?"

"Of what?"

"Of war."

"Bleeding Christ, Sam. Have you not been reading the newspapers for the past year? Germany's been busy building a navy to challenge our own. Their leaders have made no secret about wanting to expand their territory. And the industrialists in their country and ours are like pigs at a trough. They know they will fatten up on the profits that war will bring them. It's inevitable."

Sam knows that some of this is only Ned being Ned. But still, it makes his heart race. Every time they have spoken about the war, he feels the same quickening in his heart, and something cold blows through his ribs, and then a heaviness that falls to the soles of his feet as if all the blood in his body is settling there.

And now he feels Ned's hand on his wrist and hears him saying, "Steady on."

Why? Sam wonders. And then he sees that it is because his hand is shaking. The hand that is holding the razor.

"What is it?" Ned asks.

"Nothing. Hungry. I'm just hungry, that's all."

"Good. I could eat a cow. Katie's waiting for us." Ned smiles at him and looks deeply into his eyes. "Don't worry about being afraid, Sam, when the time comes," he tells him.

"We'll go in together. And when we're old men, we'll look back on it as the greatest adventure of our lives. Everyone there will be scared out of his wits. But once the bullets start flying, the anger takes over."

Sam nods his head. In truth, he's never been angry at anyone.

The kitchen is a box of yellow light and Katie is a riot of colour in her rose-print dress. She looks like she's dressed for a formal dance.

"Look," she exclaims as she points down at the floor. "Bare feet!"

"Poor little orphan," Ned says, kissing her playfully on the tip of her nose. "You've lost your shoes."

"Don't be silly," she says. "Who needs shoes when you're by the sea?"

"All right then," Ned says as he drops into the nearest chair and takes off his shoes and socks. "We'll all go barefoot to the sea. Sam, you have your orders – take off your bloody shoes."

So both of them are barefoot when they climb the cliffs above Durdle Door. Below the cliffs, Katie walks into the water. Their voices fly above her on the wind. She raises one hand to block the sun from her eyes, hoping to glimpse them.

Ned is in front, of course. Sam tries his hardest to keep up, but this is only out of habit. There's no point in trying, really. What is remarkable to him is the way Ned's bare feet keep pushing off the rocks, even the pointed rocks that appear sharp enough to puncture the skin on the soles of his feet that are as white as paper.

"Who's the sergeant in Hardy's novel? What was his name?" he calls back to Sam.

"Which novel?"

"*Far from the Maddening Crowd.*"

Sam laughs to himself. "*Madding* Crowd," he says. "Not *maddening*."

"What difference does it make? Anyway, this is where the

sergeant strips off his uniform and walks into the sea. And we think he's going to kill himself, drown himself, but then he reappears."

How does Ned remember anything about the stupid novel? Sam asks himself. Why would anyone choose to write about a beach when you could paint a beach and capture all its majesty?

"Where are we going, Ned?"

"To the top, of course, old sport!"

They are a hundred feet above Katie when they reach the top. And she has waded out into the water so that the waves are softly breaking against her back. One glance down and it makes Sam dizzy. "We'll look back on these as our best days," Ned says as he unbuttons his shirt and drops it on the rocks. Sam is thinking that Ned is either planning on climbing back up to get his shirt or he already knows that he won't be able to jump and it will be Sam's responsibility to climb down with it.

"You must jump with me, Sam. You have to find it sooner or later."

"Find what?"

"Your courage."

"Where does it come from?" Sam asks.

"What?"

"Courage."

Ned looks at him curiously. "From here," he says, knocking his fist against his chest. "And here," he says, grabbing his cock and balls with a great peal of laughter.

That is when they hear Katie calling up to them, "Jump, Sam. Jump!"

Of course she is calling to me, Sam thinks. She knows that Ned needs no encouragement.

"Take a look," Ned says, peering over the edge.

And there below them, Katie treads water. Her flowered dress lies on the shore like someone's discarded bouquet.

In a flash, Ned is off and hurtling through the air, his legs moving like he's pedalling an invisible bicycle against the empty blue sky. Sam's first thought is that one day he will paint all this.

A moment later, he looks down into the green seawater and watches Ned take Katie into his arms beneath the rolling waves. Sam doesn't possess the physical courage to throw himself off the edge of the cliff – he knows this. But that isn't what keeps him from jumping. He just can't stop looking at them, wanting to hold them in this moment of their perfection, and not to intrude upon it in any way, because he feels with a dreadful premonition that this is one of the last times he will see them like this.

cornflower

Sam is the only young man on the night train hauling itself across Northern Ireland in July of 1916 behind a cone of white light that bores into the silent countryside. The rest of the passengers are women and children and old people for whom two years of war has meant long lists of the dead in newspapers and a rationing of sugar and flour, meat and butter, coffee and cigarettes and a growing gratitude that they live on a mass of land separated from the madness in Europe by miles of water. They have also grown quite competent in sizing up soldiers in uniform, and as Sam makes his way up the aisle, the passengers who are still awake are glancing at him over their newspapers and cardboard cups of tea to determine if he is on leave or if he is wounded. Because this train is heading north, away from the war, these are the only two explanations for his presence among them.

Both are wrong.

Outside, on the narrow iron platform between the train cars, Sam lights a cigarette in the rushing air that smells of burning coal and the sea. The cigarette in his hand looks other-worldly to him and he stares at it long enough to convince himself that *he* has lit the cigarette and that *he* is holding it. This means that *he is alive* in another world in spite of everything that has transpired. It is a world made real by the moonlight that glistens on the iron rails as they slide below him endlessly. And the wooden sleepers that race past with a rhythmic clattering. A sound he never expected to hear again. A sound that reminds him of something he has forgotten. That men are capable of more than destruction. That their strength can be set upon useful occupation and purpose. The trick for him now is to want to be alive among those useful men and to concentrate on this and not allow himself to keep looking down into the black space between the train cars that seems to be waiting for him to simply step into. One half step from his perch and he will be swept down in an instant. Twisted, crushed and ripped apart beneath the iron wheels in a death so complete and so instantaneous that just the thought of it fulfils all the requirements of every image he has ever had of dying. Those dreams that comforted him and sustained him in the war when he longed for death to set him free from what life had become. Those dreams that can still seduce him so that he is suddenly there again. In the trench. In France.

France is a cesspool of steaming intestines and urine, shit and blood all bubbling in the mud. Sam stands in a line of twenty-six men, leaning against the dirt wall of the trench. His right cheek rests on a burlap sack filled with sand. He lifts one foot and then the other to break the suction. The ground is trying to eat him. Above him, dark clouds as big as continents slide ponderously across the grey sky. Since he left England, he has been dead in every way that one can measure the absence of life. These same clouds were here a hundred times before. This same day and hour of the day has repeated itself with such regularity that Sam has it all memorised. The drawn faces streaked with dirt. The hollow eyes. The foul scent of rotting corpses and cordite that catches at the back of his throat. The worst part is gathering up hunks of flesh and bones, shovelling the smaller bits into buckets, and the larger bits into burlap sacks; he always does this work too carefully, not wanting to leave anything behind in the dirt and the mud as if this were an exercise that someone would grade him on like a school project.

He is much too careful, he can't help himself, and each time he comes upon a part of a man that is still recognisable – a nose, an ear, an eyeball, a penis – he sets those pieces aside as if they were invaluable, as if they had some purpose, as if they might be used again to reconstruct a man. A new man. Those parts he was told were to be buried along with the man each part belonged to. It is absurd and ludicrous and a waste of time but there is a point to it at least because *it takes time* to do. Anything that *takes time* from the time that remains for this war to continue is a blessing. And this is an occupation that is better than the waiting, the dreading. Though the intestines, still steaming with life, are a particular nightmare for him, carrying them in buckets as if they were some ghoulish meal concocted in a butcher's kitchen that he was employed to deliver to the guests waiting in the adjoining dining room. He pushes through the swinging doors of the kitchen and finds the clientele at every table consists only of hogs and pigs grunting with pleasure. He has taught himself to throw up at will to clear his mouth of its taste for a few moments.

In the distance, there is sporadic gunfire as the Germans sight their rifles and machine guns. Soon the new lieutenant will give the 'ALL READY' in a quivering voice despite his best effort. He has replaced the lieutenant from Essex who lost everything between his thighs two days ago just after dawn and was carried away with his hand still searching inside his mangled trousers and his eyes filled with the wonder of it all, his eyes asking: *Who did this to me?* Word has come back to the unit from the field hospital that he will not die. He ordered the doctors to sew him up and send him back to the front. Then he asked a nurse for a mirror and while she stood beside him, looking away, he laughed and said, "I look just like my sisters down there now. Yesterday my mother had two daughters and one son. Now she has three daughters."

Since he heard this, Sam has tried to picture the expression on the nurse's face as she held the mirror for the lieutenant. He has wondered how she will ever share a moment of intimacy with a man that isn't drenched in the grotesque absurdity of the experience. He has pictured her face as she stood beside the lieutenant. In his imagination, he has begun painting her face. Capturing the blank look in her eyes that is meant to conceal her horror. Her face is becoming real to him when it suddenly vanishes as he sees something just beyond the wall of the trench.

He has to look again to be sure that it is what he thinks it is. A blue flower. A single cornflower is drowning in the mud. One tiny blue flower living in an appalling marsh of death. It is beyond belief and Sam inches himself up the wall, pushing off the bottom rung of the ladder, and reaches his hand as far as he can. Just far enough to clasp the flower between his fingers before a bullet whizzes past his head and makes him laugh as he drops to the bottom of the trench. His helmet has fallen off and when he picks it up, the flower is there inside it. It belongs to him. Unless, of course, it isn't real. He takes the flower to Ned, just across from him. Ned will tell him if it is real or not.

Ned is busy staring at the photograph he brought to the war. It fits in the palm of his hand. A photograph of him holding his baby daughter, and Katie standing beside them with her arm draped across his shoulders.

"Look, Ned," Sam says to him, holding the flower between the tips of his thumb and forefinger. "It's a cornflower. Can you believe it?"

Ned looks like he is in a fever dream. His eyes narrow as he stares at the flower. Sam takes the small sketchbook from his pocket and places the flower inside it. Ned watches this. He watches Sam return the book to his pocket and then he says, "She told me that she loved you first, you know. But she picked me because I didn't give her any choice. I've never felt good about that, Sam."

This is all Sam can bear of that memory that tempts him to step into the black space below the train so that his body can be swept away from him. He returns to his upholstered seat and rests his head against the window. The moon is up, sailing across the night sky, and he belongs to this world of the moon and the cool glass of the window until his eyes close and Ned is talking to him again as he slides the photograph into his pocket. "If anything happens to me, you'll look after them. I know you will." They have been in the war forever, but this is the first time Ned has said this to him.

A moment later, the call goes up the line. "Two minutes."

Ned wants him to promise, but Sam can only nod his head. He is paralysed by the same fear that accompanies him into each battle. "Promise me," Ned says again, grabbing his arm. And so Sam promises him. And this relaxes Ned immediately. "Up we go, boys," he sings. "Up we go again, boys."

Sam has learned to close his eyes as he walks into the machine-gun fire. Better not to see what he once saw, the fragment of a shell piercing a small, neat hole in the skull of the man beside him, the hole just big enough through which his brains sprayed out. Better to picture the machine-gun bullets hitting nothing, just travelling on their straight paths for miles before they lost their velocity and fell harmlessly to the ground.

When Sam opens his eyes, he sees the face of a little girl peering through the space between the two empty seats across from him. She is not looking at his face, but at his sketchbook that is open in his lap to a page where he has drawn a rat eating the nose off a corpse. Sam closes the book sharply to protect her. Now their eyes meet and he smiles at her. Before she turns away, he remembers the cornflower and gives it to her. When he places it in her hand, he realises that she is the first person he has touched since he left the war three months ago.

beach

He has been travelling all night and the moment the train stops, his eyes open. Above the sea there is the first pink light of dawn. A fishing boat with a dark green hull rides the swells close to shore. The child is gone. The car is empty now. Just as he is closing his eyes, a conductor calls to him, "Newcastle, County Down. This is your stop, son."

Nowhere to hide now. Unless he can manage to get past the man and lock himself in the toilet. Bolt the door and refuse to come out until the train is rolling again to another destination that doesn't hold the meaning and purpose of this one. But where could he possibly go that they wouldn't find him? He should have dropped into the space and been dragged to his death beneath the train. It would have been so easy just a few hours ago. His sketchbook contains the letter he has written to Katie, with her address. Surely someone would find a way to post it so it reached her.

The conductor comes towards him. He takes the duffel bag from the overhead shelf and nods his head. Sam can hear himself thanking the man, and the man telling him that he has two sons in the war, but the man's voice has a strange muffled quality to it, like he is speaking with his mouth filled with bread. "You have family waiting?" the man asks.

Sam can only shake his head and walk away from him as quickly as he can before the man draws any closer. This began immediately after the explosion that killed Ned. Whenever anyone gets near him, he feels like the breath is being sucked from his lungs. In the hospital, he hid in a storage cupboard for three days trying to decide if he should attempt to slit his wrists a second time. He wanted to. But after failing the first time, he needed a better way. There was some sort of cleaning fluid that smelled of ammonia in the cupboard in a tin can. He could just make out the lettering in the darkness and read that it was used to strip wax from floors. He drank all that was left in the container, but other than a raging bout of dysentery that lasted twenty-seven hours and left him sitting in a pool of his own excrement, he did not experience the intended consequence.

He steps off the train and watches a young lad stacking newspapers below an overhanging roof. *Will Katie find me here?* he wonders. *Will she step off a train here some day and demand that I tell her what happened to Ned?* Her husband. The father of her little daughter. Sam would prefer that they had shot him for cowardice as they had planned to do rather than have to face her.

He walks to the lad with the newspapers. "Where are these from?" he asks.

"Belfast and London," the boy tells him. "A day late from London."

Sam pays him for *The Times* and opens the newspaper to look at the names of the dead. One. Two. Three pages of names in neat columns.

"You been out to the war then?" the boy asks him.

Sam doesn't answer.

He makes his way through the village green, past the handsome stone church and the butcher's shop, and the bakery, and the store with burlap sacks of potatoes and coal stacked in neat piles outside the door.

In front of a row of whitewashed cottages, joined together at their shoulders, a woman hangs out her wash on a line. The clothes are very small. They must belong to a baby or a child.

Each time she reaches to the line above her head, her blouse lifts and Sam can see a strip of her white skin. A strange thought comes into his head: in the life of her child, how many times will the woman repeat this ritual before the child has grown and left her? And will this mother be aware of growing older herself and of the task becoming more difficult? She turns her head and pauses for a moment. Sam can tell that she has seen him. He shifts his weight nervously from foot to foot before she turns away and walks inside her cottage. If he could stand here long enough, watching her, he would paint a picture that raised the possibility that it is the ordinary and plain acts in a life like hanging out a child's washing that convey the dignity of our intentions and mark our presence with holiness. As the door closes behind her, Sam wonders if her child is a boy who will grow up to leave her for a war.

On the beach, he begins reading the names in the newspaper under his breath and doesn't stop until he has finished. It takes almost two hours and through it all he is distracted again and again by the thought that his family probably already knows where he is being sent by the army, and through them, Katie will find him.

He looks up into the warm sunlight. With his eyes closed, he can picture her arriving here some morning on the same night train that brought him to this place. There is nothing he can do to prevent her from coming here now. He missed his chance when he failed to end his life. And it was not much of a chance the first time he tried because all he had to cut open the veins in his wrists was a pencil whose point was barely sharp enough to puncture the skin. Being left-handed, the right wrist was easier, a lot easier. He watched the pencil disappear between the tendons. The blood did not stream out smoothly as he had expected it would. Instead it came in short spurts that matched his heartbeats. His right hand barely had the strength to break the skin of his left wrist. He managed only by clenching the pencil between his teeth and stabbing it into his wrist again and again.

In another hour, it is warm enough for Sam to strip off his shirt. He lies on his back in the sand and holds his hands above him. The white bandages on his wrists have begun to yellow around their edges. He will let himself fall asleep here for a little while before he makes his way to present himself at a small castle on the high street that was an artists' retreat for nearly a hundred years. The army has told him nothing about what transpires at this place, or why he was spared a firing squad to be assigned here.

castle

Despite the shabbiness and neglect, or perhaps because of it, the place is magnificent for Sam to behold. The stone parapets. The turrets with copper roofs flashing in the sunlight. Tall arched windows unlatched and swung open to balconies with scrolled iron railings. The gardens and hedges have run wild and the shutters need painting. But these are small imperfections. In place of a moat to protect it, the castle is encircled by a wide ribbon of brilliant poppies in a riotous red bloom, with narrow paths made of crushed seashells running through them. In the mud and horror of France, he had forgotten that such places still existed in the world.

The front door is open and he is making his way there when he hears voices coming from a garden beyond the hedges. He walks closer and can see two men standing with shovels. One has white hair and a matching moustache. The other is a soldier whose face is wrapped in bandages like a mummy.

What kind of place has he come to? he wonders. And as he watches, both men bow their heads.

Sam steps closer, close enough to hear the older man speaking. "Through our lives, we make the same journey again and again, from despair to hope, and hope to despair. Here is a man, a soldier who made the journey alone in the end, as we all must. May God rest his soul."

Sam listens with a pained expression. Out of respect, he does not want to intrude.

He leaves them and makes his way into a courtyard overgrown with vines. He sits at a small round table made of stone. Above him is the Union flag that has been lowered to half mast. And here is the most amazing thing. Someone has cut an open circle in the hedge, like a round window, and through it, Sam can see the sea.

He takes his sketchbook from his pocket and begins to draw. In a moment, he is lost in the details and the cast of light and shadow. It takes him no more than a few moments to capture this and then this world rolls away, and he is suddenly drawing the imagined world that Katie inhabits with her daughter, Charlotte, who must be two years old now. It is a world that Sam cannot know about, though he sees it clearly in his imagination and draws them lying beside each other in Katie's bed. The child is sleeping peacefully and tears streak Katie's cheeks. He doesn't ask where this image comes from. He just feels that it is substantial enough to trust. He believes that from the moment the telegram arrived notifying her of her husband's death, Katie would have pledged to herself to never cry in front of the child. Her daughter who is no longer *their* daughter. He draws a window on the far wall of the room. Twelve panes of glass. Lace curtains that move in the warm air as if they are breathing.

He remembers the letters Ned received from her in France. She wrote, telling him how clearly she could see Ned's profile in their daughter's. Ned shared these letters with him. In many, she wrote about how with each passing day, the child looked more like him. She wrote to Sam about her as well. She always wrote as if the war was nothing that could harm them. It was just a place they had gone to and would return from, and they would come home when it was over and their lives would pick up exactly where they had left off. If she was afraid of anything, she never told either of them. And now Sam wonders if she managed to conceal her fears from the little girl. Would she have known somehow that Ned made him promise to take care of them if anything happened to him? Surely Ned would not have written to her about this. Sam studies the faces he has drawn and wonders if he has ever been a person who could take care of anyone.

workshop

He is aware suddenly of a loud banging sound coming from inside the castle, in rooms above him. The real world is intruding as it always does whenever he is drawing or painting. Sam watches the white-haired man moving from one room to the next, banging with a hammer until he looks down and throws open a window and calls to him, "Are you our artist? I'll be right there with you."

Out of habit, Sam salutes the man when he presents himself in the garden. He in turn waves off this formality with a simple gesture. "We've suspended with all that here," he tells him. He gives the boy his hand to shake. "Call me Oliver. Just plain Oliver."

It takes a moment for Sam to realise that he is waiting for him to tell him his name. Oliver raises his eyebrows and gives him a curious look.

"Sam Burke," he finally says.

"Well, Sam. You've noticed our flag is at half mast. We're not soldiers today. We are brothers in mourning, I'm afraid." He turns away slightly, looking in the direction where Sam saw him standing earlier. "Let's get you sorted," he suggests, before he begins striding toward the castle.

Sam watches him. There is something of the aristocrat in his bearing, in the way his shoulders are pulled back neatly and how he holds his head slightly averted. But there is also something that seems to apologise for that and to draw you nearer. It is the pedestrian way he rolls when he walks, as if he had spent years working the docks or hauling fish onto the deck of a boat.

Despite this, Sam cannot move. It is a simple thing to just pick his duffel up from the ground and follow the man, but he sits down instead. It is as if he has fallen here from a great height and something has happened to his legs. He is hoping that the man will just continue walking until he has reached the door, and then will disappear inside and they will never have to see each other again in this life. That would be good because then Sam wouldn't have to tell him anything about himself and he could keep everything hidden. Where it belongs.

But this isn't what happens, of course. Oliver is not going to make it that simple for him. He stops. Then he walks back to where Sam is sitting. He places his hand on Sam's shoulder and nods his head reassuringly. "Follow me, son," he tells him softly. "There's no danger here."

Inside the kitchen, the soldier with his face wrapped in bandages stands at the marble counter, cutting carrots. He is humming to himself.

"Sergeant Lansdale," Oliver calls to him. "I'd like you to meet our artist."

Lansdale snaps to attention and salutes him before extending his hand for Sam to shake. And it happens before Sam can prevent it. The sleeve of his jacket rides up his arm so that his bandaged wrist is exposed. He tries awkwardly to pull the sleeve down, but it is too late.

"Sam Burke was studying at the Royal Academy of Arts in London before the war intruded," Oliver tells the man.

"Very fine, sir," Lansdale says with his muffled voice. "I will be in good hands then."

They are waiting for Sam to speak, but he doesn't know what to say to this. There is a brief silence that none of them rush to fill. And then Oliver says, "Carry on, sergeant. I'll give our artist the grand tour."

In the dining room, they pass beneath a dusty chandelier. There are sixteen straight-backed chairs set at even intervals around a long oak table. "If the army carries on as it has been," Oliver says, "and as long as we keep telling our boys that they can outrun machine guns, we'll fill this place before long. It will be a factory."

Sam cannot imagine what this means. He just follows as they pass through the billiards room where five small tables stand along the windows, each table containing a chessboard. The library is a circular room with floor-to-ceiling shelves of books and a wood ladder that rides around the circumference of the floor on bronze wheels like an amusement ride at a summer fair.

In the foyer, with its wide spiralling staircase, Oliver points out the umbrellas in their iron stand. "A plentiful supply of brollies," he announces gleefully like some lunatic meteorologist. "The weather here is even worse than at home, if that's possible."

They are climbing the stairs, and Sam is still behind, watching the old man's feet fall onto squares of carpet on each step. *What keeps you going at his age?* Sam wonders. *And even more important, what keeps you going from day to day, year to year, to reach an old age?* He might ask Oliver how old he is, but the effort this requires is more than he can manage. Each time one of the man's feet touches the next step, his leg wobbles slightly before his weight settles upon it. It reminds Sam of a black Labrador his father owned whom he watched grow old and climb stairs the same way.

The second and third floors are lined with rooms like a hotel. They are all empty except one that Lansdale has claimed. "Can you give me a hand with something?" Oliver asks. There is a large mirror standing on legs with carved lions' heads. "I spent my first day here removing all the mirrors from every room," he adds. "This one was too damned heavy for me to carry. And naturally this was the room that Lansdale chose. For the sea view, he said."

From where Sam is standing, the sea is a flash of pale blue light for as far as he can see. They shuffle the heavy mirror out into the corridor and into a cupboard at the far end of the hall just a few paces from Sam's room. "Well, this will be your home away from home," Oliver says as he swings open the door. "No locks on any of the doors. I took them off myself. You must have heard me hammering away earlier. I was nailing all the windows shut. Except yours. That won't be a problem, will it?"

When he turns to face him, Sam looks back at him with no expression. It is unnerving for the old man, who has the feeling that if he doesn't do something, the boy will never move again. He will be content to stand there, expressionless until the end of time. As if time has already ended.

Finally, Oliver sits on the edge of the bed and takes a deep breath. "My war," he begins, "was in South Africa. The Boer War. The Second Boer War, as they call it now. I was an army chaplain. I grew up in Hampshire where my father was a vicar. I was a good lad. I did what he told me to do. I believed in God because he told me to. I went to war because he told me to. I saw things, just as you have, soldier. I believe there is only one definition of a coward. A coward is a man who takes orders from another man. I don't care if that man is his father, or his bishop. His commanding officer. Or his king."

The way the man speaks, the rhythmic cadence in his sentences riding along on a casual tone that he is trying his best to create, is disarming to Sam in its familiarity, and so he walks across the room and stands at the window to put some space between them. He has his back to Oliver and these thoughts rush through his mind: *He must know. The army must have told the old man everything about me. He must know that Ned and I were in the trench and everyone else had climbed out, and that Ned was killed and that I was going to be shot for cowardice.*

"There's no danger here, soldier," Oliver tells him again, calling to him across the space between them. He waits for Sam to turn slightly. In those moments of silence, it is terrifying for Sam to realise that he has come to a place where everything about him is known to an old man he has never met before.

Outside the window, one fishing boat is making its way back towards the harbour with a flock of gulls above it, like a deck of cards thrown into the air. Sam could capture this in eleven brushstrokes. He begins mixing the colours in his mind. The grey that must be carefully added to the blue. The yellow of the boat's hull will require particular care.

Oliver's voice seems to be carrying from far away somewhere. "Your room is adequate I would think, for someone who's lived in the trenches. No rats. No lice. And no one trying to kill you. I'm grateful as hell that you're here. Follow me, please."

He pushes himself up from the bed and leads Sam out into the corridor.

Back down the stairway, past the kitchen, they come to a room in the shape of an octagon with the four interior walls made of brick and the four exterior walls of glass. The floor is made of honey-coloured wood planks. Light pours in. A kiln stands in one corner. Fireplaces on all four of the brick walls.

Before Oliver can say anything, Sam is already thinking how marvellous it would be to work here, at the long wood bench. He cannot stop himself from stepping closer to it. On the wall above the bench hangs a set of chisels in perfect condition. On the wall to his right, ceramic tools and glazes in jars. A rectangle box made of mahogany catches Sam's eye. He snaps open the brass clasp and lifts the lid. Inside are a set of immaculate horsehair brushes with bronze ferrules. He lifts one brush. It is an instrument of beauty and Sam gazes at it as if he has stepped into a dream that has inhabited him since he first discovered that painting had the power to transport him. The act of painting was transformative.

Oliver's voice seems to emanate from this dream. "What do you think, Sam? Everything you'll need?"

Sam looks at him and asks, "Why am I here?"

Oliver holds an envelope in his hands. He takes two photographs from it and places them on the workbench, both face down, then turns over one which shows a handsome man in his army uniform, standing with his arm around a pretty girl. The kind of picture that was taken half a million times across Great Britain as the war was just beginning. "Your orders were to travel to Newcastle, in Northern Ireland. And here you are, reporting for duty."

Sam waits as Oliver reaches for the second photograph. When he turns it over, it is impossible to tell who the man is. His face has been horribly disfigured. Raw flesh hangs where his cheekbone once was. His nose is completely gone. Horror registers in Sam's eyes.

"This is a different kind of war," he hears Oliver saying. "Mechanised slaughter. Destruction and dismembering on an industrial scale."

"Who is this man?" Sam asks in a rush of emotion.

"He's busy making our supper. It's Sergeant Lansdale. Before and after his holiday in France. You are part of an experiment, young man. Soon there will be hundreds of *Lansdales* scattered across every square mile of Britain. At the rate things are going, there will be thousands before the war is over. Some humanitarian in the war department has come up with the idea that these men should be furnished with masks so they can walk through the world again with a bit of common dignity. The first of these poor sods will be in our care – yours and mine. If things work out, then, as I said, this place will one day become a factory. Tell me, what do you think?"

Sam stares down at the two photographs of Lansdale, his eyes moving from one to the other. He can't speak a word.

Oliver breaks the silence once again. "Our job is to give them back their lives that have been shattered but spared by the enemy. If we do our job well, they can return to the people who've loved them best."

Not me, Sam is thinking. *If I were Lansdale, I would find a way to kill myself.*

Oliver's voice breaks his spell. "Here, have a look at this."

He has pulled open a drawer on the workbench. Inside, people have carved their names. *G Stubbs. Thomas Gainsborough. JMW Turner. Joshua Reynolds. John Constable.*

"I'm told that this place was a retreat for generations of artists like yourself. All the great ones came here at one time or another to sharpen their talents."

Sam looks down at the names of the artists as Oliver babbles on.

"I imagine you've studied some of them at the Academy. No doubt you're familiar with their work."

Sam knows the names perfectly well, but that isn't what interests him now as he traces his fingers over the photograph of Lansdale's wounds. The nose is completely sheared off. Gone. One ear is only a stump. A large portion of the lower part of his chin has been hacked away. The left eye is missing, the lid pulled down and sewn to the cheek. The right cheekbone is missing; the skin there sinks comically into the hollow space. His mouth is intact, which explains why he can still speak.

It strikes Sam immediately that this work will not be unlike his chores in France, carrying buckets of steaming intestines or digging pieces of men from the mud, trying to match a penis with the man it once belonged to, trying to believe that it mattered who got what. But this work will be building something. If he can do it, this work is a real occupation that will require all his focus, all his concentration, all his skill. He is beginning to construct the mask inside his mind. It could be held in place with eyeglasses. There is enough of a nub left where the ear is missing for the arm of the glasses to hook around. Because the man's lips have not been damaged, he will cut an opening for them to protrude completely through the mask. He will hammer the outline of a nose into the copper mask and, so long as it is properly positioned with the two holes left from his nostrils, it will function adequately. All of this turns through his mind in an orderly and clinical way. His sensibilities have been dulled by the war in such a way that he feels protected from the unspeakable sorrow of what he is up against. Rebuilding a man's face so that children will not laugh at him and adults will not vomit.

Sam looks up at the old man. He wants to say something, but the words won't come to him. Oliver takes a folded sheet of paper from his pocket. "Let me read you what one surgeon has written about these men he's operating on and will be sending to us… 'The jagged fragment of a bursting shell will shear off a nose, an ear, or a part of a jaw, leaving the victim a permanent object of repulsion to others, and a grievous burden to himself. It is not to be wondered at when such men will become victims of despondency, of melancholia, leading, in some cases, even to suicide. What is particularly haunting for me now are the 'healed' faces I see in this hospital, the men for whom surgery is finished and no more can be done.'"

Finally, Oliver places a hand on Sam's arm affectionately. "The War Office is calling us the Masks for Facial Disfigurement Department, to make us official, for what it's worth. But I have a question for you that is far more important, son. Can you make Sergeant Lansdale look the way he looked before the war, so that he can make the most difficult journey of all? The journey home."

names

The reason Sam can't go downstairs and join Lansdale and Oliver for supper is because he can't remember how he answered Oliver's question. This began happening soon after Sam got to France, after a small skirmish at Soissons at the river Aisne. He had stumbled upon a German on the riverbank who was wounded, but the barrel of his rifle was still smoking where it lay across his hips. Sam's own rifle had jammed and he had no choice but to kill the man with his bayonet. The first jab was not nearly forceful enough and the blade of the bayonet bounced back off his ribcage, surprising Sam so that he actually laughed out loud. The second time this happened, the German soldier laughed as well as if he believed Sam would not persist. He would turn and leave him alone. They were both being entertained by this comic opera that was unfolding between them. Finally, Sam gave up on finding the man's heart and just sunk the bayonet into his belly. When a great fart of air burst free, Sam heard himself laugh once more. He laughed until the soldier began howling in agony and tearing at the wound with his hands, trying to get at the source of his pain. Sam discovered that five minutes after he had driven the steel blade through the man's stomach, he could not remember doing it.

His commanding officer, a barrister from Manchester, called it 'protective amnesia'. Some soldiers had it, and relied upon it the way Sam had to carry them through the endless nightmare, while others remembered everything in detail and went mad. What he feared as he sat on the bed, staring at the duffel bag on the floor and then holding the photograph of Ned and Katie and their baby, was that one morning he would wake up and discover that his memory had been restored, and everything he had experienced in the war would come rushing back to crush him. "I'm grateful that you're here," Oliver had said to him. This Sam remembered. But did he say this before or after Sam had answered his question – "Can you make Sergeant Lansdale look like he did before the war?"

It doesn't matter really. He has already decided that he will wait until the old man and the sergeant are asleep, and then leave here in the dead of night. He has been trying to picture in his mind exactly where he is. Newcastle, Northern Ireland. Having never left England before he went to France, he has no feel for the geography of the world. *How many people live in Ireland?* he wonders. And are there small villages scattered across the countryside where he might disappear? And do what, for money, for food to keep from starving? Maybe starving is exactly what he will decide to do. Find a barn somewhere and crawl into the hayloft and just lie there eating nothing and drinking nothing until his heart stops. When your heart is as tired as his is, it should just bloody stop beating, shouldn't it? Well, *shouldn't it*?

That would make things a lot easier to bear.

He is fairly certain that Northern Ireland is where they manufacture steel and bricks and build iron ships for the Royal Navy. But the south is only potato farms. And fields of flax. *How far from the border am I?* he wonders.

Across the room, outside his window, the sickle of moon he saw from the train window is standing upright, caught in the branches of a tree. *How hard will the army look for me?* he asks himself. *How far will they send people to bring me back?* How long does it take to starve to death? What will his family be told? And who will tell Katie? *And how long will it be, how many years will pass before she finally never thinks of Ned or me again?* Life must go on, she will be told by the people who care about her. You have to build a new life for your daughter.

All of this is true. Sam knows that it is true. And the war will be forgotten quickly by those who didn't have to fight it. It had all been a mistake anyway. There had never been a good reason for it in the first place.

He has no idea how long he has been sitting on the bed when he hears voices from outside his window. Voices coming from above him. Or maybe he is only imagining this. He heard voices all over France. Voices from people who were not there.

He looks out of the window. Why is there so much light left in the sky? It is ten o'clock and there is still light enough to draw by. How late in the day does it stay light here in the summer? It is disorienting enough, without the voices that seem to ride the air like the voices of the dead. Sam is trying to turn over in his mind what Oliver said to him about this place. Was it possible that men would live their lives behind masks? How would a man go about this? And what about the people he was returning home to? How would they cope? He has seen the torn-apart faces, but they belonged to men who were dead, whose corpses were decomposing into the ground that had turned to pudding. The grotesque faces unrecognisable and unremarkable in a world where everything was grotesque. *Better to be dead*, Sam thinks. Yes, he tells himself again – if it were him, he would much prefer to be dead than to be sent home with a gargoyle's face. He would strike a bargain with someone and ask that person to write a letter home to his family to tell them that he had died. And then what? Maybe find his way to one of those boarding schools in England where the privileged send their young children. They would have to be very young, before they reached the age of discernment when they would be repulsed by a man without a proper face to show the world. A nursery school.

Yes, teach art to these wee children. Stay there his whole life. Grow old at the school and never leave. Hide there, a freak commissioned from the circus. Except to travel from time to time with his face wrapped in a scarf, to wherever Katie and Charlotte are living, just to observe their lives from across a street. Just to make sure that they are living on in the world without Ned. He could do this. He could manage to get money to them if he made any. He would check in on them until the day he discovered that a new person had taken Ned's place. That would be the last time he visited them.

He leans out over the window ledge and as the wind falls off, he can hear a voice more clearly. It is Oliver's voice, reciting names. One name after another. And then it is Lansdale's turn and so the voice changes to another voice, but still reading names. Lieutenant G.H. Boot. Private J.H. Collins. Private F.C. Crenshaw. Captain L.T.W. Crellin. Second Lieutenant Robert F. Damon.

Sam gets it now. These are the names of soldiers who have died. Their names are being read in alphabetical order by Lansdale and Oliver out on the turret above his window. Their voices are solemn. As if they are saying the names in prayer.

So there it is, Sam thinks. *They are remembered after all.* In the war, the commanding officers were always telling them that if they fell, they would fall with honour and would always be remembered by a grateful nation. Dying a soldier's death meant that their lives would matter in some way. And that they would not be forgotten, unlike most men who are forgotten by a world that keeps on turning as if they had never been a part of it. Sam had never believed this. The words always sounded particularly empty to him. He discovered that soldiers at war were like children, easily deceived because they wanted to be deceived. *Tell me that this will all be over and that I will go home some day and I will believe you. Tell me that I will live through this horror and I will believe you. Tell me that if I die, I will never be forgotten and I will believe this too.*

But Sam had believed none of it. And tonight, added to

the list of things he no longer believes is the possibility that a mask he might make for a man with a butchered face will help that man return home to the people who are waiting there for him.

crucifix

Not long after the war has taken Ned and Sam from her life, Katie is in church when she sees the boy who tends the sheep on the farm up the road. He lives on the farm with his mother and his older sister and he is the man of the house now that his father is away in the war. Eleanor, the midwife who delivered baby Charlotte, and who is helping Katie deal with her colic, has told her that the boy was born deaf and, at his father's insistence, was placed in a home for deaf and blind children in Cardiff when he was three years old. The day after the father left for the war, the mother and daughter took a train to Wales and brought the boy back home. "He must be sixteen now," Eleanor said. Apparently, he has a way with animals and has been a godsend caring for the flock of sheep since the baby lambs arrived this spring.

He sits between them, sister on his left, mother on his right, and they take turns tracing the words from the minister's sermon on the palms of his hands, one letter at a time. There is something mysterious and dignified about the way he sits there with his eyes closed in concentration, his hands resting in their laps, as if they are leading him somewhere beyond the borders of his known world. Or maybe it is only *my* known world, Katie says to herself as she watches. Maybe he belongs to some other world. Maybe his silent world is the world of our dreams.

Now he smiles and his sister smiles as well, and Katie can tell that she has traced something on his palm that has nothing to do with the pastor's sermon. The mother looks at both of them with a scolding glance. It is only a mild reproof, vanishing in an instant, and replaced by a flash of light in her eyes that reveals how utterly grateful she is to finally have this banished son back with her.

Whatever the sister has traced across the boy's palm, just wondering about it is enough to transport Katie from her world so completely for a moment that she forgets she is in church, with Charlotte sleeping in her arms. This baby daughter whom she and Ned named just two weeks before he went to the war. They had barely enough time together to bundle up the baby and take the train to the photographer's studio so that Ned would have one picture of his daughter in his arms to take with him to France. For those first two weeks of her life, Charlotte just slept. Day and night she slept, with barely any interest in feeding. It was as if she had just arrived from a long and exhausting journey. Katie would sometimes wake her just to be sure she was still alive. Then, a few days after Ned left, she became fussy and could not be contented. For long spells of time, she cried her heart out. Sometimes howling as if she were in unbearable pain. As if – Katie could not help but think – as if the child knew that her daddy was gone and might never return. But Eleanor assured her it was colic. Either she was drinking the breast milk too quickly and taking in too much air or she might have some kind of allergy to Katie's milk.

It took some time to find – not a cure, but an accommodation. Each time Katie fed the baby, she then walked with her for hours, carrying her high on her chest, with her belly pressed hard against Katie's shoulder to push out the gas. They settled on an equation – for every twenty minutes of feeding, they walked for two hours, marching at a fast clip. Whenever Katie stopped to rest, Charlotte began crying again from the bottom of her heart. It required incredible stamina and far more patience than Katie possessed.

Finally, Eleanor told her to just put the screaming baby down, close as many doors as she could between the two of them, and turn the radio up to a volume high enough to drown out the sound of her baby crying.

This only made Katie a nervous wreck, so she gave up and began marching again with Charlotte draped over her shoulder like a sack of potatoes.

She has marched at least four miles this morning, making certain the baby was in a deep sleep before she entered the little stone church with the slate shingled roof that stood in a narrow grove of beech trees at the edge of the Anstruther estate. On all of these marches, she carries on a dialogue with Sam, sometimes just inside her mind, sometimes speaking the words out loud. His words as well as hers. Because talking with Sam is preferable to talking to herself like some crazy lunatic. And Sam is the only person she can tell the things she can tell no one else, especially not her husband.

She has never cared at all for church and is here this morning only because of these words in the last letter she received from Sam – *Pray for us.* She had received that letter almost five months ago. There has been no further word from him, or from Ned, in nearly half a year. *Why would you write that to me?* she asks on her walk this morning. *Pray for us. Why would you write those words, Sam?* While she marches, she can see these words as he wrote them with their slight left-handed slant on the pale blue sheet of paper that is now in the teak box her father had given her, that he claimed had once held a ship's compass. The box, a perfect square with a lid that slides into place, holds the four letters she has received since Ned and Sam left her for the war. The one letter from Ned contained no mystery; it was just Ned sounding perfectly like Ned, writing blithely about what fine physical condition the army had got him into and how his appetite was good and how he was sleeping soundly, and asking her to send more Three Castles cigarettes, his brand, to augment what the army was providing. Ned's letter hid nothing and so she had not been compelled to read it again and again as she had the three letters from Sam – stopping herself from even blinking as she read them as if she were looking for something through a microscope, afraid that she might miss what she was searching for: the hidden meaning in what Sam had purposely left out. The meaning that would tell her what the two of them were enduring in the war.

Pray for us... Those words have brought her to church this morning. How strange that Sam would ask her to pray to a God he knew she had no belief in. To her, God, and all religion, are just inventions of men who are supremely afraid of dying. This, she knows, is easy to be cynical about. She came close to praying to some god, any god, to end her agony when Charlotte was stuck in the birth canal and Eleanor, with great concern, had to call for extra help. Another midwife, whose name Katie never learned, a woman who was shaped like a beer keg and seemed built to knock down walls, came hustling into the room. She shoved Eleanor aside, hiked up her dress, swung her legs around Katie as if she were mounting a horse, then reached up inside her and yanked the baby out with her broad hands. All this happened while Ned was finishing his last cricket match before he left for France.

She looks around her now in church where she is surrounded by women and counts them by their names. Amy Waterstone. Janice Hughes. Deborah Ryan. Phyllis Adams. Carole Birkehead. Ruth Cramer. Louisa Nelson. Sally Graham. Rose Blackman. Margaret Littleton. Catherine Ames. All of them except the Brunswick sisters, spinsters in their eighties, are in the same boat. All of them with husbands or sons or brothers off to the war. All of them praying that God will keep those men safe from harm, or if they are already dead, that their souls would rest in peace in heaven.

Katie regards each of them for a long time, wondering if any of them would be here were it not for the war. If some of them were non-believers like her.

The only girl among them is the deaf boy's sister, just now

sharing a knowing glance with him. The two of them are above all this, still young enough to be free of the fears that mark the rest of the congregation. They look so beautiful to Katie. So carefree. Again the boy's pose strikes her as regal. On his face there is an expression of infinite patience. She wonders about the hardship he must have endured, being taken from his family at such a young age, and how none of that registers in his face. His eyes are wide and clear, and the palest shade of blue in colour. His black hair, long and slightly unkempt, lies in thick curls over his shirt collar. His shoulders are wide and solid as if he has done hard physical labour wherever he was sent. He seems to tower above his sister and mother. As Katie is looking at him, Charlotte stirs suddenly. "Oh, please don't wake up," she whispers as she leans over and catches the scent of her baby's head, that curious mix of honey and pears. When she looks up, Christ on the cross is staring back at her with an accusing look.

It is almost as if he knows that from the hour Charlotte was born, Katie had prayed that she would be set free from this new life that had opened to her like a great dark tunnel. Each time she closed her eyes and finally began to fall asleep, she hoped that she would never be awake again. Her father and the new woman in his life would care for Charlotte until Ned came home from the war he was so eager to get into – even during their last moments together at the station the morning he left. He took her by her arm and pulled her into the shadows, dropping his hand between her thighs and touching her there while he said, "This belongs to me now. This is mine and I'm bloody going to miss it." He said this with a certain authority in his voice that made her feel violated and angry. Angry enough to tell him, "Fine then. I'll put it in the box my father gave me and mail it to you in France. I don't need it any more." He must have thought that she was joking because he dismissed her with one last kiss that barely brushed her cheek. She watched him jump onto the train and said to herself, "Let me die before this day is over."

Katie had told only Eleanor of her feelings. And Eleanor had assured her that this kind of despair in new mothers was not uncommon and that it would pass just as the baby's colic would run its course in six months' time.

Christ is looking at her now from above the altar. This Christ with his patient gaze, his arms outstretched at his sides, his hands opened in surrender, as if he were matching the pose of the deaf boy. The shepherd. The lost boy, who just might be the only boy in England returned home by the war.

CROWS

The next time she sees him, it is not by accident but by design. When she finds herself thinking about him almost constantly, she plots out a new course for her walks with Charlotte, the walks she is now calling 'potato sack journeys', that take them along the southern ridge of the pasture where he is tending the sheep. It is lambing season, mid-April, and the new babies taking their first steps in the fields beside the ewes need constant protection from the fox who slaughters them for sport, the badgers who eat them alive, slowly, and the crows who pluck out their eyeballs while they cry for their mothers who can only look on helplessly. He is walking with a rifle over one shoulder, with one lamb no bigger than a loaf of bread tucked under his arm. He takes long, purposeful strides in black boots that are caked in reddish clay while Katie watches and hears herself say out loud, "Who does he remind me of, Sam?" Perhaps the gamekeeper in D.H. Lawrence's novel, *Sons and Lovers*, that she read just before marrying Ned, partly because she knew it annoyed Ned that every moment she spent reading was a moment she was not devoting exclusively to him. "That's the truth, Sam," she says. "And by the way, how am I supposed to believe that either one of you is alive when I've not had a letter in six months? And if you are alive, then what gives either of you the right to not answer my letters?"

Both Ned and Sam are beginning to seem like people she has only invented, and everything about this boy seems exceptionally real to her for a reason she cannot even begin to understand. Especially the way he keeps glancing down at the lamb while he walks the perimeter of the pasture as if to reassure the animal that he will keep her safe from harm. He will protect her.

While Katie looks on, he crouches down suddenly, sets the lamb gently beside him on the ground, takes aim with his rifle and fires into the branches of a tree. Suddenly, there is a wild explosion of crows shrieking and flapping. Patiently, he takes aim again and with one shot sends two of the birds falling like rocks straight to the ground.

Then the child awakes and begins at once to cry. In seconds, the sound of her screaming seems to shatter the stillness and equilibrium of the pasture in a way that the boy's gunfire had not.

Katie begins marching as fast as she can walk. She glances back once and sees that the shepherd has turned and that he and the lamb are watching them.

list

If Charlotte cries through the night, Katie never hears her, thanks to three glasses of Ned's whiskey left in the bottle she found in the shed.

Once she closes her eyes, she does not open them again until well after sunrise when she awakes with a shock to see the morning light pouring in the windows across the room and to hear – *nothing*. Nothing but birds singing in the garden. It is as if she has been transported to a new continent in her sleep, or back to the world she inhabited before becoming a mother. She swings her legs out of bed and walks as quietly as she can to the baby's room where she finds her fast asleep. She leans over the rail of the cot until her cheek is close enough to feel Charlotte's warm breath. She looks down at her for a moment. In her profile, she sees Ned. No one would ever mistake her for anyone but her father's baby, that is for certain.

"Never wake a sleeping baby," Eleanor had advised her. And so she doesn't. Instead, she goes into the kitchen and leisurely makes herself some tea.

The calm is too good to last and she has barely begun to sip her tea when Charlotte wakes screaming. Katie feeds her from both breasts, changes her and bundles her up for another long march.

The pram. Charlotte hates the pram, but it would make it much easier to transport the bottle of whiskey Katie plans to purchase to help her sleep through her daughter's screams. She rather relishes the idea of shocking the townspeople by marching up Market Street with a baby in one arm and a bottle of whiskey in the other. That is a vision they will remember, and the outrageousness of it appeals to Katie. But for the sake of maintaining decorum, she wheels the cumbersome pram out onto the pavement and heads for the grocer's with Charlotte's cries echoing into the overarching trees.

Old Mr Tones has cut himself shaving and is pressing a cloth with tiny roses embroidered on it to his jaw while he helps her gather her provisions into a wicker basket. He smiles at Charlotte.

"Once she can begin eating sweets, she will find the world a much more agreeable place," he says pleasantly.

"If I thought that would help, I would give her a chocolate bar right now," Katie says.

He smiles warmly. "And how are you today, Mrs Morse?" His eyes narrow slightly as he nods his head and smiles again. "Mrs Morse," he says once more.

This means something. It means something to both of them.

They had devised this secret when the lists began appearing in *The Times*, the impossibly long lists of the names of the dead and the missing and the wounded soldiers. She had confided to him that she just could not bring herself to check the list for her husband's name. Just glancing at the list had filled her with anger.

Mr Tones had volunteered to check for her, and as long as he keeps addressing her as Mrs Morse when he sees her, she will know that Ned has not appeared on the list. She gave him Sam's name as well. If either one of them is on a list, he will address her as Katie. She has been too distracted this morning to catch the meaning in Mr Tones' greeting. "Oh," she says when she has caught herself. "I'm sorry, Mr Tones. Thank you. Yes, thank you for the news."

He touches her hand. "You're being very brave through all of this," he says, his voice rising to reach above the baby's cries.

"I don't think so," she tells him. "If I were brave, I would be reading the lists myself, wouldn't I?"

"Well, you have your hands full here," he says, nodding to Charlotte.

"And doesn't she look like her father, even when she's crying bloody murder?"

"I see the two of you in her," he tells her kindly.

He is being generous – she knows this. "What am I doing wrong?" she asks him, and the helpless tone in her voice surprises her.

"Nothing," he says. "But perhaps you should move in with your father. Is he living still in Abbotsbury?"

"Yes, but I think he rather covets his peace and quiet. Would you want to live with this siren going off at all hours of the day and night?"

He smiles again and tells her that it will not last forever. "It might seem like forever, but really when you consider the span of a lifetime, we're babies for such a small fraction of the time. It is here and then gone. Gone quite suddenly."

She thanks him again for his words of encouragement, then asks him for the whiskey which he keeps behind the counter in a wooden crate on the floor below the cash register. Outside the window, a small queue of women has formed to read through the list from *The Times* that he has taped to the glass. Mothers. Wives. Sisters.

As Katie makes her way out of the shop and passes them, she crosses quickly to the other side of the street.

Maybe the more women standing at that window, the greater the odds that someone is on the list who matters to one of them. It can't possibly be true. Her mind is becoming increasingly unreliable. It is turning through a wasteland of unaccountable ideas and foolish possibilities.

She stops for a moment and glances back at the women poring over the list on the window. There they stand, as lost as she is. Perhaps she does not want to believe that she is one of them. A company of desperate women begging God to preserve the order and continuity and equilibrium of their lives. A company of beggars. They might as well have their hands out begging Mr Tones for a loaf of bread or a rasher of bacon.

silence

Before she and Charlotte reach the top of the high street, the baby is causing such a fuss in the pram that Katie takes her in her arms and abandons the pram alongside a hedge. It is already twilight; he might have left the field by now and gone inside for his tea. But she finds him standing in the open doorway of a small rock shed, looking down at his hands, intent upon something. Finally, she is near enough to see that he is rolling a cigarette. Though she seldom smokes, a cigarette is exactly what she wants now.

Charlotte is beside herself in a squall of shrieking by now and the way his eyes fill with sympathy – and the way he places the cigarette between his lips so he can reach out his hands with such concern to take Charlotte from her – makes Katie feel so welcomed that she gratefully passes her baby to him. It is then when she sees that some of the ointment she was using to ease the soreness of her nipples is on one of Charlotte's cheeks, just a small white smear that he wipes off before she can. When he touches her, she opens her eyes, looks up at the boy and then – *her crying stops.* Just stops. Katie watches him smiling down at the child, turning his head slightly from side to side and winking at her with one eye and then the other to amuse her.

The silence is astonishing. Katie feels a heaviness lift from her. It is like she is rising from the ground. She can feel her body swaying and she reaches for his arm to steady herself. He takes no offence at this; he only shrugs slightly and smiles at her as if it were the most natural thing in the world. And this makes her want more. Something more. A more intimate exchange. "May I?" she asks, gesturing to his cigarette as she watches her hand take it from his lips. She takes a deep draw and almost immediately she feels her legs give way beneath her and she drops to the ground on her bottom. Which only makes her laugh. She is laughing like a child and he is laughing along with her in this sanctuary of silence that he has ushered her into. He kneels down beside her and looks into her eyes. "I'm fine," she tells him. "I'll be fine." She sees then that Charlotte is staring up at him, and she knows what has caused her so much discomfort. "You've taken the place of someone who's missing," she says. "You've filled a space in her life, I guess."

He seems to understand what she is saying, but she reaches for his hand anyway. She turns it over and traces across his palm, one letter at a time – *What is your name?*

He takes her hand and turns it over exactly as she had his, and traces these letters: *Finn.*

"Finn," she says. She has never met a Finn before and she wonders if his mother chose an uncommon name for her son in the hope that he might be exceptional in some way. She steps closer to him, close enough so he will feel her breath on his lips when she says his name again. There is that amazing pale blue of his eyes and, being this close, she can see there is something fragile in the colour, something that has been broken but is being repaired slowly. Charlotte has fallen asleep in his arms. She watches her head rising and falling gently against his chest with each breath he takes. And she sees that he is breathing harder now. She sees the effect that she is having on him and it thrills her in some way she never would have been able to describe, even if she lived in a world where people were permitted to speak of such things. The world. What kind of world is it where a mother could be made to give up her little boy just because he is not perfect? That is the same world that has split apart and turned the lovely countryside of France into a morgue. All the rules and conventions belong to that same world and to the men who had set them in place. Men this boy owes nothing to. Men who will reach the end of their lives and never learn a damn thing about what it means to be free. Or to touch a girl, really touch her in such a way that she will remember it in the last hour of her own life. Men who look up at the stars and wonder nothing.

What has happened to the little boys they once were, following their mothers around like the lambs following the ewes in this pasture? What has happened to the boys they had been, like this boy, before they became men who would gladly send him into a blood storm without a second thought? Maybe she wants to do something to renounce those men and to violate their rules and their conventions, something that might prevent this boy from ending up like them. How long would it take for her to spell out these words on his palms – *Promise me you will never become one of those thoughtless men.* She looks into his eyes again to be sure there is still something fragile there, something that reminds her of Sam. Then she reaches up and places one hand on the back of his head and feels her fingers moving through the dark curls. She draws his head down and stands on her toes so she can kiss his lips. She feels him start to pull away and when she looks up at him, she sees that his eyes have narrowed as if he is concentrating hard on something in the distance, something far beyond her and this place where they are standing together.

"You made me laugh," she says to him, though she knows he cannot hear her. "You made me laugh, Finn," she tells him once more. "And now I must send you back to your mother."

Her scent is on his hand when she kisses it and she wonders if his sister and mother will be able to tell what he has been up to.

Before she leaves him, she makes him show her how to

fire his rifle. He is holding Charlotte under one arm when he moves her feet apart with his hand to give her a solid base, and helps her place the butt of the gun against her shoulder. She points the gun up at the first star in the sky and is ready to pull the trigger, but he raises one finger in the air for her to wait until he has stepped away with Charlotte and covered her ears with his hands.

boots

She will realise one day that it was her boots standing on the tiled floor of the foyer, just inside the door next to the cast-iron umbrella stand, that betrayed the secret she was keeping.

Caked with mud from his field, they stand there waiting for her to step into them to return to him, the proof of her guilt, the accusation and the evidence. "Mummy puts her boots on now and away we go," she hears herself telling Charlotte one afternoon, practically singing the words. She is always in such a hurry to be on her way that one morning she puts them on the wrong feet. "Silly Mummy," she tells Charlotte, but rather than take the time to change them, she keeps walking towards him with the toes mocking her. Each time she takes the boots off when she returns home, she begins waiting to put them on again.

During the time they spend together, Katie feels free in a new way. It might be because Charlotte is so content in his company. She laughs with delight when Finn sweeps her up in his arms. It might be because their time together is forbidden. She – another man's wife – would surely be condemned even for the innocent hours they spend roaming the pasture side by side. That condemnation doesn't matter to her. She feels as if she is returning to herself after a strange journey that had taken her to a destination she had not chosen. Here she is now with someone who, like Sam, does not patronise her in the way most boys tend to treat girls: with a kind of bored superiority that she has always found infuriating. Not Sam. Never Sam. And not Finn. He is content to carry Charlotte while Katie wields the shotgun. They walk that way for hours every day. He finds an old piece of waxed canvas that he fashions into a cape for the child when the rain moves in on them. Katie grows competent with his rifle and brings down her share of crows. And she loves wielding the axe when they construct a blind in one corner off the field, where they can conceal themselves to try to kill the fox that is reigning hell on the sheep at night. They spend hours building the blind as if it were a house they plan to live in together. And they work so well together without any words, each anticipating the other's movement as if they are performing a dance they have rehearsed for years.

What she learns from him is that words really do not matter. In the end, words are just something that people say to each other, and people will say just about anything to get what they want. Of course, she would have loved to hear him say what he wanted, and that he wanted to be closer to her. But actions are what matter. Gestures. Glances. Each time they are together, Katie grows more certain of this. What could possibly matter more in this world than the way he welcomes their visits? Or the way he silently buries the murdered sheep with a tenderness and solemnity she finds exquisite?

Or how his presence always cheers Charlotte. And so, how can she be condemned for returning to him? And how can she be anything but grateful?

child

Summer is nearly lost and gone before it began. There is something about the knock at the door that makes Katie know at once that it is not the postman bringing her word that Ned has been killed. He would have knocked gently, almost reluctantly. This is someone with nothing to apologise for.

"What are you doing with my brother?" The words are as insistent as the knocking had been. They enter Katie even before she has opened the door far enough to recognise her as the girl who was sitting beside Finn in the church that Sunday morning that suddenly seems like years ago. His sister.

A moment passes while the question twists slowly through Katie's mind. *What are you doing with my brother?*

How many hours would it take her brother to describe all that they have done together, one letter at a time on her palms? What can her question possibly mean? And what answer is she waiting for as she stands there, biting her lip nervously and taking quick glances behind her as if she expects to find the answer to her question there?

"Why don't you come inside?" Katie says. It is then she sees the girl looking down at the boots with the mud from her brother's field caked on them, *right there* on the tiled floor.

"Your baby is crying," the girl says with a baleful expression.

Katie almost asks, *What baby? I'm just a girl like you.*

And then she feels some defiance rise up in her and it is just what she needs to defend herself.

"What's your name?" Katie asks.

"You'll bring shame to my mum," she says, ignoring the question.

"Shame? What are you talking about?"

"Are you daft?"

"As a matter of fact, no, I'm not daft."

"You're a married woman. You have a husband in the war. Didn't anyone ever teach you about decency?"

"Who was supposed to teach me about decency? Who taught you? Who taught you to march up to a stranger's door and accuse her of shameful behaviour? Is that something you learned from your father?"

"Maybe."

"The same father who sent your brother away? I wouldn't trust a thing he taught me if I were you. I'd break every rule he ever shoved down your throat."

"He's in the war with your husband, fighting for you," she says.

"No, he's not. He's not fighting for me. Who in God's name told you this?"

She glances over her shoulder once more and Katie sees that she is looking at someone making his way up the pavement, across the narrow street.

"Maybe I learned it in church," she says vaguely, and this is all Katie needs. It seems to be what she is waiting for.

"Oh, wonderful, so you're a religious girl. Well, let me tell you something. Religion isn't real. It was invented by the same men who started the bloody war. You've been tricked. It's all just a monstrous trick. That's why they start out telling you it was a virgin birth. They know that once they get you to believe that lie, you'll believe anything. Think about it."

"He wants to go," she says suddenly.

"Who wants to go? Where?"

"The war. My brother wants to go."

"I don't believe you. Anyway, he's too young to go."

"He's sixteen. If my mum signs for him, he can go."

The girl steps away and then walks to the pavement where she meets the man who Katie recognises now as the minister from the church. They speak a few words before the girl walks off and the man marches to the doorway. Before Katie can shut the door, he has his hand on it, holding it open. "What are you doing here?" Katie says with all the disgust she can summon through her shock.

"You've been spending time with the Thompkins child," he says, as if he were a judge condemning a criminal.

She knows that he has chosen that word – child – carefully, to inflict as much scorn as possible. "What's my sentence?" she asks sarcastically. "Am I going to hell, Father?"

"That's not for me to decide."

"No? Why isn't it for you to decide? What do they pay you for if it isn't to decide such things?"

His face reddens.

"And while we're at it, Father, what's my crime?" she asks him. "Tell me what I'm guilty of."

He begins answering immediately, but for some reason, the sound of his words does not reach her.

"I didn't hear you," she tells him. She is watching his lips move, as deaf to his spoken words as Finn would be. But she is certain of something now, something she probably should have known before. It was that part of her, the place Ned told her belonged to him. That part of her is why men invented their religion. So they could govern her desire with their rules.

When he begins to speak again, she is surprised by the sound of his voice.

"I think you're guilty of having a very high opinion of yourself," he says slowly. "You have a very high opinion of yourself, don't you?"

"I don't know," she answers. "Do you think I do?"

"Yes," he says. And his voice is very measured now, and so soft that she thinks he is going to say something sweet to her, and for a moment, she feels safe. "Yes," he goes on. "I'd say you have a very high opinion of yourself. For someone who has conducted herself like a slut."

Maybe he regrets saying that word, because he looks away shyly as if he has embarrassed himself. But he isn't finished. He turns and steps away from her door. Then he turns back and raises one hand in the air as if he were delivering a benediction. "You know that if anything happens to your brave husband, it will be God's way of punishing you for what you've done."

The tiled floor beneath her feet seems to shift slightly when she hears this. In some part of her consciousness, Katie wonders if she has crossed a line and will never be allowed to cross back. Maybe it is the line that always divides those who believe themselves worthy of being loved from those who do not.

As he walks away from her, she thinks that if this man is right, then she will be to blame for whatever horrible things happen to her husband and to Sam.

She only sees Finn one more time. The first frost has struck and the leaves on the maple trees in town have begun to give up their green. She is surrounded by motion – big clouds sailing by overhead, birds beating their wings against the wind, people walking purposefully, their shoes striking the pavement – the whole world is animated, but she is not moving.

A small caramel-coloured bus rolls past her to the town square and comes to a stop just up the street, where she sees Finn standing in a queue of boys waiting to be taken away to wherever they are given their army training. He is taller than the other lads and standing at the front of the line with his broad shoulders pulled back and his head held high. Katie feels a dull heaviness descend upon her as she watches him climb onto the bus. "Don't go," she hears herself whisper. "Don't let them take you where they took my husband and the only real friend I ever had."

BOOK II

sweetheart

The voice in the dead of night belongs to Lansdale. It is that muffled voice, and Sam doesn't want to intrude. But the voice is so persistent and so filled with desperation that he walks out into the dark corridor. He had fallen asleep in all his clothes and with his boots still on. He walks slowly towards Lansdale's room, tracing his hand along the pitted plaster wall. Then he listens outside the man's door.

Sergeant Lansdale is engaged in his nightly ritual. It is the only thing he can do to pass the hours. The hours when sleep will not come to rescue him. He strips off all his clothes slowly, folding each piece and laying it neatly on the chair by the window. He walks naked to his bedside table and takes the photograph of Amy from the drawer. He holds it in his right hand and, as he slips beneath the pale blue quilt, he carefully sets the picture on the pillow beside his head. "Time for bed, love," he says to her. Then he turns out the light. "You've had a good day then?"

"Yes, dear. It's wonderful having you home."

"Yes, it's good to be back. It feels so good to be lying next to you again. It was something I thought might never happen."

"But you kept your faith."

"Yes. Yes, I did. I kept my faith for you, sweetheart."

"Then you must tell me everything that happened to you in the war. We must talk about it one time and then never again."

"I will. I promise that I will. But first I need to ask you, are you going to sing in the choir again this Christmas?"

"Yes, I plan to."

"I'm so glad. That's wonderful. I'll sit in the front row again."

"Will you touch me now, my love?"

"I'm not sure I can. I was hoping maybe we can just love each other in other ways now."

"I don't understand."

"I know. I know. But I was just thinking how old people love each other. Just holding hands seems to be enough for them. You see them in the park all the time and they look so content, don't they?"

"We're not old, and even if we were, I would certainly want to do more than just hold your hand. Surely you know that?"

* * *

On the other side of the door, Sam hears silence and then suddenly the sound of Lansdale sobbing. At first, Sam is going to turn away and walk back to his room. But then he thinks that he will do whatever might be required just to make the sound disappear. There was a soldier dying in no man's land one evening in his first month at the front. He had been shot in the gut and he howled all through the night in pain, hour after hour until the man standing beside Sam fired one round that exploded his skull and put him out of his misery.

Sam wants to knock. He feels like he must do something. But instead, he only listens as Lansdale begins talking again, struggling with the words. "I was your little boy. You should have taken care of me, Ma. You never should have allowed anyone to do this to me. And now what are we going to do?"

In the war, Sam has heard men talking this way to their mothers. Wounded men or terrified men. The world believes that boys go off to war for their fathers, but really it is for their mothers, to prove to them that they have raised courageous sons. Sons who are as brave as the men they married. Sons who can protect them.

Who is this mother that Lansdale is crying to like a little boy? Isn't she in an army herself? One of the thousands and thousands of women who will carry her wicker basket on one arm to the market today to beg the butcher for some extra sugar, taking her place among the other women in the queue who are as terrified as she is that their sons and husbands and brothers will not return to them, and as unaware as the others that there are far worse things than being killed in war. An army of women like Sam's own mother. An army of the ignorant that also includes this girl who Lansdale calls 'sweetheart'. This girl who is waiting for him as blindly as one might wait for the plague. This sweetheart who is probably already some other bloke's sweetheart. Through everything that swirls inside Sam's mind, he has only one reference point to lead him to some kind of tentative understanding of Lansdale's nightmare. The reference point is Daisy, the only girl who has ever touched him and who he has ever been allowed to touch. She was the nude model in one of his drawing classes at the Academy and when her skin pressed against his, he became aware of his own beauty for the first time. With her face lying on his chest, and her breath rising and falling, he began to believe that he was worthy of being loved by a girl. She told him that he was lovely. Beautiful Daisy, with hypnotic eyes and curves that penetrated his sleep, told him that he was so lovely. He was too ignorant himself to understand what she had meant by that. But not too ignorant to be grateful. And now, as he listens outside Lansdale's door, he recalls what it felt like to be grateful. It was a feeling he never remembered in France. Until this moment, he thought the war had obliterated the feeling. But now the memory of it has returned. And it leaves him feeling helpless. There is nothing he can do for Lansdale except keep vigil outside his room until he has finally stopped crying. As quietly as he can, Sam drops down onto the floor.

He leans his back and shoulders against the wall and gazes into the darkness. Strangely, a calm passes through him. And while Lansdale weeps, he recalls the fine irreverence about Daisy. How she disdained rules. How she placed his palms on her knees and ran them up her dress, along the impossible softness of her thighs. Warm satin to his touch. And the surprising wetness that made him pull his hand away until she reassured him that it was all right. Unlike the army of young girls who were saving themselves for marriage, she believed this was nothing but appalling arrogance. It makes Sam smile to remember this. How lucky he had been to meet Daisy. He will pass the night like this, thinking of her and breathing deeply as Lansdale serenades him with his sobbing.

daylight

Sam has slept in the corridor outside Lansdale's room, in all his clothing, and wakes now to the sound of gunfire. A single shot startles him, shaking him violently from the sleep that he has shared with Daisy. The instant it happens, he flattens himself on the tiled floor, covering his head with his arms. A moment passes before he opens his eyes to a cathedral of silence that has fallen around him, and to the recognition that he is safe. "There is no danger here," Oliver had told him. *There is no danger here.*

It is just as silent downstairs. When the latch falls back in place as he closes the front door behind him, it is as loud as the gunshot was. He throws his duffel over his left shoulder and walks up the path toward the arched stone gate. Out ahead, the sunrise is a muted shade of red light bleeding into a colourless sea.

After he passes beneath the arch, something stops him, and he turns back. Lansdale is standing in his window. The white bandages wrapped around his face make him look like something from another world. Like his head has been dunked in a bucket of paint. He raises his hand to greet Sam.

"I can't help you," Sam says just above a whisper. And then he makes his way toward the main road.

He has gone only a few yards when Oliver emerges from the

field, with a dead pheasant hanging over his arm and a shotgun resting against one shoulder. His trousers are spattered with mud and give off the scent of wet soil.

There is something ominous in Sam's eyes as Oliver says, "Early bird catches the bird. I've been on this brave fellow's trail for two weeks now. You're up early. Enjoy a walk at dawn, do we?"

Sam looks into the older man's eyes. "I can't save anyone," he says.

Oliver turns away slightly and both men watch a few drops of blood spill onto one of his boots. "I see," he says.

Sam looks up at the sky.

"So, you're leaving us then?"

Sam nods his head.

"Well, you can walk out these gates if that's your decision."

Oliver offers his hand. Sam shakes it, turns quickly and starts to walk away.

"But don't go home," Oliver calls after him. "That's the first place the army will look for you." His voice connects Sam immediately to logic and order. Things that the war, despite all the commands and planning, made a mockery of.

He stops and slowly turns back. They regard each other for a moment.

"The boy we buried yesterday was James Lorrey," says Oliver. "He was a private from Southsea. Turned twenty-one last Sunday. How old are you?"

You want too much from me, Sam thinks. *You want to be my friend.*

"We fight a different kind of war here, Sam," Oliver says with a grave voice. "The enemy has been generous enough to spare these men their lives, but he has taken everything they need to live."

Sam is aware that the man is looking at him, waiting for him to meet his glance.

Oliver continues. "For the soldiers who come here, the war that took them from their families has ended. And the war that will take them home is beginning. This second war is every bit as deadly. And terrifying."

He can tell what Sam is thinking: *Let me be invisible. Let me evaporate into the sky.*

Oliver says his name again and Sam lifts his gaze to his face just as he produces a silver hip flask from his jacket pocket. As soon as he unscrews the top, the scent of the whiskey is in the air. Each man was always given his allotment before they went over the top of the trench. Oliver wonders if, at first, this boy didn't take his. And then he learned to take it each time it was offered. But now he shakes his head, declining.

"Just so you know, son," Oliver begins again carefully. "I've seen enough of what war can do to people. And I've had just about enough of armies and politicians who find it too easy to send boys off to fight for principles that may or may not matter. So if you want to walk away from this new war you've been assigned to, I will give you enough time to get a head start before I'm required to report you as missing in action. Let's say, I'll give you ten days. Will that be enough time for you?"

Enough time? He can tell that Sam is thinking. And then Sam asks him, "Enough time for what?"

Oliver answers, "Enough time for you to go to wherever you're planning to go. Wherever it is you would already be going to if we hadn't crossed paths this morning."

"I have no idea where I'm going," Sam finally tells him.

Oliver looks into his eyes and nods understandingly. "I've been there," he tells him with what he hopes is a reassuring tone. "Most of my life, I've had no idea where I was going. That happens to a man with no wife and children to call his home. Someday you and I are going to have to stay somewhere, Sam. And if it doesn't feel like home, we'll have to call it that anyway. We'll have to *make it* home."

A moment of silence falls.

"What does your father do for work?" Oliver asks him. It is an odd question that catches Sam off guard.

"He owns a dairy."

"Ah, cows. Enigmatic creatures, don't you think? Those big eyes drinking in the world. Great ponderous containers of silence and patience. I have vowed before that in my next life, I wish to be a farmer. I want to grow crops. Plough my fields. Plant my seeds. And then sit back and wait for God's merciful hand to sweep over my work. Think of it – what could be more opposite from a battlefield than a farmer's field? That's the ground I'll walk in my next tour of duty, Sam."

With this, he takes a swallow from the flask, returns it to his pocket and walks purposefully towards the castle without another word. He can feel Sam watching him, maybe wondering what it is like to be so old. To have lived for so long. To have outlived so many others. Like the tens of thousands of other men who died and were piled in heaps.

In time, in due course, Oliver will learn that it is something he has said that keeps Sam from leaving. It is the idea that the wounded men who come to this place are just beginning their second war. Sam feels this too about himself. There were times when he was in hospital, and when he was travelling here, when he would have preferred to be in the real war rather than this new war he feels starting up inside him. Now as he looks up at the castle, and watches Oliver make his way around to the door off the kitchen, he might be wondering if both wars will kill something essential in him. If a man can die that way more than once.

soup

Sam finds his way into the workshop and spends the entire morning setting up the tools to his liking. He is like a conductor addressing his orchestra, a sea captain stepping up to the helm of his ship for the first time. He has decided that the process of making masks will consist of strips of wet plaster laid across what remains of Lansdale's face, strips laid upon strips in a long and tedious process, with wire to build those portions of his face that are missing, until the full shape has been reconstituted. That plaster mask will then be used as the mould. Then the finished mask, made of galvanised copper, less than one thirty-second of an inch thick, will be shaped to the contours of the mould, before it is painted to match Lansdale's face from the photograph.

It will be far less complicated to make a mask that covers the entire face than just a partial mask to conceal the broken portions, trying to blend the painted tin with the man's skin. And this will make it rather simple for the mask to be held in place by eyeglasses with arms that wrap around the ears, or in Lansdale's case, one ear and the stump of the other that remains. Sam makes a mental note to tell Oliver to convey to whoever is sending these soldiers here that the surgeons must fashion some way for the eyeglasses to be held in place. They will anchor the mask.

Both of Lansdale's photographs lie on the desk in front of

Sam. In the tall windows behind him, the sun is rising in the sky. For two years in the war, he carried around a sketchbook not much larger than a package of cigarettes that fitted into the pocket of his tunic. Now his proper new sketchbook is open before him like a map of the world. The size of the blank page is slightly intimidating. It is an open field. An empty sky. He realises that what feels new to him is something he always took for granted before his world was shrunk down to the narrow slit of a trench, the width of the shoulders of two men passing in opposite directions. Space. The space to move freely. Space to be lost in. And to find yourself again. This has captivated his mind so completely that he is not aware of the charcoal markings he is making on the blank page until the sound of the pencil scratching the paper alerts him and draws him back. With just nine lines, he has captured the geometry of Lansdale's head to match the photograph of him before the war. The slope of his nose. The angle of the chin. The cut of his cheekbones and his lips. The height of his forehead. Each line he draws makes him more familiar with this man so that he can imagine his smile when he sees his home again. The joy that will animate his eyes. The crucial difference in faces is that when some people smile, their teeth show. Others, not so. He has to lean in close to the photograph of Lansdale to make sure of this. And the lips are crucial. From what he can see, Lansdale's lips are intact, which will make the task less daunting. But to make them fit precisely through the opening in the mask will be crucial. And the expression Sam fixes on the mask is ultimately the most important piece of his work. Because the expression will never change, he will have to strike a balance between happy and sad, pleased and indifferent. An expression to fit any occasion. Maybe the best thing would be to create a thoughtful expression that will not draw attention to itself but will suffice in any circumstance. He imagines Lansdale in a room filled with people who will regard him only as a thoughtful man who experienced something in life that has left him in a different kind of no man's land, an unemotional space somewhere between happiness and sorrow. It is a magician's trick that Sam is up against, and he senses this. Stare too long at Lansdale and you will see through the trick in degrees: first you will notice there is something odd about his face. Something you are not quite sure of. Then you will ascertain that what is odd is that his expression never changes. There, precisely, is where the trick must work. Right there at that point when the observer is beginning to wonder. Make the mask lifelike enough, perfect enough, and the observer will suspend his disbelief, dismissing Lansdale as a rather expressionless man with something on his mind that isolates him from the rest of the people in the room. Make him slightly unapproachable, a bit distracted, Sam tells himself. Not to the people who know him, of course, but to the inquisitive stranger.

Soon he is called for lunch. The three of them sit at the endless table over fresh bread, sliced apples and bowls of lentil soup. Each time Lansdale carefully guides the spoon to his lips, most of the soup fails to reach his mouth and runs down his bandaged chin. Despite this, he is cheerful and asks Sam if he has a girl at home waiting for him. It takes a great effort for Sam to say anything at all after listening to Lansdale weeping last night.

"I'll bet she's quite lovely," Lansdale remarks.

"No, I don't have a girl waiting for me," Sam tells him.

"Well, I do," Lansdale says eagerly. "Her name is Amy. We've known each other for ages. She was the last person I saw before I boarded the train for the war. I wrote to her almost every day when I was in France. I described for her the life that we would have together. But do you want to know what's very strange to me? I haven't been able to write a word to her since… since I left the war. The whole time I was in hospital, I never wrote anything. And the same is true here. I don't really understand this."

Oliver is quick to remind him that it's probably because now that he can actually imagine getting home to her, he doesn't feel the need to write.

"That could be it," Lansdale says agreeably. "You're probably right."

By now the soup is dripping from Lansdale's bandaged chin onto the polished table. When Lansdale discovers this, he apologises. "Oh my. I'm terribly sorry. I seem to have made quite a mess."

Oliver gets to his feet and walks around the table to place a hand on Lansdale's shoulder. "I don't think soup was a particularly good idea, do you?" he tells him.

"Perhaps, sir," Lansdale says sheepishly.

"All of this will get easier. Trust me."

"Yes. Thank you, sir."

The old man is not only attempting to offer comfort to Lansdale, but is also trying to show something to Sam. He is trying to remind him that there is benevolence in the world. Something that he witnessed before the war and believed in and, until now, thought had been extinguished.

razor

Over the white porcelain sink in his room, Sam unwraps the bandages from his wrists. There is the pink skin from the stab wounds he inflicted with the pencil that did not cause him to bleed out as he had hoped. And the white scars running horizontally like the lines on a map from the razor he used in hospital that would have caused him to bleed out if a custodian with a mop and bucket on wheels had not come upon him.

His flesh has healed quickly. How many weeks has it been now? He's lost track of the passage of time. How many days did he spend lying on his back in the hospital bed, staring up at the ceiling? How many hours did he spend with the soldier who was then taken out and shot against the pale yellow stucco wall of the French farmer's shed?

He snaps open his cut-throat razor from its black leather case and runs warm, soapy water over the steel before he lays the edge against one wrist, and then the other, crossing both tracks of scars. He recalls how easy it was to slit open the skin and the thought that had passed through his mind at the time – how ferociously we try to live or to kill, and yet what keeps the living from dying is just this little effort?

He lifts his head and looks at the face in the mirror looking back at him. He lays the blade against his jugular vein and feels the cadence of his pumping heart.

A moment later, he has lathered his face and is shaving

his whiskers when he hears an ungodly howl in the corridor, followed by thundering footsteps. Sam barely has time to set the razor on the edge of the sink before Lansdale comes crashing into him, the bandages unravelled from his head and face and streaming behind him like the tails of a kite. "It's gone! My face is gone!" he shrieks. Somehow he has the razor in one hand before Sam can react. And then they are wrestling each other to the floor. Sam is trying not to look at Lansdale's face. Especially the place where his nose should be that looks like someone sewed on a crude bow tie of raw meat.

"You don't want to do this," Sam tells him calmly. "I'm going to help you." Even as he says this to Lansdale, he is looking away from his face. He looks away from the man's eye that is missing and sewn shut. He looks too long at the other eye and discovers something he did not see in the photograph. The lid on this remaining eye has been burned away and it looks like the eyeball could just fall from its socket and roll across the floor.

Exhausted in each other's arms, they lie on the floor for quite some time before Sam dares to stand. When he does, Lansdale gets to his knees and throws his arms around Sam's legs, gasping. The fight has left him.

Soon Sam stands behind him and wraps his face properly. Then he leads him back to his bed and pulls the covers over him.

"Thank you, soldier," Lansdale tells him. His muffled voice is barely audible and Sam can see that he has covered too much of his mouth.

It takes him a few moments to peel away the bandages so that Lansdale can speak more distinctly.

Sam nods and turns to leave.

"I was wounded at Guise," Lansdale tells him. "We sent the Boche running from there. Really had them on the run. All we saw were their arses."

Sam sits for a few minutes at the foot of Lansdale's bed, listening, waiting.

"I can't see the Hun holding out too much longer," he says. "Can you, Sam?"

"It's hard to tell," Sam replies.

"Do you still dream?"

"Sometimes," Sam tells him.

"Not me. I don't dream any more," Lansdale says.

Sam hears him say this, but then, in the next moment, all the sound falls from the room, or is blotted out by the sound inside Sam's mind. A dripping sound that grows louder and louder. He is looking down at his hands that are in shackles. He can barely see them with the blindfold over his eyes. And he can barely hold the sketchbook in his hands. Someone is sitting beside him. He can hear the man sobbing, and he can see his boots on the cement floor. From somewhere outside the room, there is the sound of a man shouting the order to FIRE! The rifle fire agitates the man beside him. His boots move slightly on the floor and then the dripping sound begins. A puddle of urine forms on the floor and Sam moves his feet away from it. Shortly, two men enter the room and take the man away as he begs them for mercy. "Don't shoot me! Please don't kill me!"

Sam will be next. He knows this. He welcomes it. The end of everything. The simple act of letting go made even more simple because someone else will do the letting go for him. It will require no effort at all.

He closes his eyes and lets this thought settle in his mind. In a few minutes, it will be over. He tells himself that the last thought he will hold in his mind will be the colour of the sky that afternoon in Dorset when he and Ned stood on the cliffs together looking down at Katie. Before any of this began. Before they stepped onto the conveyer belt that carried them away from England to this place in France. Away from the girl they both loved. The order to FIRE is given again. Sam is consciously taking slow, measured breaths, expecting to see the same two pairs of boots coming across the floor for him. But instead there is only one pair of boots and they are highly polished. Sam can make out the reflection of the man's face in their gleaming leather. "Are you the artist?" he asks with a surprisingly soft and modulated voice. And his accent is one that Sam can't place. It must be Australian, he is thinking. "Are you, son? Are you the artist?" There is an odd formality in his voice.

It takes all of Sam's will to form the single word. "Yes."

"Come with me then," he says as he slides his hand under Sam's arm with surprising tenderness and lifts him to his feet. "You are now officially the luckiest bloody artist that God ever made."

morning

He has slept and when his eyes open, he sees Lansdale
standing at his window, wearing his uniform, having done
his best to look presentable. "Are you awake, soldier?" he
asks without turning around.

"I'm awake," Sam says.

"I was just wondering how a man could end it from this
height? I suppose he'd have to land just the right way to break
his neck. If he didn't land properly, then he'd spend the rest
of his life in a wheelchair. A burden on everyone. What do
you think?"

"I think we should go down and have some breakfast."

He tells Sam that his is the only window that isn't nailed
shut. "Oliver trusts you. But there are cleaner ways to do it,
aren't there?"

Now Sam knows what is coming. He hears the question
before it is asked. "You wouldn't choose to jump, would you?"

Sam can hear his heart beating. "I don't like heights," Sam
tells him.

"I saw your wrists. That takes courage."

"No. It only takes a good reason."

Lansdale turns and faces him. "You had a good... good
reason?"

Sam nods.

"Do you still have it?"

Sam wants to tell him the truth. That he is also walking along the edge. Hell, maybe the whole world is. But he doesn't. "These rough times pass," he says to him instead.

"That's what Oliver tells me."

"I think you should listen to everything he tells you," Sam says.

"Yes, he's some fellow, isn't he? An army chaplain in the Boer War. Africa. That must have been brutal fighting. Death at close range. Looking right into the eyes of the man trying to kill you. But at least they didn't have the machinery to do the kind of killing that's done in this war. Our commanding officers told us we could outrun machine-gun fire if we moved quickly enough. And then they told us not to run. Just to walk steadily into the fire. It's a wonder they got us to go over the top. Slaughter is what it is. But I've heard we may be close to inventing a kind of armoured vehicle that will crash right through their trenches and end the whole miserable affair. So it cuts both ways, right? The machinery?"

"I suppose," Sam says.

"Outrun machine-gun fire," Lansdale says with a sudden burst of mirthless laughter, mocking himself. "Do you think there's any end to the lies you can get a man to believe?"

This makes Sam realise something. He will be building Lansdale's mask for the people who are in power, the people who made this war so that when it is over, the real loss, the real horror, will be hidden away so these people can be cleansed of any guilt. Sam knows this now. The knowledge settles deep inside his consciousness, and he tells himself that he must never speak of this to Lansdale or to any soldiers who come here. He must keep the knowledge hidden because it is laced with cynicism. And he must do whatever he can to encourage Lansdale never to believe that the mask he will hide behind is meant *to hide him* as well.

old man

It is getting to Oliver now. He can feel it. The Second Boer War that ended in 1902 was going to be the last of his days in the army. But here he is more than a decade later, still serving. Serving whom, or what, he is no longer sure. And it has not been the anguish that has worn him down on the inside where it matters most. Though he has witnessed more anguish than anyone ever should in a lifetime, it is the inner turmoil that has nearly destroyed him. The turmoil of believing deeply in God's goodness while surrounded by the brutal destruction of goodness.

From the time he was a small boy, he knew that he would attend seminary when he came of age and then become a pastor devoted to carrying God's word into the world. Light into the darkness is how he always thought of it. He had imagined a small church on a hillside in the country where he would baptise babies, and marry young couples, and sit at the bedside of his dying, elderly parishioners. But somehow the marvellous order and continuity of that life eluded him. Instead of a country church, he got a battlefield, where his duties as an army chaplain included a constant struggle just to hold on to his faith in mankind's essential goodness, and to resist being swept into an impenetrable darkness. He had turned fifty-two years old when the war ended and he returned to his home in Hampshire to grow old in peace, walking the water meadows each day, stopping at the playing fields to watch the young lads dashing about on their rickety bird legs. He was not a young man then by any means, but he still possessed a certain strength that is gone now. He lived in his ancestral home in peace for eleven years before the Great War began.

In his office now, at the end of the day, he settles into the gold Queen Anne chair that serves as his bed. He has slept on one chair or another ever since he could no longer straighten his knees, compliments of a stray bullet in Africa that went through both of them. He pulls two dull green army blankets up to his armpits and places the pale blue linen scarf over his mouth and nose. The scarf that belonged to a girl he once held in his arms. He has found that this scarf works best. A few drops of ether from the blue glass bottle and he will be out for the night. As good as dead.

In some way, for some reason, he loves this room and so he enjoys his last glimpse of it before his eyes close and he tumbles down the rabbit hole into his medicated sleep each night. The tall bay windows covered by thick maroon-coloured curtains made of velvet. The dark blue and crimson patterns in the oriental carpet. The proud, authoritative oak desk. The brass floor lamps with their pale green satin shades. The intricately carved moulding around the ceiling. The drinks cabinet made of teak. The radio with its wooden scrolled case that looks like a miniature cathedral. The oak-panelled walls bleached by centuries of cascading sunlight. He always feels like a country gentleman in this room. Or a baron. Or maybe an earl. Well, at least a patrician.

In a chair like this, he once carried on with a brilliant girl who was going to be a dancer. He can remember her long hair the colour of barley, falling over his face. He used to tell her that one day he was going to write a book about everything he'd seen in the war in Africa, though no one would want to read it because it would be too grim.

"Not if you put us in your book," she had said to him.

"Everyone enjoys a love story. But of course you won't be able to write about the great sex."

She was right about the sex but wrong about the love. He was never able to love anyone very well. Blame it on all that he had seen and learned. Blame it on the sad procession of broken young men he had attended to who always cried out, or wept in the end, for people they loved.

One thing that he has learned across the years is that we cannot count the ways we can lose the people we love best in this world, but most of the time, it is our own fault.

lighthouse

For at least a week, Oliver has been after Sam to walk to a nearby farm to see if an arrangement can be made to secure milk and vegetables there for the castle. "The walk will be good for you," the old man advised him. "Take some air deep in your lungs. Get some light on your face. Work your legs to keep the blood flowing. You're a young man. You need to build this kind of daily exercise into your central nervous system so that you can live a long and healthy life."

In truth, he has sent him there because of the girl he was told was living there alone. He thought perhaps that they might get to know one another and that her company may keep Sam from running away.

As he climbs the dunes beside the sea, Sam thinks about Oliver. He finds him a curiosity. He has never lived in proximity to old people before, and is only now beginning to suspect that, though they are riding on the same train, while Sam's seat is facing forward, the old people's seats face back so that they are being drawn reluctantly, against their will, to what lies ahead.

The last few feet of dunes are steep enough for him to need his hands to ascend. The fescue grass, as soft as silk, passes through his fingers. Glancing back to the town, he can see mist rising off the cobblestone streets in the warming morning sun. From here, he can look across the fields folded softly into each other, the ancient stone walls covered in green moss, and the whitewashed cottages whose inhabitants must be trying to live long and healthy lives. Just the thought of all that *trying* makes Sam feel momentarily exhausted. Where do they find the energy? From the food they eat? And the water they drink? From the sun and the wind? Do they soak it all in, like plants? Yes, that probably explains the energy – like coal shovelled into a boiler. *But where do they find the desire? Where does that come from?*

From somewhere comes the sound of laughter. And, unlike the laughter in the trenches that was always carefully constructed to conceal terror and pain and grim apprehension, this laughter is wild with pure joy.

Two men smoking cigars, wearing black top hats and matching black capes are out playing golf. A small boy walks behind them, with bags of clubs over both shoulders. Toffs without a care in the world, playing golf by the sea with their faces turned into sunlight, at the same moment other men are being shelled into submission, burying their heads in the mud to escape the horror, staring up at the sky from fields of bones. *Who decides?* Sam asks himself. His mother would tell him that it is all in God's hands. That the Lord has a plan for each life – for the soldier in the mud and the man on the golf course. She had always said this sort of thing with a measure of calm, as if the belief brought her comfort. A comfort that she wished to pass on to him from the time he was her little boy. In France, he had searched for his mother in the night sky when he was too frightened to sleep. He tried to see her face or at least the shape of her outlined by the stars. But she eluded him there. She had not accompanied him to the war. When he was little, she was always pulling him away from the ruffians. Always protecting him.

The men on the golf course below him begin shouting at something. Shouting and waving their hands. For a moment, this unnerves Sam. He feels his shoulders pitch forward slightly. He bows his head, trying to make himself small.

That's how it always was in France. Trying to make yourself smaller so the piece of lead or shrapnel would not find you.

But then the fear passes when he sees that the men are trying to get the attention of someone out ahead of them who is walking behind a grass cutter. He is in their path and they are trying to get him to move aside so they can continue on with their game. It is a small drama that plays out almost, it seems, to Sam's amusement, so that he can apply his mind to discern the logic in what is taking place before him. There is a beauty in the logic. A simple beauty. It was very different in France, where any logic at the start of each assault soon fell away to bedlam. There was a more resilient and determined logic in the shelling, the result of decisions and calculations made miles away. The person with the grass cutter moves off to the side and the men strike their balls forward and the boy carrying their clubs hurries to keep up. Logic. It is all so sensible. It occurs to Sam for the first time that there is still a logical world and that he has somehow washed ashore there. For now, though, he feels like he is trespassing.

Sheep with their heads down are eating their way across a green field. Hundreds of them. "Pick up your heads and have a look around!" he shouts to them. The sound of his voice surprises him, but not the sheep. They ignore him. And the words – where did they come from? And the humour behind the words? How strange it all feels to him. Well… strange, yes. And it *is* strange because *he* is strange. How strange *he* is. A moment later, he is mimicking the sheep, down on all fours, moving along with them. He is aware that this is the sort of unpredictable and comic behaviour for which he could be counted on as a young boy. He had almost forgotten this. The sound of his mother and father breaking into laughter at the sight of his antics is something which left him in France, but here it is again, the impulse reinstating itself.

He sits there for a while before he gets back on his feet and walks on to the farm.

It stands on the windswept headland, high on a promontory

looking out to the sea. There is the ramshackle main house with its dull clapboards that desperately need paint. Two small outbuildings in similar disrepair, both with their rooflines sagging slightly and weeds growing through cracks in their stone foundations. At the west end of the property, there is, of all things, a lighthouse, washed with pale pink paint that must have once been red. He is drawn to it immediately and finds himself practically running towards it, until he *is* running and feeling a marvellous velocity as the ground below his feet flies away behind him. As he runs, he keeps glancing behind him to be sure he is actually doing this. He is aware of his own incredulity. He is aware that he exists somewhere in the space between himself and the place where he stands watching and considering himself.

There is a steel gate at the base of the lighthouse with a rusted latch and a bronze padlock that has been left unlocked. He drags the gate open carefully and then climbs the steel stairs, slowly at first, the iron railing sliding beneath his fingers, spreading the dull cold of coins across his palm. At the top, he steps into a small glass room. A cone of white light and silence. Everything in the world below is now the size of toys. He sees some small children running along the shore like a flock of birds on their legs that seem too thin to hold them up. He remembers the children in France as his unit marched past them, always calling to them in their awkward English – *Tommee, give me B-U-L-L-E-E beef, please, Tommee!* Almost all his memories are from his first few months in France, before his mind closed out most of what was happening around him.

Something makes him turn suddenly, sharply. And he sees her through the sunlit pane of thick glass. A girl in one upstairs room of the farmhouse, standing at a window in a white dress that flows around her like a cloud. He leans closer for a better look, and to be certain he isn't imagining this. At the same instant, she turns her face slightly and he is sure that she has seen him. He feels their eyes meet and there is almost a sound to this, a sound inside his mind like a key turning in a latch.

paris

The delivery man has a great big pot belly that he manoeuvres like a man walking behind a wheelbarrow filled with cement. He and Sam make three trips from his truck to the workshop with boxes of supplies that have come all the way from Paris. He is breathing hard by the second trip and this reminds Sam of the soldiers who suffered most in the trenches. The soldiers who had grown heavy before the war. It was not just the extra weight they had to lug around; it was that they made big fat targets for German snipers. Better to be as skinny as a rake handle like Sam. There were times when he proceeded across no man's land with his body turned sideways to narrow himself further. He found that he could even run sideways, shuffling his feet quickly enough to keep up with the others when order broke apart and running was the only thing left to do.

"So is it true what I heard about what goes on in this place?" the delivery man asks.

"What have you heard?"

"I heard about the masks."

"Yes, it's true."

"And you're one of the artists then?"

"I am."

"Well, I guess you got lucky then."

"I guess I did."

"Imagine this stuff coming from France as if there was no war on at all."

"Imagine."

I'm carrying on a conversation, Sam realises. *Things are changing.*

There are boxes of plaster, tin, wax, wire, and paints in colours that are rarely found on the open market. Sam waits until the man is gone to open them because he does not want to share this bit of pleasure with a stranger who knows so little about him that he would call him *lucky*. They are packed in glass jars beneath straw in a wooden crate he opens with the claws of a hammer. Cadmium blue. Yellow ochre. Burnt sienna and Venetian red. Sam lines them up on his workbench, then moves them around into different positions, at first in no discernible pattern, but then in the shape of as many constellations as he can remember. Virgo and Gemini. Leo, and Orion with his hunting shield and bright belt. A galaxy of colour to navigate this strange place by. When he opens the box of gauze, he feels something tighten beneath his ribs. He is going to have to make a mould of Lansdale's face with the gauze soaked in plaster. In some places, this will require careful improvisation and a wire frame to create the bones that are missing in his chin and cheek. He will have to build the frame of the nose with wire as well to hold the plaster strips. He will sculpt the plaster form and then he will gently hammer the copper mask over the completed mould to capture the topography of the mould. Then paint. Then two thin coats of enamel.

He takes the photographs of Lansdale from the drawer and lays them on the workbench. He no longer looks like a stranger. Some attachment to the man's life has already been formed in the crucible of Sam's first weeks here. It is not unlike the bond that formed in the war. What were those lines from Shakespeare that the lieutenant from Wales was always reciting? *This story shall the good man teach his son…*

From this day to the ending of the world. But we in it shall be remembered. We few, we happy few, we band of brothers.

Happy? The word had always struck Sam as odd. To be happy when you are surrounded by the dead, and the suffering of the dying, and when yours may be the next corpse added to the piles. And yet there were moments when he and Ned laughed together. As if they hadn't a care in the world. They laughed the way they had laughed as boys at the end of the day when they ran home to the sound of their mothers' voices calling them for their tea.

He holds the photograph of Lansdale under the light to study the shape of his nose. His next thought is that Lansdale will never grow old. In the town he returns to, he will always be the young man he was before he went to war. Everyone will grow old around him, but the fineness of his youthful face will never fade. He will remain the thoughtful young man. Forever young.

grave

It is late when Sam stands outside watching clouds race across the stars in the western sky. It seems like hours ago that he was in his room trying to sleep, listening to silence from Lansdale's room, waiting for some sound to tell him that he was still alive. Before he gave up and made his way down the stairs, he stood outside Lansdale's door, listening again. But there was nothing. The stillness and the silence unnerved Sam, and he was grateful the moment he stepped outside and heard the wind rushing through the stand of ash trees beyond the garden.

Now he lights a cigarette and as he watches the moon and stars brighten after the clouds pass, he cannot help but wonder if Katie is awake at this hour across the sea, 500 miles from here or more, looking up at the same stars and trying to imagine what her life will be like without Ned. He cannot help but wonder how she might think of him if she thinks of him at all. She will be waiting for him to come see her – he knows this. Already more than three months have passed since she would have received word of Ned's death. She will be waiting for him to return and this is something he will never do. He will never return to answer her questions. There will be too many questions that he *must never answer.* It will be far better to send her the letter he has carefully written. In that letter, he composed for her a story she can believe in. A narrative that will answer the questions racing through her mind when she looks up at the night sky. A sky like this. A night like this. But now he decides that he is not ready to post the letter.

He is walking towards the grave when he hears Oliver's voice.

"What's on your mind, son?" he asks.

Sam is hesitant to answer. He has not decided to tell Oliver anything and so the sound of his own voice comes as something of a surprise to him. "This man you buried here. Why did he kill himself?"

"He couldn't wait any longer."

"What was he waiting for?"

It is obvious from the way Oliver looks away. Finally, he says, "He was waiting for the artist to arrive."

Sam had suspected as much. And it makes him angry. Instantly angry. But he only knows for certain that this is anger rising through him when he can't remember the name of the man who bought the farm next door to his father's. The man whose name he said out loud when he awoke this morning after a dream about his childhood. Damn it! This is the thing that unnerves him. This amnesia that can sweep over him without warning.

He hears Oliver saying his name, asking him something. But before he can finish his question, Sam raises his voice to drown him out. "How do you expect me to save a man's life just by making him a mask to wear?"

"The war department believes it's worth a try." The reply is so reasonable that it angers Sam even more.

"The war department believed Gallipoli was worth a try," he says.

This makes the old man laugh. Just one short bark of a laugh.

How did I manage to do that? Sam wonders. How did he manage to make someone laugh?

"Good point, son. Gallipoli was a fool's errand."

Sam is thrown off balance each time Oliver calls him

by that word – *son*. He finds it hard to believe that anyone who has done the things that he's done could deserve to be someone's son. It is a common belief for men who have been at war. Particularly young men who have never been separated from their mothers before.

"I can't save anyone," Sam says insistently.

Again, Oliver responds right away. "The army is hoping that you can. And so am I," he tells him as he rakes his thick white hair back with one hand.

What do you know about me? Sam wonders again. *What have you been told? Why don't I just come out and ask you if you know that I've been spared a firing squad to come here?* He can almost hear himself asking Oliver these questions.

Oliver has turned back toward the castle where a light is on now in Lansdale's room. "It's about hope, Sam. Remember? Hope. Look up there to that window. You've already given one man hope."

He sounds so certain of this that it turns Sam's anger up another notch. "What do you think hope is, anyway?" he asks. "Why do you keep using a word that isn't real?"

They stand there, a few feet apart, for a long time before Oliver answers. "I've seen what it can do."

"You tell me then. Tell me what it can do."

He watches Oliver narrow his eyes as he stares at him. "You're too young to live without hope. You're going to need to get through the years ahead of you. The disappointment. The betrayals. The ways your heart can be broken. Without hope, you don't stand a chance."

"A chance of what? Surviving? Look at me – I'm a survivor, remember? I survived when so many others were slaughtered. I can survive anything now. They should have issued us white aprons to wear instead of uniforms. The white aprons that butchers put on. That's the business we were in."

His voice is rising above them. It is clear that he feels that he has said enough. And so Oliver changes the subject.

"What I would like to do is knock down that brick wall over there and rebuild it properly. Are you any good with cement?"

Sam shrugs. In truth, he has rebuilt walls around the farm with his father since he was six years old.

"It will be good for Lansdale," Oliver tells him. "Keep the body strong. The body leads the mind."

"What makes you think he wants to go on living?" Sam asks, his voice quieter now and calmer. Perhaps because the man's name has suddenly come batting into his head. The man who bought the farm beside his father's. *Goodwin. Yes. Goodwin from Yorkshire. See, I can remember things. It just requires a bit of patience.*

"Ah, living, that's the thing, son. And there's a difference between surviving and living."

"A difference? Tell me what it is. Tell me."

"You don't know?"

For some reason, he wants to fight the old man. He needs to lash out at him. He is waiting for his answer and if he says the wrong thing, he might just grab him by the throat.

Oliver can see this. When did talking reside so close to physical violence? he wonders.

"The difference is called *feeling*. That's how we know that we're alive, Sam. That's the only way we know for certain."

girl

Each time Oliver watches Sam walk away from him, he worries that one morning he will just be gone, that he will have given up on everything and left in the night. That is why he wants him to meet Lily. Though he does not know her story and several years will pass before he learns it from the baker's wife in town, the only person Lily ever confides in while she lives alone in the old farmhouse and waits, Oliver hopes that Lily might help Sam *feel* once again. He tries to believe that she might pull him from the nightmare he has been through.

Lily has seen Sam in the lighthouse, and she is already wondering who he is. Even as she steps away from the window so that he will not see her, she is already turning him into someone else. She is turning him into the boy she has lost who had left instructions for her to find her way to this farm and to wait for him for as long as it took for him to come meet her.

His name is Brian Callahan. Thirteen months ago, he was supposed to meet her here. They would have been husband and wife for more than a year by now. What that would have been like is something she wonders about through the days alone. She imagines the details of her wedding night. His hands resting gently on parts of her that have never been touched. Something strange and unidentifiable moving through her like light through a quiet room. At the market when the clerk places her change on the counter, she sees the boy's hand reaching for hers. He takes her by the hand and leads her up the stairs to the tiny room that faces the lighthouse. Slowly, she undresses for him in the turning band of calibrated white light that makes the room go from light to dark, light to dark, light to dark in even intervals. Eleven seconds in between each transition. Enough time for her to remove more clothing, so that each time she reappears in the light, she is more exposed, and closer to giving herself to him.

She has only imagined all of that, and it makes her angry that she keeps thinking this way. Even as she watched the boy walk away from the lighthouse, wondering about him, transforming him into the other boy, she was angry with herself for ever believing anything he told her before he bought her first class passage on the ocean liner from New York to Liverpool, thirteen months ago now. Before he took her to the bridal shop on 57th Street in Manhattan to buy the dress. Before he sat beside her while she sewed the folded scraps of cloth into the hem of the wedding dress, telling her that a wedding dress would be perfect; no one would suspect a lovely girl travelling to England for her wedding. "But we *are* going to be married, aren't we?" she had asked him several times in her insecurity. Each time he had smiled at her with his eyes narrowing and answered yes, of course, just as soon as the rebellion was over, just as soon as the rebellion had forced England to agree to leave Ireland to her own affairs and never to return. He had never even told her how old he was, though she suspected him to be maybe ten years older than herself. She had turned nineteen on the passage across the Atlantic. The first night out, somewhere off Nova Scotia, the bakery chef had prepared a cake for her with sparklers. She had watched a man walk across the dining room, clapping softly for her, looking so much like a penguin in his black and white coat and tails. He had introduced himself to her below the crystal chandeliers when he wished her happy birthday. He told her that his name was Vanderbilt. "A.G. Vanderbilt, miss," he had said as he bowed gracefully from his waist.

Though she had only lived two years in America, the name already meant something to her. He waited for her to tell him her name.

"Lily," she said. "Lily Connolly."

"And you're travelling home?"

This question was to let her know that, though she might live in America now, he knew which part of the world she was from. He knew where home was for her. He knew she was an outsider in his America.

It wasn't until Mr Vanderbilt was walking away from her table that Lily remembered she was not supposed to tell her last name to anyone who didn't need to know it. This was part of the secrecy that had filled her with electricity. It was part of the adventure. The first time she had crossed the Atlantic she was fifteen years old, travelling in a steerage berth below the waterline, on her way to Ellis Island. Travelling from east to west. Now she was travelling west to east in a first class cabin that was as fine as any New York hotel room, or any of the rooms in the elegant Brooklyn brownstone where she worked as a domestic, thanks to an uncle, her father's brother, who was organising the rebellion in Dublin. Her uncle, James Connolly, whom she had no memory of but had apparently met as a small child when her father and mother took her and her siblings from Galway to Dublin one Christmas.

The boy who was going to be her husband had come to New York to pick up instructions for the rebellion that was being planned across Ireland. These instructions that he had come from Ireland to New York to pick up were so secretive and important that they could not be transmitted any other way than by scrawling them on scraps of cloth and sewing them inside the hem of her wedding dress. He and Lily did the sewing together one rainswept morning in the parlour of the Brooklyn row house where she was employed by the German family who owned it. This was on April 29. Two days before she boarded the world's largest passenger ship to carry the instructions to Ireland. She had asked the boy to tell her what information the scraps of cloth were meant to convey, but he refused. "After it's over," he said with a half-smile.

"After we're married?" she replied, not wanting to say that again, or at least not to say it in the form of a question as she had, but unable to keep from saying it because she wanted him to reassure her that this was not all some ruse cooked up by the men who were always drinking their whiskey and smoking off by themselves and plotting with their big dreams of independence.

"Yes," he said, "after we've been married." To which he nodded his lovely, proud head with the thick shock of auburn hair she was looking forward to running her fingers through in time. There was something irresistible about him and the mystery that surrounded him. And something even more irresistible about the fact that she had been chosen to be an important part of whatever it was they were planning. Chosen only for her innocent appearance, she knew this. She was eighteen but with her hair down could easily pass for fourteen. But still, it was something. And in the three weeks she and the boy had spent getting to know one another in New York City, she had fallen in love with him. She was certain of this because from the first walk they had taken together along the docks where she had walked a hundred times, she could not imagine taking the walk again without him at her side. She could no longer hold in her mind a clear picture of her life without him in it. And it would be a life with him in Ireland. A life back home where she longed to be.

But she had not longed to be here alone as she is now – and as she has been from the hour she arrived by train in clothes that rescuers had provided her at the dock in Kinsale. It was there they pulled survivors from the lifeboats that had made their way to shore after the great ship, the *Lusitania*, had disappeared below the waves. She had been watching that word, that name, slip beneath the water. Only the enormous *L* was still visible when her eyes closed, as she began to drop down in the seconds before someone pulled her from the water.

She was stunned, of course. Frozen stiff practically, unable to feel her feet or move her arms, but still determined to find the person who had saved her life. And maybe it was the wedding dress that saved her. She had been modelling it in front of the gold-framed mirror in her stateroom when the first explosion tore through the ship. She felt the floor shudder beneath the soles of her bare feet.

When she threw herself into the sea, the dress had filled with air on her way down from the third deck as she fell, and it ballooned around her like a mushroom. That was her thought. She was a white mushroom floating on the sea, surrounded by terrified and screaming people. All strangers to her.

On the dock in Kinsale, two men carried her over the bodies strewn across the pier. There were bodies everywhere. All of them lying patiently with ghostlike white faces. In the weeks that followed, she read in the newspapers that someone in America was paying one pound sterling for each American body that was found. And 1,000 pounds sterling for the body of Mr A.G. Vanderbilt, who had spoken to her in the dining room below the crystal chandeliers that had left a pattern of shadows on the bald spot on top of his head.

Whoever this boy is in the lighthouse, she has watched him walk away across the hillside and disappear beyond the dunes. Now she sits down and opens the tin box that she found in a drawer in the kitchen when she first arrived at the farm, embossed with a picture of Princess Mary's head and the words *Christmas 1914*. Apparently, British soldiers were given these with an ounce of tobacco, cigarettes and a lighter inside before they boarded their ships to cross the Channel for the war in France. In this box, Lily has put the folded newspaper clipping:

MAY 8, 1915. LUSITANIA SUNK BY
SUBMARINE. PROBABLY 1,000 DEAD. ONLY
600 SAVED. TWICE TORPEDOED OFF THE
IRISH COAST. SINKS IN 15 MINUTES.

136 AMERICANS ABOARD DEAD OR MISSING. INCLUDING A.G. VANDERBILT.

Also inside the box are the scraps of cloth that she removed from the hem of the wedding dress. Each is marked by an outline of a small section of the Irish coast. Before she boarded the ship, she had made Brian tell her. She had leaned into him as they waited in the queue at the pier. She told him again that she loved him and that she would follow the instructions and do as she had been told for the sake of the revolution, for the sake of freedom in Ireland, but she would not tolerate being kept in the dark just because she wasn't a man.

He looked down at his feet and shook his head slightly, saying, "I don't know. I don't know, Lily. Why are you asking me this?" She almost relented, just to make it less difficult for him. He tried a different tack then, kissing her on the top of her head and whispering, "No more banister to polish for you." She felt him laugh lightly. She had told him of the brass handrail that ran the length of the staircase in the brownstone where she worked. The staircase dominated the centre of the building and went up six storeys, and she had been instructed to polish the rail every time someone either ascended or descended. The German family ran some kind of export business out of the building. There were always people coming and going and there were some days when Lily did nothing but climb up and down the staircase, polishing the gleaming rail that showed her face reflected in miniature all the way up and down as if it were mocking her.

"No more banister to polish," she repeated. But then she held her ground with Brian, and in the end, he told her that the scraps of linen with the coastline of Ireland drawn on them marked locations where guns and ammunition would be dropped off in advance of the uprising. He told her gravely that without these shipments, there would be no chance for the uprising to succeed.

"The Brits will crush us like cockroaches, Lily," he said

sorrowfully. He told her that soon after she arrived at the farm on May 7, men would come for this information. He insisted on this with a kind of determined confidence in his voice that assured her no part of his plan would fail.

He sent her on her way then. She climbed the steep steel ramp into the great ship and hurried through the crowd to the nearest deck where she stood at the railing, searching for him in the distance.

postman

A soft morning rain falls over the town at dawn. Sam has walked in darkness from the castle and is sitting on one of the benches in the village green, smoking, when a postman wanders over to join him. Sam is looking at him. He is a boy really and can't be older than fifteen or sixteen. He has startling green eyes and a spray of freckles over his nose in the shape of a butterfly. His name, he says eagerly, is Tommy Falcon. He was appointed postman for the town as a kind of gift when his father, the normal postman, went off to war. He is drowning in the dark blue jacket with the straight red collar and brass buttons, obviously his father's uniform. There is something so innocent and pleasantly disarming about him that Sam catches himself smiling at the kid, and for the first time since Ned's death, he is talking openly, no longer choosing words as an act of concealment.

"I'm looking forward to Christmas," the boy tells him.

"Christmas?" Sam says. "Why Christmas?"

"Cards and packages," he answers. "You know, good news for a change."

He explains how depressing it has been for him to deliver letters from the war. "People hate to see me coming in their direction. You wouldn't believe it, but I've held envelopes in my hand that were smeared with blood. Jesus, it gets you down after a while. And the telegrams are the worst part. I had one woman faint when she saw me coming up the walkway to her door. She just dropped to her knees and then keeled over. I had to pour a glass of water on her face and drag her back inside. Mercy. That's something my da never had to do."

"Was it a wife?" Sam asks him.

"Mother. That's worse, I think. A wife can always find another bloke, can't she?"

"You're wise for your age," Sam says.

"Never did well in school. But my mother has always told me that I'm dumb like a fox." He laughs heartily at this. Then he says, "Actually, I fancy working for the railways when I'm old enough. I love trains. How about you then? I've never seen you in town before. Where do you stay?"

"I'm up the road," Sam tells him.

"Yeah? Which road?"

"I'm in the old castle."

"Oh Christ, they're putting wounded soldiers up there, I heard. I imagine I'll be delivering more sad letters there. What about you? Were you in the war?"

It is a question that Sam won't answer unless he has to. Instead he points to the row of whitewashed cottages across the street. In the garden behind one of them, the young woman he saw when he first arrived in town is hanging laundry on the clothes line in the rain. "See that," Sam says. "That takes faith."

"That's Maude Kennedy. What do you mean?"

"Hanging laundry out in the rain. You have to have faith that the sun is going to come out before the day is through."

"I guess so," the boy says, too young to comprehend the full meaning.

"She must have little children."

"Three of them. Troublemakers, I can tell you. Always running wild in the streets."

"Her husband?"

"France, like my da," the boy says.

And with that single word – *France* – Sam is suddenly

pressing the soles of his shoes hard against the ground to try to stop the dizzying sensation that is rising through him. He can feel his mouth going dry. He wants to stand up and say goodbye to the boy, but he's afraid he will fall over. "How old are you?" Sam asks to try to pull himself back from the edge.

"Fifteen. Two more years and I'll be in the war with my da. He was in the big battle at Verdun."

There it is. A cold spark at the base of Sam's spine. The tightening of his ribs. And all the light falling out of the world at once so that Sam is suddenly on his knees in the same darkness that surrounded him as he knelt over Ned's body in the smoky trench in the place this boy has somehow named. Verdun. What are the odds that this boy's father would be stationed in the same place? The Great War with heaving oceans of men and machinery moving ponderously across vast continents, and with such exquisite indifference, in every conceivable direction has been reduced to one place by a dark river.

The thing that Sam must do now is figure out a way to stand up and smile at this boy and shake his hand and wish him a good day so that he does not suspect he has something to hide.

His father will know. He already knows the story of the soldier whose heart was shattered by a piece of shrapnel from an exploding shell when he returned to the trench for his friend who was paralysed there. He may even know Sam's name. A name he will forever associate with Verdun.

The words Sam finds to excuse himself are these: "I hope Christmas arrives before you know it."

He looks into the boy's eyes as they shake hands and the boy replies eagerly, "Maybe someone will mail you a package, sir."

As Sam walks away, he turns back one time to make sure the boy is not watching him and wondering. "Tommy Falcon," he says to himself as he watches the boy make his way up the road to begin his work day, lost inside his father's coat. Oddly, Sam wants to call to him. Call him back so he can tell him something that his father will never know about what happened at the river Marne. One end of the metal shard that was shaped like the twisted handle of a spoon and that tore the opening in Ned's heart came to rest against one of his ribs, and the other end lay beside a tuft of grass the size of a penny that held one small piece of the faded shell of a robin's egg.

search

Sam has just stepped inside the front door of the castle when Oliver rushes towards him with a look of panic in his eyes, a look that Sam knows well, and it seems for a split second that the war has returned to claim him. "I've looked everywhere," he cries. "I can't find him."

They set off together and walk down every street in town while Oliver explains that Lansdale had been talking about going home. "Twice yesterday, he told me that he thought it would be best just to go home and let everyone see him the way he is. I tried to make him understand that he couldn't do that."

Shopkeepers are just opening their doors to a new day. None of them has seen a man with his face bandaged and they regard Sam and Oliver suspiciously. At the station, the man who has been on duty through the night saw no one. "Are you sure?" Oliver asks him again. The second time, the man answers, "Bleeding Christ, man, I'm not blind."

They climb into the hills beyond the town, resting every few hundred yards so Oliver can catch his breath. He bends over at the waist, with his hands on his knees. "We have to make this work here, Sam. It's a long road, but if we lose Lansdale, I'm afraid that the people who came up with this idea will give up on us. I don't want that to happen. And we're being watched. If we fail with Lansdale, there will be no place for these poor sods to go for help."

The trail they are taking leads into a forest where the trees are thick enough to block out the blades of morning light. It feels like dusk as they walk along and the only sound is the wind tossing the trees except when they take turns calling out, "Sergeant Lansdale!" every few moments. They can both tell by the tone of each other's voices that they do not expect to be answered.

They have walked a long way when Oliver decides to ask him about Ned. "Tell me about your friend," he says as if this is the most natural thing in the world to ask, and when Sam doesn't answer, he goes on. "I've lost too many friends myself. Sometimes I feel like I'm cursed. Do you feel that way?"

"Maybe I do," Sam answers, because *cursed* is exactly how he feels.

"People say it gets easier as time passes, but that's not necessarily true."

"We were like brothers," Sam says. Their eyes meet and he can tell that Oliver is both surprised and encouraged that they are finally talking about Ned.

"He was one of those people you think the world can never destroy," he says.

"There's no one that war can't destroy, son. The weak, the strong, they all fall. But it can help to talk about these things."

"How? You just said it won't get any easier."

"Not easier. But talking can help us make sense of these things."

"How do you make sense of something that was senseless? The whole war is senseless."

"You're right there. War only makes sense to the men who plan it and never fight themselves. It makes such perfect sense that they can't resist doing it over and over, no matter how enlightened they believe they've become. My personal opinion is that history will condemn our commanders who ordered men to advance in frontal attacks and be mowed down by machine guns. They'll be condemned for lack of imagination at the very least."

"I never would have gone if I'd had a choice," Sam says.

"Who took away your choice then?"

They look at each other for a moment.

"I promised his wife that I would look out for him."

"That's another thing that is believed only by people who aren't there. You know that there is no logic to it. No one can look out for anyone. It's just luck in the end. Good luck or bad luck."

"That sounds like the philosophy of a gambler, not a man of faith," Sam tells him.

"Tell me what faith means to you, Sam."

"Why are you asking me? You must have had faith. You must have believed all of it in order to become a pastor."

"I suppose I did. Perhaps because it was easier than not believing. Just as it was easier for you to go to war than having to explain to everyone why you didn't go."

"What do you believe now?"

"What I believe is that life is amazing."

"Amazing?"

"It's amazing to me, the things that happen in people's lives. Just look at your life and how old are you, son?"

"Twenty-four."

"Twenty-four and you've already lived so much life." Oliver pauses with this thought before he says, "You must have been very frightened."

"I wasn't afraid," Sam replies. "After the first day, I told myself that I was already dead."

Oliver nods his head. He has heard this before. It is the common denominator of the soldiers who are bravest in battle. "You cheated death," he says. "And then you decided to take your own life. Why?"

"I wanted the pain to end."

"Of course you did. You lost your closest friend. And you felt responsible because he'd come back to the trench for you."

There it is, Oliver thinks. Now Sam will know that he knows his story and that he has accepted it as the truth. He wants Sam to believe this despite his own doubts. And he can tell that this is immediately satisfying to the young man. His story has caught on and proved sturdy enough to follow behind him all the way from France. His story has become the truth and this is satisfying to him.

"Someday you're going to have to talk about what happened," Oliver tells him.

"Talk about what?"

"What I see in your eyes."

With that, Oliver is on his feet again. Determined to leave it there. To push no further.

"What?" Sam asks. "What do you see in my eyes?"

Oliver glances at him, as if he might answer this question. "When you're ready, we'll talk."

"Ready for what?"

"In time, Sam," he says again as he starts walking. "All in good time."

Lansdale isn't running away. He isn't running anywhere. They know this as soon as they see him. It has taken almost the whole day for them to find him squatting on the ground beneath a stand of beech trees. He has stripped off all his clothes and there is blood smeared on his hands and arms from the small animals he has killed with a knife and fork from the kitchen. His head is bowed over the dead squirrel and rabbit and he is gently rocking on his heels, forward and back, forward and back, in a steady cadence. There is something so exquisite and compelling about the composition of this image that Sam can feel the pathway opening in his mind where the shapes and textures and colours begin to sort themselves out. It happened to him so many times in the war. It is nothing less than his mind preparing him to capture the image. It has been happening to him this way since he was five years old. It is both his curse and his blessing that he is not able to walk past an image like this and that he must process it at the deepest part of his mind. And his heart. He can feel it in his heart, like something dull being dragged across it. It is always the same feeling. And that is when he knows that he has the ability to transform the image into something meaningful.

Oliver steps in and disrupts the image to gently pull Lansdale to his feet. Together, he and Sam dress him. Before they leave the woods, Lansdale buries the animals. It is then, as they watch, that Sam knows what he will do to help this man.

That night, Sam stares at Lansdale's photograph for hours, trying to find what is in the picture that you don't see until you bear down on the image hard enough to make the real world outside the photograph less real than the world of the picture. A world Sam enters.

At a glance, there is nothing remarkable about Lansdale and the girl standing at his side. But there is always something that defines the subject. It is something that Sam has learned to identify and to trust. It is his way of seeing that separates him from the rest of the world and that he has not lived long enough to fully comprehend.

He takes his paints and brushes and easel up to his room and stands in front of the tall mirror that he and Oliver had carried from Lansdale's room. The overhead light and the bedside lamp are adequate. And with the first brushstroke, he is sure.

By morning, he has painted Lansdale's face on the mirror. It is a perfect rendering and when Lansdale stands in front of the mirror, Sam can hear the breath rush from the man's lungs. He pulls his shoulders back and turns slightly from side to side like a man trying on a new suit of clothes. Then he stands motionless for several minutes and in the silence, Sam can feel him assenting.

"We're all wearing masks," Sam says, and he lays a hand on Lansdale's shoulder to reassure him. "We almost never take them off."

Lansdale nods his bandaged head. "Can you make me look like that, Sam?" he asks.

"I will make you look just like that," Sam tells him.

calipers

It was only an abstraction to Sam before – that horrible image the nurse at the Red Cross station must have encountered when she stared at the sutured pouch of flesh between the lieutenant's thighs where his private parts had hung. The flesh drawn together like an empty leather change purse. The human body transformed to a grotesquerie. But the moment he unwraps Lansdale's bandages and sees his wounds in full, it is no longer an abstraction at all. The horror makes it very real. Until this moment, he might have believed that what he saw in France had numbed him so that nothing like this could ever reach him. He has just raised his calipers to make the first measurement when he feels everything in his stomach roaring up into his throat, and he rushes to the sink to vomit. He gags twice before he manages to catch his breath. "Must have been something you ate," he hears Lansdale call to him through his laughter. It is this laughter that Sam is most grateful for.

"You owe me for that one, soldier," he says when Sam resumes his work.

"I do," he answers. "I'm sorry."

"I did the same thing," he says. "Not to worry."

Not to worry, Sam thinks. What he *is* worrying about is that Lansdale will be able to discern what he is thinking once again – that this poor man would be far better off dead. That the merciful thing to do would be to put him out of his misery with a bullet to the back of his head like a farm animal, or to send him to eternal sleep with an injection of cyanide. Where are the generals who cooked up this war that mutilated Lansdale's face? Sitting behind their big desks out of harm's way, of course. It occurs to Sam that *Oliver* must know their names. *Oliver* must know where they go for lunch each day at their private clubs in London. Maybe Sam will drive a hard bargain with him and demand to know where they live. He will do what he has been ordered to do here and then, before he leaves, he will get their names so that he can spend the rest of his life tracking them down and murdering them one at a time. But murder would be too easy. What he prefers is some way of making certain that these men behind their big desks are haunted by Lansdale's mangled face, and by the faces of every other soldier who comes here. Maybe it is his duty to memorise their mutilated faces and to paint them all and then to one day fill a gallery. A memorial to war unlike any that England has ever seen, to put the lie to whatever cemeteries will one day line the fields of France and Belgium and England. Cemeteries with handsome crosses that complete the deception. They make it possible to believe that God has simply called these men home. *What God?* Sam wonders. *The same God who sanctioned their murder? Let me paint their ruined faces on their gravestones and it will be enough to make even God turn away.*

It is his anger that enables Sam to finish his work this morning, covering what is left of Lansdale's face with petroleum jelly and then laying on the first wet strips of gauze that he has soaked in plaster and warm water. What they talk about during these hours is the future. It begins with Lansdale telling him that if he lives to be the age his grandfather is now, he will live another sixty-one years. "Can you imagine 1977?" he exclaims, adding, "1977. Do you suppose anything will be left of the world by then?"

What a question, Sam thinks.

"My God, I can't imagine there will be, can you?" Lansdale

exclaims. "Cars will be faster, I guess. Tyres will be better so they don't puncture every thirty miles. What else? They say the next war will be in the air instead of the mud."

"That sounds better," Sam says.

They have an hour to just pass the time while the plaster turns hard enough for Sam to take the cast off Lansdale's face. "So, they let you out of the war so you could come here and do some good then. It's almost enough to make you think not all the mucky-mucks who run the show are bleeding idiots. I don't want to pry, but can you tell me what happened to you in France?"

Sam is inserting two-inch-long straws in the plaster for the nostrils, around which he will shape the nose. With each moment that passes, an intimacy establishes itself that Sam does not want to defile with his lie.

"Were you with your friend when he died?"

"I was."

"You blame yourself. For surviving, I mean."

"I suppose I do." Sam is thinking – *Well, at least you don't have to feel guilty for surviving. Compared to what you are going to have to live with, the dead should feel guilty.*

"It's just war, Sam. If you need to blame someone, blame the bastards on the other side. And he had a wife waiting for him?"

"Yes. And a child. He and his wife had a little daughter. *Have* a daughter, I mean. Two weeks old when we left. Now probably walking and speaking."

"Jesus. That's rough. My girl and I always talked about having a lot of kids. I wonder how that's going to work out now. You know what I mean? I figured that I would either die in the war or get through without a scratch. Was it the same with you?"

"Pretty much."

"What can you tell me?"

"About what?"

"About where you are now. I mean, when it comes to living on."

"I don't really know about that. I'm just here with you."

"My father was in the Boer War like Oliver. He told me that all men return home with secrets. Your friend's secrets died with him. Yours are safe with me." Lansdale waits patiently. Respectfully.

"I don't want to go home," Sam tells him. "I don't want to see her."

"Your friend's wife?"

"That's right. I haven't written to her since…"

"Does she know where you are?"

"No one knows where I am."

"Better that way. Easier, I guess. Everyone at home thinks I'm in hospital recovering from my wounds. I imagine you could be some comfort to her, though? Being her husband's best friend."

"I don't know what I would say to her."

"You're afraid of what she will ask you?"

"Yes."

"You don't want to keep the truth from her, but you don't want to be the one to tell her something she will never be able to forget?"

"That's it. Yes."

"I think about that, you know? At home, will I always be trying to keep my secrets safe? Will I always be hiding something from everyone? Is that any way to live?"

A way to live, Sam thinks. He quotes Oliver then: "Everyone has to find a way to live, Oliver says."

"You're speaking about his wife and the little girl?"

"I guess I am."

"People forget. Time rolls on," Lansdale says. "She'll meet someone new. And that new man will be the only father the little girl ever remembers as she grows up. The dead have no claim on the living. What is it that makes us think we can't be replaced? It's entirely possible that Amy has already met someone new. When I would read her letters, I was always trying to see beyond the words she wrote. It's excruciating, isn't it, though – the thought of another bloke touching her the way I did? I believed that she belonged to me. What makes a man believe such foolishness? No one belongs to anyone."

Sam can hear the despair seeping into Lansdale's sentences. The despair that must have torn through him as he slaughtered the animals in the woods. Oliver has told him that it is the despair that must be drained from him before he returns home.

"Before the war, who were you, Sam?"

"No one," he replies.

"Same with me. I was no one, wanting to become someone. Like everyone else, I suppose. That's probably the reason I went off to the war – so I wouldn't be *no one* forever."

Sam turns away to his workbench. "You're not going to be able to talk for a while," he tells him as he shapes a slice of an apple in the approximate size of Lansdale's mouth with a paring knife, then sets it carefully in place in the wet plaster gauze. At first it isn't precise enough to create a hole that will naturally accommodate the shape of Lansdale's lips. He removes it and shaves it until it's perfect.

potatoes

All she asks is that he is kind and gentle. At nearly fifty yards away, he could be anyone. He could be the boy who was to meet her here at this farmhouse and marry her. There is something about the way he moves in space, with tentative steps as if the ground is trembling beneath his feet, and his shoulders pitched forward slightly so that his head is bowed. This tells her that he is vulnerable in the same way she is, and that she has nothing to fear from him. He has not been sent to arrest her for her part in the uprising that is now being called the Easter Rebellion, that failed so miserably on the streets of Dublin just seven weeks ago. Her uncle Connolly was wounded in the post office building before he was later shot by a firing squad of British soldiers, along with others whose names she has read in the newspapers. Names that so far have not included Brian Callahan. In truth, she knows that she was a fool to trust him. To trust any of them, or their dreams of independence. They left her here alone for more than a year with the scraps of linen in the hem of her wedding dress. What kind of men would do such a thing to a nineteen-year-old girl who was just trying to be – *to be what?* She was just trying to be what they wanted her to be. She was just trying to do what was expected of her, the way she always had from the time she was wee, when she first began to understand that it was a man's world. If you had trousers on, then you counted for something and you were not told what to do. You made your own decisions. You determined your own fate. Her fate had been to hide inside this dusty old house for all these months, peering out the windows at anyone who approached, wondering if this was the person who had been sent to finally tell her what had happened and what was expected of her now.

But as the boy draws closer, she can tell that he is not going to tell her anything she doesn't already know. She can tell that he is in the dark just as she is.

And then she recognises his face.

Or, at least, she seems to recognise his face. He sees this as she opens the door. "You were in the lighthouse," she says. And she is aware that she is accusing him of something. Trespassing, perhaps, though he doesn't seem capable of this. He doesn't seem capable of committing any violation. "Well then, what is it you want?"

He looks surprised by her question. And when he answers, "Potatoes," she nearly laughs out loud.

"Well, that's not a great deal to ask for," she tells him, "but I have no potatoes. It's the next farm just beyond the stone wall that you must be looking for. The owners are feeding me and most of the town from what I can tell."

He looks so confused and frightened that she keeps talking just to try to say something that will reassure him. "I saw you in the lighthouse. And you saw me. You saw me in my wedding dress."

Even this is not enough to make him raise his head and look into her eyes. She takes a deep breath. Off in the distance, fat black clouds are shouldering their way across the sky above the sea. She is aware that she is walking a fine line here with exasperation on one side and curiosity on the other. It would be simple to turn him away. To send him back to wherever he came from. And then he would be no more to her than just another boy who had brushed against her life before he disappeared. She watches him standing in front of her, shifting his weight anxiously from one foot to the other, with his head still bowed. What is he waiting for? He is like a little boy waiting for instructions from his mother. Go wash up before supper. Don't go clomping through the house with those muddy boots on! He doesn't look like he's been out of his mother's care for too long. *Or maybe he is just slow*, she thinks. And then she decides that is it. There is something wrong with him, something broken inside him. A boy who climbs up lighthouses alone and looks at girls trying on their wedding dresses. Maybe she isn't the first girl he has spied on that way. Maybe he is from around here and had first climbed up into the lighthouse as a little boy to gaze down into the house.

Maybe he has returned for a reason that has nothing to do with potatoes. Maybe he is as curious about her as she is about him.

Still, she knows it will be best to set her curiosity aside. Far better to do that than to start to believe in another boy who will just end up disappointing her. Far better to turn him away than to start down that path once more that led to her being disappointed with herself. For much of the past thirteen months, she has considered just how many more times she can be disappointed in herself before it becomes an affliction that will prevent her from ever trusting her judgement again. She has wondered if there is a line you can cross in that regard, and once you have crossed it, you are never able to cross back.

Yes, better to send him on his way.

Better perhaps.

But not easier.

She feels like screaming at him. And she might have screamed if he had not reached inside his coat pocket and taken out a small book that he then holds open for her to see the page where he has sketched her in her wedding dress, framed in the broad, curved window of the lighthouse. He keeps his eyes averted while she takes the book from him and stares at this picture of herself.

"Look at me," she says. "You wouldn't know by this

drawing that I was a foolish girl, would you?" And then she sees that he is looking at her. And she sees something resting deep in his brown eyes. Something she cannot comprehend, but whatever it is makes her feel calm for the first time since she jumped from the deck of the ship and fell through the air, into the sea. Until this moment, she had not realised that she was still falling.

BOOK III

notification

It is the first Sunday in July of 1916, and from the front window, Katie stands behind the lace curtain and watches them make their way up the hill under a cloudless sky towards the station in Dorchester with their heads bowed like mourners. Her father has begun to look frail and old for the first time. These visits are difficult for him, she knows. His companion, Doris, wore a new pleated dress for their visit today and Katie knows that it is to be some kind of signal that she too must begin to get over her husband's death. The dress with its gaudy red belt and yellow flowers delighted Charlotte and assaulted Katie in equal measure. She has not had the heart to tell her father that these visits always leave her feeling so lonely she wishes they would never return. She much prefers to be left alone in her grief so she doesn't have to summon the terrible, statuesque reticence that the bereaved in this country seem to pride themselves on, and pretend that she is going to be all right for the sake of everyone off fighting the war, or home waiting for news from loved ones.

Now with the child down for her afternoon nap, Katie takes the notice from her bedside table and reads the words again:

Army form B10482 April 1. 1916
Madam (It is my painful duty to inform you that a
report has this day been received from the War Office
notifying the death of)

(No.) 19747
(Rank) private
(Name) Ned William Morse
(Regiment) Royal Lancashire
(which occurred at) Verdun France
(on the) 22nd (of) February 1916
(and I am to express to you the sympathy and regret
of the Army Council at your loss.) (The cause of
death was) killed in action.

By his Majesty's command, I am to forward the
enclosed message of sympathy from Their Gracious
Majesties the King and Queen. I am at the same
time to express the regret of the Army Council at the
soldier's death in his Country's service.

I am to add that any information that may be received
as to the soldier's burial will be communicated to
you in due course.

Application regarding the disposal of any such
personal effects, or of any amount that may eventually
be found to be due to the late soldier's estate, should
be addressed to: "Secretary, War Office, London,
S.W." and marked outside "Effects".

I am, Madam,
Your obedient Servant,
Sgt. Larsen
District. 3
Officer in charge of records

By now she has each word memorised. She closes her eyes and reads them like the words of a prayer, recalling the soft sound the letter made when it fell through the letter box in the cottage door to the tiled floor two months before. A sound as delicate and intimate as a whispered kiss. And how she saw the postman hurry away up the brick path before she could reach the door. She never blamed him for this. In fact, she was grateful that he had granted her privacy even though he was probably still close enough to the door to hear her scream in anger when she realised that Ned had been dead for weeks before she had been notified. It made her imagine piles and piles of bodies that someone had to climb through to identify. Nets on a dock filled with fish is the picture that came to her consciousness.

The words, she knows, except for Ned's name and number, could be describing anyone from his unit who died at the same place, on the same day, and could appear on all these letters to survivors. *Is that what I am now*, she has wondered, *a survivor?* A survivor once again. She was three years old when her mother died and it was easy then to believe what her father and others told her, that her mum was waiting for her in heaven to join her at the end of her own life. This is different. Now she wonders what it means to be a wife who has survived her husband's death. She has questions about this that she knows she will never share with anyone because they are much too private. But almost from the moment she learned of Ned's death, she began to recall the closeness they had shared at the start of their marriage, before the strange darkness began to haunt her after Charlotte's birth. It was a darkness that somehow seemed to diminish her affection for him and replace it with disapproval.

For some reason, it is what they shared *physically* that haunts her. The way she quickly began to wait for Ned to touch her again after he touched her the first time. How surprising this anticipation was to her. That she could spend whole days waiting for this as she had never waited for anything before. His touch had set something turning inside her that made her reach for his hand whenever he was near her. No one ever spoke of these things, but she had found a book in the library that explained it partially with a calendar that showed how a woman in her childbearing years will feel a certain desire each month just before her bleeding begins when she is ovulating. This was as close as she came to understanding why she wanted to pull Ned into her and why she wanted to pour her desire on him. Really what she wanted was to incorporate his body into hers so that there was no margin of space between them. In the days when her longing for him was just beginning to familiarise itself inside her, she often felt slightly off balance. Needing someone for the first time had changed the ontology of her life. And it seemed that nothing would ever be the same again for her. She had been frightened of what it meant *to need Ned* the way she suddenly did. Ever since his death, she has caught herself looking at couples wherever she goes, trying to discern the governing dynamic of their love stories. Does he touch her the same way Ned touched me? And does she wrap her legs around him and arch her back to try to draw him deeper, closer? She never spoke with Ned about these great changes she was experiencing, though once she had awakened him in the night and whispered to him, "Why do I want you this way?" As if he might know the answer to this question that she should have been able to answer herself. He had simply smiled at her. His triumphant smile. And why shouldn't he have been triumphant about this? After all, he had won her so completely. *But what happens now?* she wondered.

She sits at the dining room table, folding the letter and ironing its creases while she wonders if her deep feelings would have lasted with Ned. Would the two of them have become like the married couples who seem never to need to touch? How well do you need to know someone before you can talk about these things? Are they the things her mother would have talked with her about if she had not died? And what language would she have to learn to be able to talk with Charlotte about these things when she comes of age? How will she ever describe for her this period of time when their lives were turned inside out? There were the four letters from Ned and Sam in the early autumn of 1914, in the weeks after they had gone to war. Then there were those terrible months with no word when she suspected Sam and her husband were both dead. That was the time of Charlotte's screaming that stopped one morning as suddenly as it had begun soon after Finn left her life in May of 1915. Over a year ago. Instead of crying, the child began smiling at her in the most comforting way so that Katie began telling Charlotte everything. And, as if to bless this new companionship, at the same time, letters from Ned and Sam began reaching her again. Apparently, there had been some mix-up at a depot in France, but soon enough, the old letters arrived with new ones and Katie read them all aloud to the child, over and over, when she put her down for the night, as one would read bedtime stories, until all of that ended suddenly with the notification of Ned's death.

She tells Charlotte everything, knowing that she is too young to understand and to remember. She tells her all her secrets. She confesses all her fears to her. Except for one. The one that especially troubles her when she is in her father's presence as she has been today. She is afraid that because he knows her so well, he knows that before the war killed Ned, she was often afraid that she would lose him to another girl. She was afraid because she had already felt him withdrawing from her. She thinks about the way he used to take her face in his hands when he was making love to her at the start of their married life, and how he stopped doing that eight months later. She was keeping track of the number of times he made love to her. She was already testing his desire for her in small ways like the way she walked through a room or hesitated when she dressed in front of him. There was something disturbing about how the more she gave herself to him, the more she wanted him, and the less he seemed to want her. That wasn't fair. And she was afraid it would only grow worse. This bothered her so much that she contemplated speaking with Sam about it. He was the only person to whom she had ever felt comfortable confiding her fears. Because she knew that he would never judge her harshly. He loved her too much for that. Dear Sam, who now would blame himself for failing to keep his promise to her to bring Ned home. They had spoken of this just days before they left for France.

"He is going to need to be a hero," she had said to him. "And you must tell him that I don't need him to be a hero. And neither does his daughter. We just want him to come home to us. Promise me, Sam."

"I promise," he said.

He had said this with such a serious expression that she realised what she thought was a simple request was not simple at all. They were sitting on the porch. The stars above them were close. And for the first time, she recognised the difference between loving someone and being in love. *There it is*, she thought. Ned was already beginning to love her and to no longer be *in love* with her. Meaning that, if he had lived, if he had survived the war, then one day he would be touched by someone, but it wouldn't be her. It would be someone new. But none of that mattered now that Ned was gone. All that mattered was that he was dead because she had betrayed him by consorting with the shepherd boy. And if there was a God who had taken her husband, then he had taken Sam as well.

benches

She has told Sam that her name is Lily, and as he bends low
over his workbench where he has clamped the mask in a vice
beside a bright lamp, smoothing the plaster with a tiny strip of
wet sandpaper wrapped around the tips of two fingers on his
right hand, he thinks about this girl and how he wants to return
to her just to be in the presence of her innocence. Whoever
she is, whatever she has experienced, her innocence is intact
and it is intoxicating to him. And that thing she said about
herself, that *she was foolish*, there is something irresistible
about that as well, because he has felt the same thing is true
about himself. Thinking back now to the way her eyes lit
up and she nearly laughed when he said he was looking for
potatoes makes him feel that if he spends enough time in the
presence of her innocence, he might forget the boot he picked
up with a foot still in it, and the squealing horse racing across
no man's land between the trenches whose ears had been set
on fire.

* * *

While Sam works, Lansdale and Oliver play chess in the
library. It has been a clement day and they have opened all
the windows on the first floor to let some warm air blow
through the rooms. Earlier, wearing a battered brown silk

bowler hat and his most respectable tweed jacket, Oliver presented himself at the council meeting in town to settle a matter concerning the benches in the village square. Now as he sits across from Lansdale and his wrapped head, he thinks that he did the right thing by pressing the issue with the town council. He had petitioned them quite forcefully to set aside two of the benches for the soldiers from the castle. He suggested that the benches be painted blue as opposed to the others that were dark green, and mothers with their children would be advised to stay clear of the blue benches to spare the children exposure to horrors, and soldiers the embarrassment of being stared at. One of the council members had vociferously opposed. "Why couldn't the resident soldiers restrict themselves to the grounds at the castle? Townspeople go to the square for a few minutes' escape from the war that is suffocating them in their homes."

Oliver had pressed hard, explaining that the soldiers needed to learn to be part of the flow of normal life again so that they could regain their self-confidence. And everyone knew how unintentionally cruel small children can be, simply because they are curious. Saying this had been a mistake on his part because it only undermined his argument for the soldiers to be assimilated into the town. "Do you imagine these men in the pubs and shops as well?" he was asked.

"Indeed, I do," he replied. "I want them to learn to move freely in your beautiful town so that they may do the same when they return home."

Someone suggested they wear some kind of armband that could be spotted at a distance so people could give them a wide berth. Oliver objected. "They're already marked men. I don't want to give them one more reason to feel they aren't normal, and like everyone else who is just trying to go about their lives."

In the end, he got his way at the meeting but not without a good deal of haggling and finally a rather stern rebuke to remind the council members that they enjoyed the privilege of living a peaceful existence in this town because of the extreme sacrifices made by soldiers. None greater than those men who had become horribly disfigured by the war that was going to disrupt and destroy the lives of a whole generation, who gave up their peaceful existence in order to protect the rest of us from tyranny. He considered it a small triumph that the room was silent when he finished. He did not stay around for the small talk that would follow.

"You and I will have some painting to do in town soon," he tells Lansdale.

"My father used to tell me I was hopeless with a paintbrush," he says.

"Well, you can always learn, sergeant. It requires a certain measure of patience. Like this game."

He watches Lansdale move his knight on the board, then check for threats before he takes his hand off the piece and looks up at him. "I'm sorry about what happened the other day," Lansdale says.

"Out in the woods, you mean?"

"Yes, sir."

"Yes, I'm sure you are. But we all do things we're sorry for. And in your case, feeling sorry is a sign of healing. But we must talk about what happened. Did you know where you were? I mean, did you realise that you were here in this place, and not in France?"

"Yes. Yes, I believe I did."

"And were you angry?"

"No," he says, bowing his head.

"Look at me, please." Oliver waits for him to lift his head, then thanks him. "It's important for you to always look into the other man's eyes."

"Yes, of course."

"You're still the same man you were before the war, Sergeant Lansdale. You must do your utmost to keep this in mind at all times."

"Just so, sir."

"Tell me then what you were feeling."

"I think I just wanted to see what I would feel. When I killed that squirrel, I wanted to feel bad about it. I never could kill anything on the farm. That's what prompted my father to tell me that I wouldn't make a good soldier. I could never slaughter a pig. Maybe I wanted to prove my father wrong. I guess that's part of it."

"And when you were in the woods, when you were killing the animal, was your father there with you?"

He nods his head slowly. A moment passes and then he is crying.

Oliver takes hold of his wrist and grips it for a little while. "You are your own man," he tells him. "There's nothing more that you have to prove to your father, or to anyone. Do you believe me?"

Lansdale nods silently before he speaks again. "I did feel sorry when I killed the animals. It made me feel ashamed."

"All right then," Oliver says. "That's a good sign. It means your conscience has survived. Conscience is the first casualty of war, son. A man has to build his life upon what he brings home from war, but without his conscience, it's a feckless proposition. So, there's reason for us to be hopeful."

"I have to tell you, sir, that I'm worried."

"I know you're worried. You're entitled to be worried. But you have to keep going. You have work to do here in this place. Much is at stake. Not just for you but for all the men who will follow you here."

"I hope that I don't let everyone down."

"Don't think about everyone else. Think about yourself now. This is a time in your life when you're permitted to be selfish. It's only fair, after what you've been through."

Lansdale seems to be thinking this over. Then he speaks again. "I'm mostly worried about what this is going to do to Amy. I've been thinking that I should write to her and tell her I'm not coming home."

"We'll talk about that, son," Oliver tells him. "We'll have

a long talk about that soon." In his mind, he believes that once Lansdale's mask is finished and once he grows comfortable wearing it, then they will talk about his girl.

Later that night, after he has stopped at the bottom of the stairs and listened to Lansdale talking to Amy in his room, Oliver stands outside the workshop watching Sam shaping a piece of tin over the plaster mould. He has been working for eight or ten hours by now. He thinks of entering the room, or making Sam a cup of tea. But he is so engrossed in his work, and it is such a beautiful thing to observe, that he is unable to move away from the window.

Oliver can't deny that he is drawn to this young man and to what has been broken in him. And he feels uneasy as he considers the secret that he is keeping from him. All his life he has hated secrets. You place two people in a room and one of them has a secret he's sworn to keep from the other, and soon enough, you have a conflict with one person fighting to expose the secret and the other fighting to protect it. And for what purpose? Usually, it is just vanity or pride or greed or one kind of stubborn desire or another guarding the secret.

It has never been easy for him to be deceitful. He has always prided himself in his honest and fair treatment of people, regardless of their station in life. For him it is a simple matter of living by the scripture he has heard his father preaching from the time he was a small boy. *Do unto others as you would have them do unto you.*

But now he has entered a peculiar region of his life that makes him feel like a stranger to himself. He accepted a commission to run this operation at the castle for king and country because he believed that the mission of rehabilitating broken soldiers was a noble one. Indeed, the moment he first learned what was to transpire here, he believed that he was not only the perfect man for the job but that his whole life had been a preparation to do this work. But when he was notified that the first artist assigned to him would be a soldier who had been condemned to death by a firing squad for cowardice during a forward advance into no man's land, he had immediately been suspicious. He knew the army's method of operations well enough to know that this soldier had been carefully selected for what someone high up in the chain of command had considered a good reason. It was really a simple matter of the chance to kill two birds with one stone. So his job, as it was presented to him, is therefore twofold: first, he is to make the soldier comfortable and do whatever is necessary to encourage his work in the production of masks. And second, he is to crack him open and get inside his psyche for the purpose of helping the army understand why certain men behave as cowards under fire. This has become a burgeoning problem in the trenches. In some units, it is near epidemic levels. Answers have to be found and remedies applied as quickly as possible. The report on Sam made clear that his cowardice had caused his friend's death. He had been paralysed in the trench and his friend had returned and pulled him out just as a shell exploded and took the brave soldier's life. This had compelled the coward to try to take his own life on two occasions, first at the front, and then in hospital.

Oliver's instinct had been to refuse to be part of this secret inquisition for either king or country, or both. But by the time he learned of it and read Sam Burke's file, he had already seen the photographs of Lansdale's pitiful face that had left him desperate to do something. And so he agreed to play this role.

Tonight, as he watches Sam pouring himself into his work, he feels a deep and disturbing regret that borders on a sense that he is doomed internally for what he is taking part in. He can barely catch his breath as he settles into his chair and waits for the first drops of ether to transport him to the bottom of the world.

teacup

"We're not going to worry ourselves at all about this," Lily tells Sam as she takes hold of both his hands and leads him inside the front door of the farmhouse when he returns to her. She feels his resistance. He is pulling back from her, but she will not take *no* for an answer. Not now. Not after she has told him all her secrets the last time he was here. By confiding in him, she has made him an accomplice in the role she played in the failed rebellion. She has told him that it is only a matter of time before they will come looking for her here. Unless Brian comes for her first.

She has told him about Brian. It took her only a few minutes to tell everything she knows about him. She has described the three weeks they shared in New York City. The walks they took. The afternoon they went to the bridal shop to buy the dress. How they sewed the scraps of linen into the hem. How he told her nothing. And then how she made him tell her everything. If he is still alive, he will come for her and take her away from here. If he is dead, then she is sitting here for no reason and is only making it easier for the British authorities to find her.

She makes Sam a cup of tea and this time she folds a small handkerchief and places it on the saucer to keep the teacup from rattling the way it did the last time she made him tea. His hand was trembling and she could tell that it embarrassed him.

She sits beside him at the table and says, "This is our time now, Sam. This is all we have."

The last time, they made it almost to the staircase that led to her tiny bedroom before he stopped and apologised. Her eyes were already on the stairs and she was already imagining the two of them climbing the steps together, being drawn on by a feeling they shared. It was the sharing that she wanted most. And the warmth of him. She wanted to draw on that warmth and to give it back to him in a greater portion.

She is wondering if she might make him laugh, if that will make things easier. "It will be as easy as shelling peas," she says. "That's what my best friend, Cara, told me the morning after her wedding night." She says this with a smile, but his expression doesn't change. Whatever he has been through in his war has left him with a far-off look in his eyes that seems to reflect from some place that has been hollowed out inside him. She can't help but imagine the worst. That he might have been wounded so that he can't be with a girl again. If he ever was at all.

A moment passes. And then she says, "We have arms, Sam. Can't we hold each other and just invent a world together? We can pretend, can't we? For just a few hours. It must be a little like dancing. Surely you've danced before." She is aware that she is chattering away like a magpie. Each thing she says is another key that she is trying to fit in the lock. "When I was a little girl, do you know what I used to pretend? I used to pretend that I lived in a place where there were no potatoes. I did. I really did. And that's why I laughed when you first came looking for potatoes. I despised potatoes because we had them at every bloody meal. So I made up a place where apricots replaced all the potatoes. I loved apricots. I'd only had them once at my nana's, on my birthday. Her sister had sent them from London. But they were the best thing I'd ever tasted. And whenever I sat down to more potatoes, I just pretended they were apricots with that beautiful orange colour."

There is something sad about the way that he is just taking

this all in, all this nonsense that he seems to be listening to and even concentrating on as if she were telling him something deeply meaningful. She can tell by his expression that it has nothing to do with her. She could be anyone babbling away like this. He could be listening to anyone telling him anything and he would just sit there respectfully because it was easier than having to speak himself. As long as she keeps talking away, he will feel safe. She can tell this. And she can also tell that he has been raised properly by a mother who taught him to sit up straight and to always convey to people that you are interested in them and what they have to say.

She wonders about his mother for a moment as they sit in silence and she studies his face. What kind of woman is she? And is she waiting for this son of hers to come home, waiting someplace far away from here? He has told her nothing about himself and she has no reason to think such a thing, but she cannot help but imagine meeting her someday when he takes her home to tell her that this is the girl he met in Northern Ireland, in the farmhouse below the dunes where the lighthouse stood. *This is the girl I've written to you about, who somehow survived the sinking of the* Lusitania.

How silly of her to imagine such a thing. To picture a future. A new future to replace the one that she has lost across these last thirteen months of waiting.

Suddenly she is finished waiting. She sets her teacup on the round table, then turns to face him as she drops down on her knees just in front of him, close enough so she can then lay her head in his lap. She feels him trembling. She tells him that there is nothing for him to be afraid of. "Nothing at all," she says, barely whispering. She has a powerful sense that it is her turn now to get her life started again after all the hours she has sat alone in this house. "Let's not be afraid of anything ever again," she hears herself telling him. And then she sees the scar on his wrist. A fine white line where the skin is raised slightly. His hand is delicate and soft and this scar is the only imperfection on the beautiful body that his mother gave him. She runs her finger over the scar and looks up at him. His eyes have closed and she wonders if he might be praying, asking God for something. Maybe he is praying that she will stop touching him. But she has made her mind up. And whatever he has been through, whatever terrible things have happened to him, she feels quite certain that she can heal the broken part of him. She is just a girl, on her own, adrift in a world of secrets and mysteries, and yet she feels a power racing through her that he has confirmed in silence simply by returning to her the way he has. There is something he wants from her, something he longs for that he may not even be conscious of. It is beyond speaking. Beyond words. Even if she could find the words to describe the longing, she would not say them out loud. "Let's take a walk," she says instead. And he is immediately on his feet as if she has just set him free from something he was dreading. "You wanted to see New York City," she says to him as she takes both his hands in hers and leads him a few steps before she stops to describe what it was like to come in from the sea the morning she arrived at Ellis Island. The great Statue of Liberty rising up across the water. "I was surprised that she was green," she tells Sam. "Bright green." A few more steps to the foot of the stairs where she describes the Flatiron Building that rises into the sky almost 300 feet high, blocking out the sun at certain times of the day. "Here's the entrance, just here," she tells him. "Let's you and I go up and have a look from the top, shall we?"

She leads him up the stairs then, like a blind man. *The blind leading the blind*, she tells herself. *It will be as easy as shelling peas.*

On the landing, there is a circular window that looks north to where the lighthouse stands. She has never asked him before what it is that he does at the castle. And now, when she asks and he tells her, it takes all her willpower to suspend her disbelief and to believe him. To believe him is also to feel blessed in some way, for how many girls in the history of the world have taken a boy into their beds who made masks for men who have lost their faces?

This makes Lily believe in herself and in her place in the world in a way she never has before. Someday she will be telling this to someone when she is an old woman – *Think of it. The very first boy I ever made love to was an artist who made masks for soldiers who had lost their faces in the war.*

foyer

Here is where Katie sits at sunrise writing her first letter to her daughter. The early gold light of dawn slants in through the stained-glass window above the door, and spills across the tiled floor whose coolness she feels on the backs of her thighs. Here is where her boots once stood, caked in mud from the shepherd's field – in another lifetime that has receded from her, like something glimpsed briefly from the window of a moving train.

It was Mrs Tones, the grocer's wife, whom she barely knew at all, who suggested that she might better cope with her grief by writing everything she is feeling in letters to her daughter so that one day, when the child has grown, she will have an account of what transpired after her father's death.

Katie has tried to follow this counsel that she knows was given to her out of affection and concern, but something is keeping her from writing about herself. Maybe it is because her grief is slowly being outweighed now by her anger. Sometimes, all she can feel is anger, and in a strange way, it is the anger that is helping her cope with the grief. Anger consumes the grief to prevent the grief from consuming her. That seems fair enough. And why shouldn't she be angry that the minister was right, that her transgression has led to her husband's death? *Let there be a God*, she thought, *just so I have someone to be angry at.* This was far better than being angry at herself for allowing her girlhood to be laid to waste, for allowing herself to be transformed into a grieving woman. A widow. She is consciously holding on to her anger because she can sense that, once it passes, she will be drained of everything except the longing that will replace it. A longing that will define the rest of her life and that will cripple her.

There is also some pride or vanity involved. These things that she writes down now about herself when she is broken in pieces will be available for public consumption some day when they belong to Charlotte, after she has died. They will become the property of her daughter, and who could say what type of woman this little girl will turn out to be, or whom she might choose to share these letters with? The idea of being on display is intolerable to her. *Here on exhibit is a young woman who became unhinged.*

And so instead of writing about herself, she writes letters to the war department demanding to know where her husband's body was buried. Each time she sees the name of a government official in *The Times* who has anything to do with the war, she writes to him, always ending her letters with the same defiant sentence: *Until I have proof that my husband is dead, and I can stand at his grave and know where he is buried, I will continue to tell his daughter that he is coming home to her someday.*

The difficulty is that so many men are missing. In *The Times* each day, the families of the missing post small advertisements instructing how anyone who has information about their loved one should contact them. She knows exactly how desperate you have to be to believe even for a minute that this might actually lead somewhere. You place the notice in the newspaper and hope some other family in England reads it and writes to their son or husband in the war and asks if they know anything about your son or husband. It is like dropping a small pebble on the beach and then returning a year later to reclaim it. She knows that some of these men will never be found. Their bodies will be left to rot away until nothing remains of them that can be identified. Or they will be blown into tiny pieces by artillery fire from the Germans.

She wants Ned's body back even if it is in pieces that someone has collected with a shovel and placed in a sack. And she feels entitled to this. Ned's body. The body she chose to share with her own body for a few months. When she thinks of it this way, she always feels that Ned's body should be returned to his mother who had created it from her own body and caressed it and bathed it as she had Charlotte. Shouldn't all these men be returned to their mothers who were the first people to behold their majesty, the first people to hold them when they came into this world? The mothers who remembered them best when they were in all their glory, when their feet were as wide as they were long, little square feet you could wash in a teacup. And what a forsaken world it had turned out to be for these mothers. It makes her so angry that she can barely breathe. And in her anger, she thinks that the pieces of these dead boys *should* be returned to their mothers so that they can try to put them back together again. It is not a task she wishes to do herself, though she had used her time as Ned's wife to commit to memory every inch of his body. She did this consciously when war seemed inevitable because she knew that Ned would insist on going to fight in it.

The way he was so determined to get into the war had been the point of origin for her anger. How could he be so eager to leave her? How could he be so eager to leave their child? She had written to Sam about this at the Royal Academy in London, pleading with him to write to Ned and try to talk some sense into him. *Perhaps your father would hire Ned to work on the dairy farm so that he would not be required to go to war*, she had written in one letter to Sam. But she knew that this too was a hopeless proposition. Nothing would deter Ned.

She knew as well that nothing she could offer Ned matched the excitement he felt for the war. This made her even angrier, and determined to know what had happened to him. For months she had written letters to Sam that were unanswered.

His family did not know where he was and they suspected that soon they would be notified that he was missing. Which meant that he too was dead. But after Ned's death, she had never missed a single edition of the newspaper when the lists of the dead were printed; and because Sam's name had never appeared on these lists, against all reason, she posted a notice in the newspaper asking that anyone knowing the whereabouts of Sam Burke, an artist from the Royal Academy in London fighting in France, kindly contact her at once. A message in a bottle, dropped into the ocean.

moustache

A week of work, most of it tedious and solitary as Sam sculpts the plaster mould of Lansdale's face, leads to a moment in the workshop late at night when he peels off the man's bandages for the last time and places the mould on his face, hooking it on with arms from an old pair of spectacles that reach behind Lansdale's left ear and the stump that remains on the right side of his head. Sam is thinking that Lansdale will have to let his hair grow long to conceal the stump. This mould will be only temporary. The finished mask, made of copper and painted to capture all of Lansdale's features, will be held on the same way with a pair of gold-framed wire-rim government-issue glasses whose steel arms will be fused permanently to the copper.

Lansdale examines himself in a hand mirror. "It's going to be bloody easier to breathe, I can tell already," he says.

"Are you sure?" Sam asks him as he moves the plaster mask slightly to make certain the openings for his lips and what remains of his nose are perfect.

"Positive, old sport," Lansdale replies.

Sam hears the excitement in his voice and hesitates; he doesn't want to say anything to diminish Lansdale's enthusiasm. "I want you to wear it for a few days to make sure it fits properly," he tells him. "Then I'll need to borrow it for ten or twelve hours a day to build the copper mask to match it exactly. That will take maybe two weeks."

"I hope they're paying you well," Lansdale says.

Sam smiles at this. "I'll do most of my work at night while you're asleep. I'll want you to wear the copper mask to make sure you like the way it feels. Once we have it shaped perfectly, I'll start the painting. Are you all right with this mould being blank for all that time? Or, if you prefer, I could paint a little colour on it."

Lansdale moves his head from side to side while Sam adjusts the arms to make the mask more stationary. Suddenly, Lansdale asks him if he would be keen on a little fun.

"What do you have in mind?"

"I would like you to paint on the mould… Drum roll, please! The face of none other than Horatio Herbert Kitchener."

It catches Sam off guard and makes him laugh. "Secretary of state for war?"

"None other," Lansdale says giddily.

"Are you serious?"

"I am, Sam. Big bushy moustache and all. The way he looks on all the poster boards above the words *YOUR COUNTRY WANTS YOU!* I should think it would bring me great pleasure to stomp around this glorious ruin of a castle for the next few months impersonating the bugger."

"You could get us both in trouble," Sam objects mildly. In truth, he is already imagining the brushstrokes on the plaster to make Kitchener come to life.

"Fine," Lansdale says. "What are they going to do to us? Send us back to the front? I'll take my chances. How about you?"

Sam manages a short, wry laugh, but inside he feels something heavy and cold drop into the pit of his stomach. To steady himself, he tries picturing Lily's face, but instead he sees the horse with its ears on fire dancing in circles, flesh melting off its head. When he grimaces, Lansdale leans close and tries to apologise. He places his hand on Sam's arm.

"That was in poor taste, old chap."

Sam looks away, then turns back. A quiet deeper than silence falls over them. "Do you ever wish you were back there?" Sam asks.

It is a question that puzzles Lansdale at first, and then makes him contemplate its implications deeply. He leans back against the workbench. He bows his head. When Sam sees the mask slide down slightly from his forehead, he reaches forward and straightens it. "The arms aren't working properly," he complains. "I'm going to have to make some adjustments on the tin version."

"Do you?" he hears Lansdale ask, drawing Sam back to his own question.

"Some things were simpler there," Sam says.

"Living and dying were simpler," Lansdale remarks. "Separated by no more than a few seconds. Inches. And both were out of your control. The living and the dying, I mean. Now, the living part takes such an effort. I'd go back tomorrow if I could be guaranteed to be killed quickly by Fritz. One bullet, clean through the brain. Followed by a long, uninterrupted sleep."

Oliver has been lingering outside the open door to the workshop with a bottle of whiskey to mark the occasion and when he hears this, he immediately sets out to alter the mood, raising the bottle high into the air and exclaiming: "To the turret, gentlemen!"

There is a clear sky above them, and stars pierced with light. Under torchlight while they pass the bottle, they read the names. It takes well over an hour. There are 312 names, five of them quite familiar to Sam, and twice that number familiar to Lansdale. It takes so long to get through the list that they have nearly finished the whiskey, and Sam and Lansdale are drunk enough by the end, after they lead Oliver to his chair for the night, to stumble into town, and take a poster board of Kitchener off the wall of the train station above the locked ticket booth.

Back in the workshop, Lansdale sits in one chair wearing

his blank plaster mould with the poster of Kitchener propped up on another chair beside him.

The dominating feature in Kitchener's face is the bushy moustache and Sam paints this first while Lansdale seems to relax like a man in a barbershop having his hair trimmed. "Someday you'll have a girl talking to you about getting married the way Amy talked to me, old sport. Girls never seem to tire of that conversation, even though in most cases it's more of a monologue than a conversation. It's a fairy tale that appeals to them. Did you know that the Romans were the ones who began the ritual of throwing rice at the bride and groom? Actually, it began with wheat. But then they switched to rice. It's all meant to be a wish for fertility. There's nothing I don't know about weddings, thanks to Amy."

"How do you suppose she would feel being married to Horatio Herbert Kitchener?" Sam jokes.

"I don't think she's terribly fond of moustaches." He thinks about this in silence and then says, "But then again, Sam, what do I really know about her? She might have taken up with a moustache in the twenty-six months since I was with her. How would I ever know?"

Sam rushes to reassure him. "I'm sure she's kept a candle burning just for you."

"No, but honestly, Sam, how would I ever know unless someone told me? All we ever did was kiss and, you know, touch each other. I'm quite certain she was a virgin when I left her. Only been kissed by one other fellow at a charity fair in a church. But how would I know if she's still a virgin? I don't know anything about what goes on *down there*, do you? It's all a damned mystery to me."

It makes Sam uncomfortable to engage in this conversation, but he knows that Lansdale is waiting for him to join in. "Maybe it's better that way," he says. He is thinking how war had been a mystery to him before it revealed itself in unimaginable ways. "Maybe they keep it a mystery for our benefit."

"I guess it depends on the bloke," Lansdale goes on. "I

don't think personally it would make that much difference to me if she's a virgin or not. I could see myself marrying a widow who lost her husband. But I suppose the greatest advantage to marrying a virgin is that she doesn't have any kind of high expectations of you."

This makes both of them laugh.

"I'm no Don Juan myself, truth be told," Lansdale says. "I'd prefer not to be measured against someone who actually knew what he was doing. But I've been thinking about something else, Sam. Since it's probably true that most of the time when a girl and a fellow make love the room is dark, do you think I should keep the mask on, or take it off? What would you do?"

Keep it on, Sam thinks instantly. *Don't ever take it off!* But he keeps this thought to himself. And then, as he applies his brush to painting one of Kitchener's eyebrows on the mould, he decides that what Lansdale wants from him is truth, no matter how painful that truth might be. That is what he is waiting for. He begins slowly. "All I know about being with a girl, I learned from someone at art school. She wasn't a virgin and she had to show me what to do."

As soon as they begin talking openly like this, the workshop feels transformed to both of them. It is almost as if music has filled the room and is carrying along their sentences while they talk and filling those sentences with meaning.

"What was her name?"

"Daisy."

"And was she a student like you?"

"No. She was a model. In my drawing class."

"Undressed?"

"Yes."

"Completely?"

"Yes."

"Oh God. And was she lovely?"

"She was."

"And she chose you, Sam?"

149

"Yeah. But I wasn't the only one."

"So she didn't think it was a sin then? I mean, to do it with a man who wasn't her own husband."

"No. She was her own boss. She didn't live by anyone else's leave. She took orders from no one. And she treated it like it was a blessing. Not a sin."

"A blessing. Oh my. And did you feel blessed?"

"I did. She made me feel worthy of being touched that way."

"You must think about her all the time?"

"I used to. But ever since France, I can't get a clear picture of what my life was like then. With her, I mean. I have only a dull recollection."

They speak this way for a long time as the night goes on. Finally, Lansdale admits that he can't keep his eyes open any longer. Sam asks him to leave the plaster mould so he can finish Kitchener's face. "I'll have it ready by breakfast," he says.

On his way out of the workshop, Lansdale stops and asks him if Daisy is still in London.

"I believe she is."

"Do you have some way of getting in touch with her?" Lansdale asks.

"I could write to her, I suppose. She might have forgotten me by now."

"Do you think you could ask her if maybe I might come see her?"

Somehow Sam has not seen this question coming. He tries not to say anything for fear of sounding alarmed. And perhaps Lansdale senses this and that is why he speaks quickly to fill the silence that has settled in the space between them. "In all of Amy's letters to me, do you know what she used to call me?"

"Tell me," Sam says with relief.

"She said I was her 'Christian lionhearted man'."

Sam looks at him and smiles. "Well, there you go."

"See you in the morning, Sam," Lansdale calls as he leaves.

A moment later, Sam hears Lansdale singing. He watches him mounting the stairs and marvels at this. After all this man has been through and the struggle that lies ahead of him, he is encouraged enough to sing his way to bed. He is indeed what his girl had called him – a Christian lionhearted man. This makes Sam remember the look on Katie's face the day she and Ned were married. The way her eyes closed just before Ned kissed her at the altar. It was as if she were silently surrendering to him. That had been the moment when it dawned on Sam that Katie belonged to Ned. And that the world he had ushered her into, the world of her desire and her belief in him, was where the meaning of both their lives would reside from then on. *Will Lansdale's girl ever look at him that way?* Sam wonders. *Will Lansdale ever get to see any girl look at him the way Katie had looked at Ned?*

This makes him think of Lily, alone in the farmhouse. He feels that it would have been cruel of him to tell Lansdale about her, but he wants to tell him about how he insisted that she blow out the candle before they lay down on her bed. Not so much because he didn't want her to see him, but because he didn't want to see someone trusting him when he felt so manifestly unreliable. He doesn't know if he is being unfair to her, returning to her as he is, and yet he can't resist her acceptance of him and the feeling that he has been crippled in just the right way, his arms and legs broken in just the right places so that he fits perfectly in her embrace.

ghosts

It takes only a week for the copper version of the mask to take shape, about half the time Sam thought would be required to match its contours to the plaster mould. The work progresses quickly because Lansdale is so agreeable and accommodating. He never has any complaints. He never points out any imperfections. He claims that the mask fits precisely enough even when Sam can see that it doesn't and there are sections of it that still remain to be hammered into shape. Oliver observes this and it worries him that Lansdale might just be humouring Sam, pretending to go along with the plan when, in fact, he has no intention of ever wearing the finished mask. But gradually he lets go of these concerns and tells himself that, after nearly three months in the castle, Lansdale is just eager to be finished so that he can make his way home.

Soon Sam begins rising before dawn to paint the mask. After preparing the copper by cleaning it with vinegar and sanding its surface lightly, then applying two coats of enamel, he is pleased how the acrylic paint adheres.

Normally he will keep at his work until evening, but today Oliver sends Lansdale to get him so the two of them can begin knocking down a crumbling brick wall in the courtyard while he sits sunning himself and delivering his sermon.

"Listen carefully then, lads. Here is the architecture of life. We are born unwittingly. We grow up steadily. We betray our dreams reluctantly. We turn old inevitably. We become ghosts permanently. The important thing is to find a way to feel at home in the world. And the best way, is physical action. Knock down a wall and rebuild it."

Lansdale is breathing hard through his mask. "Easy for you to say, sir," he manages to remark.

Sam has never really welcomed physical labour. Perhaps the result of too many chores at the farm growing up. His arms and legs are still as thin as rake handles as they were in his boyhood. The first time he lifted a sandbag his second day in France, he staggered under its weight before it knocked him over backwards and he ended up sitting on the ground with it in his lap. A couple of men had a good laugh from that. He had been trying hard to look the part of a soldier, but he was fooling no one.

Now as he lays into the brick wall, he thinks how Ned would delight in this task. He always loved knocking things down. From the time they were little boys, he talked about being a steam shovel operator when he grew up. He would be swinging his sledgehammer so hard at this wall that his feet would leave the earth. And Sam would be trying for all he was worth to keep up.

In an hour they have hit their stride and are soaked in sweat. And Oliver was right; they both look as if something has been lifted from their shoulders. They look as carefree as little boys.

"If I turn into a ghost," Lansdale says with complete joy, "I'll return to haunt this old place. Every castle needs at least one ghost, doesn't it?"

"Ah, you'll make a fine ghost, sergeant," Oliver assures him.

"What about you then?" Lansdale asks.

"My plan is to go look up a woman in Devon, and haunt her through eternity," he confesses pleasantly. "I'll stay in her dressing closet."

This makes Sam smile when he hears Lansdale giggling behind his mask.

Oliver calls them closer and speaks just above a whisper. "I'll let you boys in on a little secret. Most men experience the supreme pleasure of undressing a woman. And its joy is not to be underestimated. But this girl bestowed upon me the exquisite privilege of *dressing her.* Every morning after her bath she would sit on the edge of the bed with the sunlight streaming in on her beautiful body and I would start with her stockings and work my way up to the top. And very *slowly,* boys. I always proceeded slowly so I would commit the whole proceeding to memory and never forget a single detail. At first, I had some difficulty with the snaps and catches, but I grew to be quite competent. I was a king in those moments. I was on my knees, but I was a pope. A prime minister. A bleeding, bloody czar! Pardon my French."

They work away through the morning. Sam happens to turn and see the postman's son in his father's uniform, with the mail sack slung over one shoulder, standing behind a hedge, watching them curiously. Sam thinks that it must be quite a sight for the boy to behold Lansdale in his Kitchener mask. But soon he discerns that the boy isn't looking at Lansdale. He is looking at *him* instead. And this sends a chill up his spine. He feels his hands trembling on the handle of the sledgehammer. With the boy's father sending him letters home from the war, Sam is suddenly quite certain that he is going to find out about what had happened to him at Verdun. Maybe he already knows.

But this day goes on like every other day and ends with Lansdale stopping by the workshop before climbing the stairs to bed, to see how his copper mask is progressing. Tonight Lansdale suggests they sing Harry Fragson's song, 'Hello, Hello, Who's Your Lady Friend?' that has become popular with the troops. Lansdale begins with a booming voice:

"Jeremiah Jones, a lady's man was he. Every pretty girl he liked to spoon.

*Till he found a wife and down beside the sea, went
to Margate for the honeymoon.
But when he strolled along the promenade with his
little wife just newly wed,
He got an awful scare when someone strolling there,
came up to him and winked and said—"*

The chorus they sing together:

*"Hello! Hello! Who's your lady friend? Who's the
little girlie by your side?
I've seen you with a girl or two. Oh! Oh! Oh! I am
surprised at you...
It isn't the girl I saw you with at Brighton.
Who? Who? Who's your lady friend?"*

"He's some fellow, isn't he?" Lansdale says when they finish. "Our old man here. I can't imagine it was a stroll through the park in his war in Africa. But still, I doubt he ever saw the sort of things you and I saw. I think there must have been some decency to the war he fought."

"Maybe a little more decency," Sam says. He tells him then that he has written to Daisy. "I posted the letter the day before yesterday."

Lansdale takes his hand and shakes it with both of his. "Can't thank you enough, old man."

Then, as soon as the initial excitement passes, he asks with a worried tone if Sam thinks she will respond.

"If the letter reaches her, I'm quite confident that she'll reply."

"And can I ask... what did you tell her about me, Sam?"

"Oh, I told her all about your beautiful moustache."

This makes them both laugh.

"But seriously, do you think it's too much to ask?"

Sam can tell that he is going to struggle to finish what he really wants to ask and he wants to spare him that.

"She's not a fragile soul. She knows what she wants and she takes it."

"But will she like me? Do you think she'll like me?"

"Of course she will. But I don't think that liking you is the most important thing to her. I think she'll understand the purpose in your meeting."

Lansdale seems to be considering this. "Of course. Look, Sam, you have my word that I won't... I'll conduct myself like a gentleman."

"I don't think she cares a great deal for gentlemen. Gentlemen seem to keep finding ways to make a mess of life for everyone. She's a free spirit, Lansdale."

"How will I know, though? I mean, if we do end up with each other, how will I know if I'm conducting myself properly?"

Sam has a momentary image of Daisy rising up beneath him with her elbows pushing into the bed, to draw him deeper into her. It is an image that had abandoned him the whole time he was at the front and he thought was gone forever. But now that it has reinstated itself in his mind, he recalls it in all its intimate detail, and he wonders if he has Lily to thank for restoring these memories.

"I read somewhere that if you do it properly, the girl cries," Lansdale says. "For joy, I mean." He turns away when he says this.

This catches Sam by surprise. "That never happened with me," he says. "Let's see if she writes back."

"Good enough," Lansdale says.

They say goodnight. After another hour, Sam finishes working and stands outside Oliver's door. This night he has fallen asleep in his chair before he managed to turn out the lamp on his desk. When Sam crosses the room, he sees the blue glass bottle on the floor beside the chair. And the strange sight of the linen scarf draped across the older man's chin. If he were able to smell the ether when he stands directly above him, it would remind him of the smell inside hospital tents behind the front lines.

Sam covers Oliver with the blanket that must have slipped off onto the floor. On the desk, the newspaper lies open under the lamp, and perhaps if he weren't so thoroughly exhausted, he might have lingered there longer. Long enough to notice a small paragraph on the open page of the newspaper that Oliver had circled with a pencil. A few lines of print that include Sam's name.

In his room, he looks at his photograph of Ned with Katie and the baby. He has the feeling that something is vanishing. Something he will never recover. Something that cannot be measured now. Something that he should have weighed and protected when it still belonged to him.

He lies down and tries to sleep, and when sleep will not come to him, he goes outside and starts running. He runs as fast as he can run without purpose or destination as the night closes in around him. At dawn he is sitting on the beach while the tide pulls away from the shore. And he acknowledges something there. In the months he has been at the castle, a darkness has begun to lift from him. Maybe it is the result of Lansdale's courageous hope in spite of everything. Or maybe it is Lily's innocence. As he watches the dawn light rest upon the sea in front of him, he realises that he has begun to no longer feel like a stranger to himself, and he wonders if this means that he is alive again.

clock

This time she sits at the window, waiting for him to arrive, watching for him to appear. There are streaks of lightning in the distance over the sea and the fescue grass on the hillside leans away from the gusting wind, and she can hear the dull concussion of waves pounding the shore beyond the lighthouse. Maybe in the morning she will find that the storm has dredged up the body of Mr Vanderbilt and dragged it onto the beach and she will collect the thousand-pound-sterling reward. She has read in the newspaper that bodies are still being recovered though it has been over a year now since the great ship went down.

He arrives by bicycle this time and this makes her smile. She can see that he is pedalling hard, pushing himself through the wind to reach her door. She can see the eagerness in his movement. His intention and his earnestness. And this pleases her. She has given him something and she has held something back the last time they were together. He is close enough for her to see the determination in his eyes and this makes her wonder which he is returning for – what she gave him, or what she held back.

She has already decided that this time she will make it different for him. This time she will ask him to undress her so she can watch his hands moving over her body, so she can have the memory of her body revealing itself to him by degrees. If he does this too quickly, she will take hold of his hands and whisper to him to go slowly... *Slowly. Slowly, please.* The last time they were together, there was a gathering momentum that swept them both along.

This time it is delirium. It is as if a switch has been thrown and a great engine starts. It is as if they have been moving in slow motion all their lives until now. They are devouring each other. Pressing into each other. Pouring over and through each other. They are being pulled along by a tide of dreams. Pushing off from the bottom, and rising together to burst free and gulp the air. The sound of them has never been heard in this house before. The heat from their bodies is changing the cast of light in the room.

When he kisses her eyelids, it feels like the end of loneliness. His lips on her breasts are a latch falling, a gate swinging open.

When she parts her thighs for him, it is like a sudden reversal of fortune. All that has been denied them is being fulfilled. All that has frightened them is being driven away. It is the beginning and the end of longing. It is the illness and the cure. He has made the other boy disappear from the world.

The boy who promised himself to her and broke his promise no longer matters. He no longer has a name of his own. And the world he disappeared into no longer exists for her. There are enough mysteries in this room to spend a lifetime contemplating and unfolding them.

This boy is now at the centre of these mysteries. He is placing one unexpected thing after another into her hands. They are returning to a place they have never been to. A place where the answers precede the questions. Where meaning is something they can touch.

And then he falls asleep beside her. Feeling him disappear is a revelation to her. She can almost see who he was before she knew him this way. She can almost see who he was as his mother's little boy. *Maybe this is the only way we ever know a person*, she thinks. In the darkness, she has managed to map the contours of his body and learned to anticipate his desire, but that counts for nothing when he is sleeping this way. When he is sleeping, he does not belong to her at all. She wants to give him a dream to accompany him wherever he goes when he is sleeping. The dream is the two of them dressed in fine clothes, eating dinner beneath the chandeliers in a great ship like the one that sank beneath her. They are travelling the world's oceans on this ship. Up on the top deck he leans her against the railing and kisses her. In the cabin with the round window, he is down on his knees, peeling her stockings off her legs. The thought of this makes her shudder. It rolls through her and her hands twitch on the bedspread. "What have you done to me?" she asks him. She has the strange desire to walk through town with him, holding hands, so that they can be seen and acknowledged. And how grand it would be if the two of them were to spend the rest of their lives in this room. If the world beyond were to disappear. A life circumscribed by the dimensions of their physical touch. The window with its dark green curtains is another country. The wood door with its glass knob opens to a continent they will never walk in. Someone has sentenced them to remain in this room until they can assemble, from only the furnishings present, a clock that actually works. The brass knobs on the bureau. The steel springs on the bed. The threads of the carpet. The cotton wick and the glass globe of the gas lamp.

But before their sentence begins, let them take that walk through town, to the village green, holding hands, just one time. So that someone might remember them together. Because she knows they will not be together for long. Who they were before they met is who they will be again. Nothing lasts. The only thing she was ever told about being with a boy was this: *When you first marry, you will want to wear nightgowns to bed, to make things easier. And after a little while, his enthusiasm will disappear, and you will catch up on the sleep you've lost.* If this will not last, then there is no time to waste, and she must wake him to start up the engine again.

But first, she thinks a bit longer about all this. About Brian and his promise. And her uncle Connolly and the revolution. And Mr Vanderbilt with his gleaming bald head rolling from side to side in the currents at the bottom of the sea. And Sam with his sketch pad and paints. As sweet as this time is with him, and as intoxicating as it is to feel this electricity race through her, she is already deciding something. She will not allow this to become an addiction. There is another world inside this one and that is the world she will inhabit through the years ahead. It is a world where her solitude encloses her and reassures her. She will depend upon no one ever again – she knows this. She will rely upon her loneliness to nourish and sustain her. And in this world inside the world, she will keep the memory of Sam lying beside her this way. And Sam below her looking into her eyes, as she looks down at him – this collection of moments will remind her that she had a choice, and she chose to go it alone, and never again to depend upon anyone or to rely upon anyone to keep their promises to her. She wonders if he knows this, if he can sense that what she is giving to him is not the centre of her. It is not the part that would sustain him in the long run, nor is it the part that will define the worth of her life. That part she will protect and put to some other use.

tickets

One of the ways your life changes when you are a young woman and word gets around town that your husband has been killed in the war, is that other women with husbands still fighting will cross to the opposite side of the street when they see you coming, or leave the market when you step inside, before they have finished shopping because they are afraid to get too close to you. They fear that the scourge that has ripped the natural progression from your life can be spread like a virus from you to them as the umbrella of immunity that has so far protected them during the war is lifted from above their heads if they get too near you, or linger in your presence. And so your life takes on a deep and perplexing loneliness that is enlarged each time you discover another thing you cannot share with anyone.

For example, there is no one Katie can talk to about how her desolation is made worse by her child. People would expect the opposite to be true. *At least she's not alone, at least she has her child*, they must think when they see the two of them on the street. There is no one she can tell the truth to. No one to help her understand why Charlotte makes it worse each time Katie looks at her and sees the child's father. How can she look at her without seeing her husband? The child, her constant companion, is an unwitting reminder. Now that she is speaking her first words, she even sounds like Ned. And it makes her worry that she will grow to resent her daughter.

Maybe it is already beginning. Doesn't she already resent this half-life that her life has turned into? This half-life that her daughter has condemned her to? If she weren't here, looking up at her with her imploring expression, maybe Katie would pack a bag and go as far away from this life as she could. She has enough money saved to go to Canada. She and Ned had spoken of making this trip together. In the library, she had read about Halifax, Nova Scotia, where the boat would land. She had been reluctant because of the sinking of the *Titanic* a couple of years earlier, but Ned had insisted that this would make the voyage more thrilling, and she had gradually endorsed the idea. There was wide-open land for the taking in Canada and Ned had told her that he would make a go of it as a farmer, growing wheat.

Maybe she will leave Charlotte with her grandfather and his companion, and take the ship to Canada and pray that it hits an iceberg and sinks in the North Atlantic, all the way to the bottom of the sea. For this to happen, she imagines that she will have to wait for winter to make the crossing. Winter is months away. Far too distant, with far too many days to get through first.

In better moments, like this morning when Charlotte helped her carry the washing out to the garden, taking one handle on the wicker basket and marching along proudly in step with her, Katie does the mathematics in her head. She is twenty-five years old now, which would make her forty-three in eighteen years when Charlotte turns twenty. Forty-three seems like a dreadful age to be. Much too old to still be young. And yet, *not old*, really. Unless she considers that her mother was only in her twenties when she died. Forty-three is neither young nor old. Another kind of half-life that this present half-life will have prepared her for.

It is really a matter of getting through these terrible days and living far enough beyond them so that they become the *past*. The past is something she can manage. As she had managed her mother's absence. And her father's despair. And her father's lady companions across the years, who were often too solicitous or too indifferent.

The past will be Charlotte's past as well. It consoles Katie when she reminds herself of this, that the past will belong to both of them equally. She draws strength from this. If only she can lead them both through the storm, there is the possibility that their suffering will make them both stronger. And what the war has taught her is that she will do whatever is required to make certain that Charlotte is never placed in the position that *she* placed herself in by her own choices. She knows that she has been an accomplice in her own misery because she had been willing to take up the role of the dutiful wife, watching stupidly while all the young men she knew went marching off into the great and glorious fight for England. It had felt so *wrong* when it was happening, and even more wrong as her life was reduced to waiting. Waiting for word. Waiting for the war to be over by that first Christmas. When she read that the French army had lost 200,000 men in the first month of the war, she knew that her waiting would be feckless. The waiting had quickly left her feeling diminished. Each day she lost some piece of herself. Some of her will and determination vanished in those days. In her letters to Ned, she wrote of how she wanted to hold him in her arms, but in truth, she wanted to strike him with her fists for placing her in the useless and helpless position she was in. And it took all her forbearance to keep from shouting at the mothers she encountered, women in their middle age who had waved their sons off to battle. *What is wrong with you! You created these lovely baby boys. You spent years of your life pouring your love into them and teaching them to be gentle and imaginative, and patient, and then you smiled and waved and handed them over to old men who led them away from you into the blood storm, where their perfect bodies that formed inside you while you were in all your glory were butchered while you did nothing to stop it. You do exactly what I do – you wait. Like imbeciles. And you pray to a God who exists only in your imagination.*

It is enough to make her want to scream. To scream at the old men who started the war that they were never going to have to fight themselves. And at the young men who they sent to fight it for them. Young men who wanted more excitement than they could find at home with their wives and children, and boys like Finn who had simply vanished from Katie's world without a trace.

These young men like Ned had grown *ungrateful*! That's what it came down to. She knows this. These men had grown bored at home with the wives and children who had showered them with love and affection. These men who would not be made to ache for anyone, or to wait for anyone, or to grieve for anyone. It is something Katie can't talk about. It is one of those things that everyone knows is true but no one will acknowledge. There are too many things like that in life and they make her furious enough to pledge to herself that she will not keep these secrets forever. She will tell Charlotte everything. She will tell her never to acquiesce in her life the way she has.

When she hears the child stirring from her nap, her first thought is of the five hours that lie ahead before it will be time to put her to bed for the night. Time carries such expanse, and such dread with it now. What will they do to fill the next five hours?

She walks into the child's room, and as is Charlotte's practice, she greets her mother with words, the first little sentences she is learning to say. She always seems to awake with words on her mind, as if the words have woken her from her sleep. "Bunny, Mummy. Sky, Mummy," she says, pointing first to her Beatrix Potter Peter Rabbit and then to the dark sky outside the window.

"You are such a clever and sweet little meringue pie," Katie says in return.

This makes Charlotte giggle as she stands up in her little bed, clutching the small stuffed rabbit to her chest.

Above her head on the top of the chest of drawers is the photograph of her father. Katie has placed it there so he can look down at his daughter. She has thought back over her own childhood many times since Ned's death, trying to place a memory in time. She was in the garden watching her father burn leaves in the tin barrel. He had on his tan work trousers that were held up by pale blue suspenders. Over the years, with his help, they decided that she must have been four years old, the same year of her other memory of him falling asleep in his night vigil at her bedside. No memories before the age of four means that Charlotte will remember nothing from these days. So it will be up to Katie to keep Ned from vanishing. She's had nothing to say about his death, but it is completely in her power now to keep him from vanishing from his daughter's world.

Katie picks Charlotte up into her arms. "Shall we see if the postman brought us any letters today?" she says.

"Yes, Mummy," she replies. "And sweets, Mummy."

"We will have a sweet, because you're such a good girl. Mummy's very good girl."

In a narrow band of sunlight, there is one envelope lying on the tiled floor below the bronze slot in the front door. Katie sets Charlotte down and watches her dash through the sunlight, thinking solemnly how lovely this sight is and how sad it is that Ned will never see it because the world is dead to him. Charlotte picks the letter up in both hands and carries it back to her.

Katie reads the return address. Newcastle, Northern Ireland. She knows no one in Northern Ireland. She opens the letter with a wary anticipation and reads Oliver's words:

Dear Mrs Morse, I trust this letter will reach you and that in these difficult times of war your spirits will be lifted by the knowledge that your search for Sam Burke has not been in vain. He is presently here, having survived the fighting in France. Without betraying the confidence that I share with him, I can report to you, ma'am, that he is safe here and doing important work with his prodigious artistic talent. I am hopeful that Mr Burke will one day write to you himself. But for now, in consideration of the trauma he has endured as well as the responsibility I hold for his well-being, I ask that you kindly explain to me the reason you are searching for him. You may rest in the assurance that I only desire what is best for Mr Burke, a desire I am certain you share. I remain respectfully, Oliver W. Blackburn.

It isn't until she considers tearing the letter into pieces that she realises the depth of her anger at Sam. This person whom she had adored and with whom she had shared her deepest thoughts – speaking to him as if he were beside her through the most difficult months after he and Ned had gone to the war and left her alone with her baby – is now someone she wants to lash out at. How in God's name has he run away from the bloody war and not told her where he is? How could he *not* have written to her in the six months since Ned's death?

She might have torn the letter into pieces if Charlotte had not worked her way between Katie's legs and laid her head against one thigh. "Letter," the child says, perfectly enunciating the 't's.

"Sam," Katie says.

Suddenly, Katie is smiling despite herself. "Mummy's friend," she says. She strokes Charlotte's head and feels the anger subsiding.

Her next reaction is to consider how odd it is that in a time when men from every corner of Europe seem determined only to murder each other, Sam has somehow found his way into the company of one man who is determined to protect him.

She is grateful for this and she finds herself singing and speaking sweetly to Charlotte through the rest of the day. But then, when she is alone in the night, reading Oliver Blackburn's words over and over and trying also to discern what he might be withholding from her, it seems brutally unfair that he is trying to protect Sam from *her.* What does he know of her affection for Sam, and Sam's for her? What gives him the right to be the arbiter of their relationship?

It angers her so that she barely sleeps at all, and in the

morning, as soon as she has Charlotte dressed and has fed her breakfast, they walk together to the station. It is only when she is standing in the queue that she realises the last time she had been in the station was on the morning when she watched her husband leave for the war.

She had planned only to ask for the timetables so that she might study them and calculate the distance and route from Dorset to Newcastle, Northern Ireland, and the time it would take should she one day travel there. But when she sees that the only people in the station are women with children, as helpless as she and Charlotte are – women and children left behind to wait – a defiance rises through her. It takes her a moment to realise that her hands have tightened into fists, and that her jaw is aching because she is clenching her teeth so hard. She had waited for letters from Ned and Sam. From the early autumn of 1914 until April of 1916, her life had been defined by waiting for word from them. Her sanity had seemed to hang on every scrap of information she could learn about the war. What in God's name is she waiting for now? And who is he – *this Oliver Blackburn* – to prolong her waiting?

It is almost a 500-mile journey. A train to Liverpool. A ferry across the Irish Sea to Dublin. Another train from Dublin to the north. It will take sixty-seven hours. Her child will travel free, provided she holds her. Considering the length of the trip and how uncomfortable it will be for both of them, she buys a second ticket for Charlotte. She can see the derision in the eyes of the elderly stationmaster who sells her the tickets. Maybe he believes that women should remain at home. Or maybe, at a time when everyone is being so frugal and living with every manner of deprivation, the fact that she is splurging on an extra ticket rankles him.

Katie leans in close enough to him to see her own reflection in his glasses as she scowls back at him. "Her father died in your war. I haven't told her yet. Perhaps you would like to tell her for me?"

Their eyes meet and then she turns and walks away.

church

Sam is in his room with the window open, looking down at Lansdale, who is mixing cement in the rain for the new brick wall while he sings happily to himself. For the first time, he is wearing the mask that he will wear for the rest of his life and from the second-floor window, it is impossible to tell that it is not his real face. The transformation is complete and persuasive enough for Sam to suspend his disbelief. For a few minutes, there never was a war. There never was this place.

"Well then, son, is this not a fine day?" Oliver calls to him as he enters the room. They stand side by side, looking down at Lansdale. "You see that fellow down there? Do you see what he is? *He's himself again.* Because of you, Sam. You can see by the way he moves. He's a man with a life to live. And you gave him back his life. The mask is life."

It was Oliver's idea to mark the day appropriately by dressing up in their uniforms and attending church in town. They arrive a little late with Lansdale leading the way up the central aisle. He seems determined to compensate for not being on time by singing louder than anyone else. His impressive tenor voice ricochets off the rafters. People in the congregation glance at them, welcoming them with pleasant smiles, before they turn back to their hymnals.

Because Sam's mother had always taken him to church while his father tended to morning chores on the farm, church was a place where he felt like a child, sitting among the imperious and perfumed ladies with their chins held high in that self-righteous way they had, and today is no exception. He remembers Katie whispering something to him once when she saw how uncomfortable these ladies made him. "Undress them with your eyes, Sam. That's how you get back at them. Take their clothes off right down to their bony knees and sagging breasts."

This memory makes him smile to himself. How he had marvelled at her ability to always summon the appropriate measure of defiance. And he knows that she would have made a far better soldier than he had ever been.

The pastor is a diminutive, grey-haired man with matching eyebrows and a delivery that is anything but diminutive. He reads the Beatitudes with great force, and then circles back to the fourth one as the subject of his morning's sermon. "'Blessed are they who hunger and thirst for righteousness, for they shall be satisfied.' Who might we say Christ is speaking about here?" he asks passionately.

The church falls into a stony silence as his eyes scan his devoted parishioners, like a king surveying his subjects, before he provides the answer to his question. "I believe we may be absolutely certain that he is speaking about *us. Here. Today.* In this great war. We are on the side of righteousness. We thirst for it. We hunger for it. And we are in the process of tearing it from the hands of those who have made a mockery of it. From the start, our enemy has revealed their moral deficiency as their storm troopers slaughtered innocent women and children by the hundreds during their onslaught through Belgium. The only thing they could have done to make this vile act even more vile was to deny it – *as they have!* But we know better. We have not been fooled. And as Christ proclaimed, we will be satisfied! We will not be denied the satisfaction of seeing Germany crushed beneath the boot heels of our valiant soldiers."

The moment he pauses, the silence in the church deepens. He knows precisely how long to pause for the full effect of what comes next. He gestures with a simple nod of his head to a man in uniform in the front row who may have been unnoticed until now. He gets to his feet and, with a walking stick in each hand, begins to make his way to the altar.

The pastor opens his arms to welcome the man, then he speaks in a voice just above a whisper. "We are most gracious to have with us this morning one of those valiant soldiers who has offered to speak to us about the recent fighting. To remind us of what it is that we are fighting for."

With a handshake, they exchange places, and the soldier stands behind the altar. He is constructed like a stevedore with wide shoulders and a thick shock of black hair. Sam rises slightly in the pew and leans towards him. He has seen a hundred men like him, men who looked so resolute and strong before they went over the top that he actually pitied the Germans on the other side of no man's land. Men, he was certain, who were too mighty for the world to ever tear apart. Men, unlike himself, who seemed made for war. *Real* men. Men like Ned.

The soldier begins with a steady, forthright manner, reading from a sheet of paper. "I have just returned from the side of a ridge in a village called Hulluch where the Germans used chlorine and phosgene gas. The gas came over us as clouds. The clouds filled the trenches. Below the clouds, men twisted and turned in every imaginable posture of agony, ripping their clothing off them as they tried desperately to breathe. The trenches became their graves. And the Germans think they have us now. They believe that they are safe. They live under the illusion that they are safe. Now those who are left of us are climbing the hillside, up to the ridge, to kill them, to make them pay for what they have done to us with their murderous gas. To... to annihilate them."

Suddenly, the sheet of paper falls from his hands and his whole body begins to tremble. He looks at once like he is only a cardboard cut-out of a man, not a real man after all, and as though he will suddenly fold in half.

The pastor rises from his seat and the silence in the

congregation is lost to the rustling of people trying to find some way to be comfortable where they are now most uncomfortable in the pews. Something is coming. They can feel it and soon it is upon them all, like a sudden gust of wind. And the soldier's voice rises as if to climb above the storm so that he is shouting at the congregation while tears pour down his face.

"Men are groaning like animals in the mud. They are tearing out their tongues to try to breathe. Their tongues are knotted at the back of their throats."

The pastor has reached his side and when he tries to take the soldier's arm, he is flung off with such force that he stumbles and falls to the red carpeted floor. Women gasp at this. "I must tell it!" the soldier stammers. "I must tell it all. I must show you this war!"

With that he tears open his jacket and then his shirt. He turns abruptly so that the congregation is staring at the horrible shrapnel wounds that run from his waist to the base of his neck. They look like a string of sausages has been sewn under his skin.

Sam is about to get to his feet when Lansdale moves first and makes his way up the aisle with one hand placed against his mask self-consciously as he strides purposefully. Sam rises, but Oliver tells him calmly that it's all right. "Lansdale can manage," he says.

"There is no righteousness in this war!" the soldier bellows to the congregation. "There are only rats the size of cats eating the flesh off boys. And my pal, Walter, begging me to put a bullet into his head. My friend Walter. My friend—"

As soon as Lansdale reaches him, he tips his mask back for the man to gaze upon his face. This stops him in an instant. The man bows his head, and with great gentleness, Lansdale helps him back into his shirt and jacket and then leads him from the altar to a side door behind the organ with one arm draped across his shoulders.

babies

There are some moments of such stunning intimacy that even time will not diminish them. It is a warm evening just after dusk settles. A pale sickle of moon lies on its back in the empty sky above them. With Sam's promise not to let go of her the whole time, Lily is able to summon the courage to go into the sea. Swimming had always been one of the things Lily loved doing best. From the time she was a small child, the feeling of being weightless thrilled her and she delighted in every occasion to swim, particularly in the rolling swells of the sea. But in the time she had lived at the farm, even glancing at the water filled her head with the terrified screams of her fellow passengers grabbing hold of each other in the waves. She had swum away from them quite calmly, curious in a distracted way as to why they were wasting their strength on screaming instead of swimming. The shoreline had been visible, the sun above them strong at mid-afternoon, and she had managed to convince herself that this was just an inconvenience. Until the ship began its final plunge beneath the water, pulling all the screaming passengers down with it in the whirlpool of suction it created. She had felt herself being sucked towards the others just before someone in a lifeboat grabbed her by her armpits and lifted her from the water. But she had not been terrified like the others were and so it seems unfair to her that she is frightened now.

But Sam promises not to let go of her and so she lies face

up in the sea now, feeling one of his arms behind the backs of her thighs, and the other beneath her shoulders. He holds her this way for quite some time before she says, "When I tell you, please let go, Sam."

Her eyes are locked on his the whole time and she never stops talking, as if her words will help in some way. She talks right through her fear, telling him everything she remembers from that day when the great ship went out from under her. There was a man whose head exploded when it struck a portion of the giant propeller. And a woman who jumped from the top deck with a baby under both her arms, but somehow turned upside down before she struck the water. "They went into the water and they never came back up," she tells Sam. "I kept watching for them to come to the surface. And that was where I jumped as well. To the same place. Because I thought I might find them and pull them up with me. I don't know why God would save me and not those wee babies. But then, when you think about it, God didn't save me, did he? I saved myself because I've always been a strong swimmer. And those babies were just babies. So it makes sense. I think almost everything we think doesn't make sense ends up making sense if we think about it carefully enough. Do you believe that, Sam?"

He responds by smiling at her. His eyes are smiling at her in that way of his when he is hoping that she will accept his silent smile as a kind of assent that will make his silence acceptable.

After a while, her words have brought a calm to her. "You can let go now," she tells him.

"I let go a long time ago," he confesses.

Indeed he has. And now she lets her body drift slowly from him, keeping her eyes open and on his face.

* * *

They are sitting in the dunes with the lowering sun across their backs when she tells him this: "There's a part of me that's in you now, Sam. And the same is true for me. I will carry a part of you with me from this place when I leave." She lets the silence fall again, waiting to see if he will respond to what she has told him. And when she can tell that he isn't going to say anything, she searches his eyes for some hint of how her words have struck him. And then, finally, she decides that she .will make him talk. "Do you believe me, Sam?"

He nods his head to this question.

"No," she says gently. "Tell me. Please."

"I believe you."

"And do you understand that I will have to leave?"

"Yes."

"Will you come with me?"

This has startled him. "I can't," he tells her. "I'm still in the army."

"We could run away. You can run away from the army. You've already done your bit for king and country."

"I didn't do it for king and country," he assures her.

"I know. I didn't mean it that way. I know you went to war for Ned."

He looks up at her, and she can see his eyes darting, unable to settle on her face. This always happens whenever she mentions that name. She takes his hands to calm him. For a long time, there is only the silence between them and the waves drumming along the shore.

"I'm only a girl," she says, almost as if she has just discovered this. "Do you think our lives matter at all, Sam?"

He answers reluctantly. "I don't know… Anyone's life can be destroyed so easily."

"But before the war, before everything you went through, what did you believe?"

"I don't know. I honestly can't remember. I can't remember before the war."

Suddenly, he turns and looks into her eyes as if he has just remembered that she is there with him.

"I wish I could remember," he says.

She takes his hand and presses it against her breast. "You'll remember this, won't you?" she asks. He nods and she smiles at him and tells him, "If there was a room where we could live together and if someone just slid a plate of food under the door once a day, I could live there with you for the rest of my life. That's how I feel when we're together."

She waits for him to show her that he feels the same way, and when he doesn't, she accepts this and tells him that she knows it is asking for too much. "Far too much," she says. "I'm just being foolish. I know that."

He shakes his head slowly and says, "You're not being foolish. I don't think you're foolish at all. You've just been through something terrible and you're trying to find out what is…" he takes a few seconds to come up with the word, "…*real.*"

She tells him that she knows he is real but she isn't certain about herself.

He finds this remarkable and tells her that he feels the same way. "I know *you* are real, but I'm uncertain about myself."

They both think it astonishing that they have somehow found one another and that they can see in each other the thing they cannot see in themselves.

She ventures a difficult question while she has his attention. "Do you think this means that we are meant to be together?"

She watches him lower his head and turn it slowly. "Nothing means anything, Lily," he tells her. "Not any more."

She looks at him again, this time pretending that she is seeing him for the last time. What will she remember? What will she forget? The way his dark curls rest against the tops of his ears? The pinkness of his nipples? His thin, unmarked fingers? The softness of his palms? The depthless brown of his eyes? The bow of his lips? Her own anticipation as she pressed his hand against her that first time, assuring him that it would be as easy as shelling peas? The way she drew him inside her? The fierceness in his eyes when she brings him to his pleasure? An outbreak of texture and sound. Now, it seems as if she has made it all up inside her imagination.

And now, it seems quite possible that it will never happen

again. She will grow into an old woman, trying to remember these details. Trying to persuade herself that she didn't miss her life. She tells herself something as she looks at him – *We're far too young to ever grow old.* She doesn't realise that she has said this out loud until he turns and looks at her. And when he smiles sadly, and his eyes widen, it is enough to convince her that what they have shared is as close to real love as she will ever come.

singing

Sam sits in the morning sunlight reading the letter that has come from Daisy. After he finishes, he finds Lansdale at work again, laying bricks to finish his wall.

"Ah, replacements," he exclaims when Sam appears. "Just in time. I'm about to drop." He has something to show Sam. He walks to a glass of water on the bench. "Watch this," he says cheerfully. Then he drinks the glass empty without spilling a drop. "Tell me, do you see the magician's trick?"

"I don't know what you mean."

"Ha! Success!" he cries out.

Then he shows Sam the short straw that he has cupped in his hand. "You remember Oliver was turning the place inside out searching for a straw? Well, there was method to his madness."

"Brilliant," Sam tells him. "I've heard back from Daisy."

"Oh, Lord," he says. "Listen." He reaches for Sam's arm. "No matter the verdict, I'll always be grateful that you were willing to do this for me, old sport."

They sit together on the bench while Sam reads Daisy's letter to him.

Dearest Sam, I cannot tell you what relief I feel knowing that you have survived and are safe in Northern Ireland. Did I ever tell you that my grandfather on my mother's side of the family once owned a farm in Carlingford, which cannot be terribly far from where you are in Newcastle.

Soggy old London has not been the same since you left, but I am managing to keep from drowning, having found work as a stenographer's assistant after the Academy made me redundant. It seems that the combination of fewer students and my having gained just over a stone in the wrong places conspired against me. I am walking everywhere every day now to try to drop the weight. However, I believe it was at my same age – 31 – when my mother began to lose her figure, so I may be heading straight for the glue factory.

I should like very much to meet Mr Lansdale, as I am certain any friend of yours will be fine company for a lonely, ageing former model. But in the interest of total honesty (something you know I insist upon), I think I should express my feelings in this letter.

I will be harshly judged, and no doubt called 'promiscuous' for my beliefs that when a woman makes love to a man, she is bestowing a gift upon him, as he is upon her. And with the world such a cold and brutal place, I am of the opinion that they should exchange this gift as often as is practicable. I also believe that whenever we make love to someone, we are also making love to everyone we ever cared about enough to make love to before. And so, if it comes to pass that I should take Mr Lansdale into my embrace, I will also be embracing you again, Sam. I hope you believe this.

And if I can help Mr Lansdale gather the strength and courage he will need to return home to make love to the girl who is waiting for him, I shall consider this a privilege, start to finish. It rather pleases me to think that when I am old and covered in dust and not

a single man in the hemisphere wants to touch me, I
shall have the consolation of my memory of helping
a soldier wounded in battle to survive his wounds.
Please remind him that we are all wounded in one way
or another and we make love to heal those wounds.
Also remind him that we are all wearing masks most
of the time to conceal our vulnerability.

Very good then, my old friend and lover. I long to
see you again. Perhaps I will come visit you in your
castle one day after I have dropped my stone.

All love to you, Sam. My telephone number is
below.

Ever, Daisy.

Lansdale is gazing up at the sky when Sam finishes reading.
"Good God, man," he exclaims. "There are such things as
angels after all. Can you imagine, Sam? What have I ever
done to deserve this?"

"It's a gift, like Daisy says," Sam reminds him as he folds
the letter and returns it to its envelope. "Keep this," he says,
handing it over.

Three days later, it is time for Lansdale to catch his train.
He has a few moments with Oliver in the music room where
he pours some whiskey into two cut-crystal glasses and
they clink them together. Oliver nods thoughtfully. Despite
himself, his eyes quickly fill with tears as he tries to find the
words he wants. "Well, soldier, is there anything you need for
your journey?" he asks.

"No, sir. Thank you."

"You need some money. All young people need money,
sergeant."

With that he digs into his pockets. He places the notes in
Lansdale's hand. "You'll give yourself some time then?"

"Sir?"

"Take it slowly for a while. You're entering the world for
the second time, you see? And this time without your mother

to guide you. Try to see a little of the world's beauty each day. Take it in deeply. Don't waste a moment."

Lansdale nods solemnly.

With some time to kill, he and Sam walk the long way along the shore. Lansdale skims the first stone across the water. Sam picks up the challenge and skims one a little further. Playing this little game seems to remind both of them that they are young. It is something they have forgotten, and it goes on until Lansdale steps to Sam's side and puts his arm around his shoulders. "You must have been a great friend to Ned," he says.

This surprises Sam. He has spoken so little of Ned to him. He tries not to seem alarmed. He doesn't want to spoil Lansdale's bright mood.

"Oliver told me what happened. I'm sorry you didn't both make it."

"Me too," Sam says.

"I know you are. But I want to say something to you. Most of the time when we disappoint people, we're just doing the best we can. I believe that. And I also believe Oliver is right about cowards. He told me that there's only one definition of a coward that has any meaning. A coward is any man who takes orders from another man. You're not a coward, Sam."

Sam lets this pass. "Have you got your straw?" he asks him.

"Two extras," he says. "I plan to have a pint on the train. Maybe more than one." The two men embrace for a moment in that awkward way men do, neither of them knowing why they feel awkward, and both of them wishing they didn't.

At the station, there is a little time to speak some more.

"You'll see me again," Lansdale tells him.

"I hope so," Sam says.

"No, you definitely will. I'm coming back through this way before I head home."

Sam doesn't understand.

"So I can give you a full report about Daisy. And even if things don't work out, I'm going to tell you that it was all grand. I'm going to lie to you if I have to. So that's fair warning."

"All right," Sam says. "But I don't know why you would lie to me."

"Men always lie about women, don't they? Because the truth is too difficult to share. And I'm going to lie to Amy as well, you know? I won't ever tell her about this time in London. It will be one of those lies about love."

Lansdale looks away. When he turns back, he asks Sam if he is doing the right thing.

"Going to London to spend time with Daisy?"

"Yes."

"Of course it's the right thing. Don't be daft, man. You're just a little nervous. That's completely understandable."

"You always know the right thing to say," Lansdale remarks. "I'm sure glad the army didn't shoot you."

He laughs and Sam laughs along with him, although inside he is troubled over this. It makes him wonder how much Oliver knows about him and why he would have shared any of what he knows with Lansdale.

They have time to share a corned beef sandwich. Lansdale breaks his half into small pieces which he then slips quite effortlessly through the opening in the mask to his mouth.

"I feel like I'm off to visit an old friend," are the last words Lansdale says as he boards the train. He waves once, then Sam watches him disappear, and then reappear at an open window where he pulls himself to attention and salutes.

Sam's shoulders pull back reflexively. He steadies his gaze and returns the salute.

lies

They are down on their knees, putting a coat of bright blue paint on the benches in the village square when Sam finally confronts him. "Why don't you tell me what you know about me?"

For some reason, this doesn't take Oliver by surprise. He glances at Sam and then quickly looks back at the bench.

"What do you mean?" he asks.

"I think you know what I mean," Sam says.

Oliver feels awkward suddenly. He moves to the second bench. "Why don't you finish that one and I'll get started on this one," he says.

He hopes that with their backs to each other, it might make it easier for both of them. "What the army told you about me," Sam goes on.

"I have already told you, son. I know that they were going to stand you up in front of a firing squad for desertion because they found you in the trench with your friend who was dead. The rest of your unit had gone over. But the army needed an artist. That is all I was told. Is it correct?"

Sam barely whispers, "Yes."

"Oh yes, and the report said that you were an exemplary student at the Royal Academy before the war intruded."

"That seems like a faded dream."

"It will come back to you. This war can't go on forever."

"Can't it?"

Oliver takes a deep breath and wipes the sweat from his forehead. "I do hope Lansdale's journey goes smoothly," he says.

"What about my time in the hospital?"

"I know that you tried to end your life there. That would have been because your friend died, and you survived."

"Correct. And personally I would have chosen death rather than what Lansdale is up against now."

"But he has something to live for."

"What is that exactly?"

"His dear girl."

"And how do you think his *dear girl* feels about things? Do you think she believes she's lucky to have him coming back to her?"

"That's not for us to say, is it?"

"Put yourself in her shoes then." As soon as Sam says this, he can sense Oliver turning to look at him. Their eyes meet briefly before Sam looks away.

"I guess time will tell," Oliver says.

"Time will tell. Is that what you said to Lansdale?"

"I said nothing to discourage him. My assignment here is to get our soldiers home. And if I must lie to them, then I will do that."

"Lies about love," Sam says, repeating Lansdale's words.

"*Lies about love*. That's good. Very poetic."

When Sam fails to respond, Oliver tells him that was meant to be a compliment.

"Thanks," Sam says. "*Lies about love* – belongs to Lansdale. He said that to me before he got on the train."

"You could have claimed the credit and I would have begun to think of you as a poet as well as a damned fine painter and sculptor. But you're far too honest, aren't you, Sam?" He doesn't wait for an answer. "Yes, you're too honest," he goes on. "So let me be honest with you about something. I know precisely how difficult it will be for Lansdale to return to his girl. This business between men and women isn't very complicated, but it takes most of a lifetime to understand it. A man can make love to any woman. All that is required of her is that she possesses the proper anatomy, if you get my drift. But it's different for her. She needs to be attracted properly. And what attracts her is a man with self-confidence. A man who believes in himself, and feels his power. That is the necessary ingredient. So, do you think your friend in London can make Lansdale believe in himself again?"

Much of what Oliver has told him is probably still a mystery to Sam, but he answers nonetheless. "I guess time will tell," he says.

This makes the old man smile. "We have two new boarders arriving this week. You're going to be very busy, I'm afraid."

"Good," Sam says. "I like being busy."

"It's the time to think that wears on you, I suppose?"

"Something like that, yes."

Oliver watches him painting for a moment. Even though he is just slopping paint on a bench, there is a fineness to his work. And something delicate. What he wants more than anything else is to find some way to ask Sam about this girl whom he has written to in response to her notice in the newspaper. This girl named Katie Morse. He has gathered from her last name that she is the widow of Ned Morse, named in his reports as Sam's friend who died in the trench. But he knows nothing more. And as the days pass while he waits for her to reply, he wants very much to know more. In truth, he had dashed off his letter to her under the influence of some heavy drinking in his room that had persuaded him he was doing the right thing. But with every passing day since he has posted the letter, he grows less certain of that.

Now he decides to take his chances. "You've never said anything to me about your friend Ned," he says.

"What do you need to know?"

"*Need to know?* That's a cheeky way to put it, don't you think?"

Sam paints for a few moments in silence before he apologises.

"It's all right," Oliver tells him. "No apology is necessary. I know it can't be easy for a young man like yourself to endure the presence of a doddering old fool. It's just that I had hoped that after the considerable time we've been together here, you might want to talk about this friend you've lost. And I don't mean this the way it might appear."

"I don't understand," Sam says.

"I'm not advocating that you talk about your friend so that you can put him behind you and move on in your life, though that would be the prevailing wisdom about such things, I suppose. My idea is that we keep alive the people we've lost by talking about them. Telling others about them." As he explains this, Oliver believes Sam knows that he means it and that he is not trying to trick him into talking.

"Who told you that?" Sam asks.

"It would have been my father. As a parish pastor, he spent most of his time trying to console the bereaved. He taught me the value of talking about loss as a way of healing."

Sam says nothing. Oliver looks at his face, a face that shows no signs of what he has endured. Then he looks down at his own hands, covered in brown spots. *When did this feeling begin*, he wonders, *this feeling that life is unacceptably long?*

"You're right," Sam says, "what you said about *time to think*. That was the worst time in the war. Waiting. Thinking."

"What would you think about?"

"The farm. My father doing the chores there without my help. I always did them with him – inside my head. But whenever I tried to draw the place from memory, there was just a blank."

We are talking to each other, Oliver realises. *Now is the time to ask.* "And Ned's wife? You were close to her?"

Sam answers with some reluctance. "Yes. The three of us were close."

"And her name?"

"Katie," he says.

There, that question is answered, Oliver thinks. "You've written to her?"

"No," he says immediately.

"Why wouldn't you write to her? Why wouldn't you want her to know—"

Sam stands up before he can finish. "I'm done," he says.

Oliver looks up and sees him standing with the paintbrush at his side. He looks like he is going to turn and run. *The truth*, he thinks. The truth has never really been of any value to anyone. Still, we want to know it. Maybe just so we can stop wondering. "Any wife would want to know what happened to her husband," he says. "So would a friend. If you hadn't been there with Ned, you would want to know too."

"How do you know what I would want to know?" Sam replies angrily. "How do you know what she wants to know? Her husband is dead. I promised to bring him home. That's all that matters. And she already knows both those things."

"All right then," Oliver says. "You don't want her to know that her husband died because he came back to pull you from the trench. He came back to save you from a firing squad. And a shell exploded and killed him. It was bad luck that killed her husband."

"People don't die from bad luck," Sam says.

"Of course they do!" Oliver insists.

"Look," Sam says with a sharp edge in his voice. "If I… If Ned—"

"Who is it then? Who's to blame then, you or Ned?"

"Why are you asking me this? *I'm to blame*. I've already told you. Isn't that good enough for you?"

"No. As a matter of fact, it isn't. It isn't good enough for me. But I don't really matter, do I? You're the one who matters. You and Katie."

Oliver sees Sam flinch when he says her name.

"There's nothing I can do for her now," he says as he turns to walk away. "There's nothing left."

"Nothing left?" Oliver calls to him. "What do you mean?"

"I don't hear you," Sam calls, without looking back.

Oliver watches as something rises in him. "No, no!" he shouts. And then he is charging after him. "Don't you do that!"

He grabs hold of Sam's shoulder and turns him around forcefully. They are looking into each other's eyes. "I always thought that if I'd ever had a son and we fought, I wouldn't let him walk away from me until we'd settled things," he tells him.

He can plainly see the pain in Sam's eyes.

"What do you want from me?" he asks. And it is less of a question than a surrender.

"Everything," Oliver answers. "I want to know everything about you. I want to know the dreams inside your soul."

Sam looks at him and shakes his head. "You've got the wrong person," he says. "And I'm not your son."

orders

Oliver insists that the meeting take place in town rather than at the castle to avoid raising Sam's suspicion and in deference to the two new soldiers who have just arrived by train that morning, looking exactly as Lansdale had first looked with their faces wrapped in white shrouds like mummies who have escaped from an ancient tomb.

The colonel is over an hour late and Oliver has spent the time at the front gate, pacing back and forth, waiting for his arrival so he can intercept him and steer him to the Whale and Dove pub on the high street.

Sitting across from each other, he quickly tries to take the measure of this man who the war department has dispatched to see how things are progressing at the castle – meaning, has he learned anything about Sam's cowardice that might prove useful to the army?

A guess would place him in his mid-forties. The impeccable cut of his uniform, his perfectly manicured hair and sideburns, and his immaculate fingernails give him the impression, not so much of an officer, but of a fop.

Foppery is the word in Oliver's mind when the colonel begins to speak by asking him if he is sure he doesn't want a drink.

"Tea is fine," he insists. He knows the colonel is testing his willpower and decides that he might just as well put forward a good impression, rather than give the man a reason to sack him.

"I understand you have two residents at the present time," he says.

"Yes."

"Is there anything you need?"

"Need?"

"Yes, I'm instructed to ask how you're getting along and if there is anything you need in particular."

"Instructed by whom?"

"My superiors. There are a great many people interested in your enterprise. And hoping for your success."

Oliver is torn between telling him the truth and concealing it. "Straws," he says.

"Straws?"

"Yes, we could use some more straws. You see, without a straw, you can't drink through a mask. It's too difficult to find your mouth."

He thinks he might have seen the colonel grimace before he lights a cigarette and says, "Your Private Burke is not the one I would have selected for this experiment. To be frank, I suspect he might be a queer."

"Why?"

"I've known a few of these artist types in my time, major. All queers. And even if they're not, I think you will find that their sensibilities don't match with the average soldier. Too thin-skinned. Lacking in physical stamina."

Oliver feels a great urge to defend Sam. "I don't believe that applies to Private Burke."

"Yes, well, in any event, I was overruled by the powers that be, and so, here we are discussing Burke."

"I think you may be right, though, colonel. I think he is the wrong sample."

"And why do you say that?"

"Because I don't think he's a coward. I think he possesses great internal fortitude. Perhaps he just stopped believing in the cause. King and country – maybe they began to sound hollow to him."

The colonel sits back and straightens his shoulders as if to brace himself for a blow.

Oliver goes on. "I'm sure there are a great many men who have come to doubt the efficacy of this war. You probably know a few."

"I do not," he says forcefully. "And in any event, plenty of men who doubt the cause still go over the top. Still follow orders."

"Have *you*?" he asks him sharply.

"Have I *what*?"

"Have you gone over the top, colonel?"

"Twenty years younger and I certainly would have. But we're not here to discuss my courage, are we?"

"Or lack of courage," Oliver says, holding his ground as he presses the soles of his shoes hard against the floor.

The colonel stubs out his cigarette and immediately lights another. "They are there to do their duty for king and country and to follow orders. I've heard that some officers have had to threaten to shoot anyone who refuses or who returns before the attack has concluded."

"And have they done it?" Oliver asks.

"Of course. They have obeyed orders."

"That's a hell of a way to win a war, don't you think, colonel?"

"So long as we win."

"And I guess I don't need to ask you if you would obey such an order," he says.

The colonel cocks his head slightly to one side and narrows his eyes. "And I guess I don't need to ask you the same question," he says. "But I have some other questions to ask you, and I'd like straightforward answers."

"Go on, ask."

"Does he have a girl at home who was writing to him?"

"No."

"You're sure?"

"I'm doing my job. He has no girl at home who is writing to him."

"And his friend who was killed when he returned to the trench."

"Ned."

"Private Morse."

"Private Ned Morse."

"A friend from boyhood?"

"We could save time if you were only to ask me questions that you don't already know the answers to," Oliver says, by way of issuing a complaint.

The colonel glares at him. "I could remind you of my rank, major."

"No need. And just for the record, I couldn't give a damn about rank. I consider it one of my greatest failings that something as artificial as a man's rank once impressed me. Boyhood friends, yes. Very close. And no buggery. Go on, colonel."

He does, immediately. "He tried to kill himself on two occasions. First when he was being held behind the lines—"

Oliver interrupts. "About to be led to a firing squad."

"And a second time when he was in hospital. After he had been spared the firing squad," the colonel says.

"Yes. And that proves something, doesn't it?" Oliver insists.

"What does it prove?"

"That he wasn't afraid of being executed. He was afraid of living. Living without his friend." His mind wanders for a moment. He begins thinking of the soldiers who were left behind in the trenches, ordered to shoot anyone who returned. How dreadful a duty to perform. "He was just scared," he says. "We do things when we're scared. Things we can't always account for."

"Not if we're properly trained," the colonel objects. "And that is the purpose for this…" he uses the word again, "… *enterprise*. We need to learn if there's something lacking in our training of these men that accounts for acts of cowardice.

He allowed his best friend to go over the top without him at his side. Something corrupted his loyalty to his friend."

"I suppose you're right."

"It's not enough for me to be right, major. We need to find out what it was. And don't tell me again that it was fear. Every man in the trench that morning was afraid."

"But perhaps not equally."

"And again the question – *why not equally?* What made this Burke fellow more frightened? It's your task to find the answer to that question. You have your orders and I'm sure you will meet them. For King and country."

stitches

The baker's wife who has sold Lily bread for the last year tells her this morning that there were two men in the shop asking if she and her husband knew her and showing them a photograph of her. "We told them nothing," she relates to her. "But I watched them go up the street and step into every shop."

Lily is sure she is telling her the truth. "They knew my name?" she says.

"Yes."

"And they had a photograph of me?"

"Yes. I recognised you immediately."

"Why did you lie for me?"

"My husband and I are Catholic," she tells her.

"And you're sure they were British?"

"They were not in uniform, but I know a wolf in sheep's clothing." Her eyes narrow and her voice falls to a whisper. "I know a British soldier when I see one," she says.

So Lily must take a different route back to the farm, walking along the golf course, across the dunes, running all the possibilities through her mind. Maybe the woman is wrong. Maybe they weren't British soldiers. Maybe they were on Lily's side and they learned from Brian or one of the other men he was in league with that she has been waiting in this town for over a year, and they have been sent to help her. But surely, whoever they were, they would have no way of knowing she hadn't drowned in the Irish Sea with the great ship. Maybe they were only guessing. Maybe they were looking for her to confirm what they already suspected – that she had drowned in the sea. But why go to the trouble to confirm this now, when the rebellion had failed? What difference could it make to them whether she was alive or dead? They had to be British soldiers, snooping around, trying to tie up loose ends to their investigation. Someone had given them her name and photograph.

The photograph! It hit her finally. Only Brian had a photograph of her. She had given it to him in New York. It was the only photograph of her on this side of the Atlantic. So then, the Brits had him in custody someplace and they had extorted the photograph from him, and the location of the farmhouse as well. Brian had been forced to name her as his accomplice. A conspirator in the planning of the uprising.

At first the thought of it fills her with such dread and fear that she can barely place one foot in front of the other. But she has only gone a little way before her fear turns to determination and sends her racing across the dunes, hoping the British soldiers are at her door so she can demand that they tell her what has become of this boy who was supposed to marry her. She can feel her heart pounding beneath her ribs, and the roots of her hair feel like something is pulling at them.

She bursts through the front door and searches the house for signs of them. For a few minutes there seems to be a different scent in the air, an oily scent that has risen above the smell of the peat she burns in the fireplace for warmth. It is enough to make her certain they have been here. It is enough to make her push a chair to the front window where she can see a long way, and sit there in the chair sewing the scraps of linen with the coastal maps back inside the hem of her wedding dress. This work, this tedious chore, is something she wants to do for Brian. And for herself. It is her way of saying goodbye to him, and letting go of the memory of him. He is dead. She knows this. She has known it for the year she's been waiting for him. And it is only a matter of time until British soldiers, or some kind of officials, come for her because her uncle James Connolly was their enemy. He led the rebellion. And she doesn't want them ever to know the secret of these scraps of linen. Let that remain a part of the story that they never learn. Let that part of the story belong only to her and to the boy who trusted her with it. It seems right to her to deny them this and to keep this hidden. She has not told Sam or anyone else.

She had hoped that Sam would return to her long before she had to light the lamp so she could see her stitches. But there is no sign of him out on the main road or coming up the long walkway. No sound of his feet on the gravel stones. Maybe she will grow old here, sitting at the window. A spinster sewing the hem of a wedding dress she never had occasion to wear. The thought makes her smile wryly because she knows something about herself now. It is something that she has learned over the past months. She has learned to be alone and to prefer it. Despite the sweet embrace of the broken soldier from the castle, she prefers her solitude. It has occurred to her that certain people are born to be alone and to make their own way in order to achieve whatever they were put on this earth to achieve. Like poets, she imagines. Living inside their own words. And artists like Sam, living inside their visions. And the priests and nuns she used to see shuffling along the streets of Galway as a child.

Maybe I'll become a nun, she thinks. And how odd to have these thoughts while her wedding dress is unfolded across her lap like a cloud that has fallen from the sky. She can look at it now without recalling how it billowed in the air as she jumped into the sea. This means that the months she has spent alone in this house have healed her. No. She has healed herself. And this, she knows, is essential if she is going to spend her life looking after herself, and depending on no one to care for her. There is a deep satisfaction in knowing this. In knowing that she is self-sufficient. She has heard people say before that everything happens for a purpose. Until now, she never knew whether or not to believe this. And before it was always said in the context of religion and of a belief that God's hand was in everyone's life. That was something she seemed to sense was just not true. But this is different. This knowledge is something she has fought for every day of her solitude from the time she awoke each morning until she closed her eyes at night. It is something she will never yield. To anyone.

shears

This is the last time they will make love. Neither of them will speak of this, but it is there with them like the flickering candle when he lifts up her sweater and places his lips on one nipple. Or perhaps he doesn't feel it the way she does. Maybe she is out ahead of him a little way in this regard. He is a few years older, but from the beginning, she has been aware that she has been leading the way since they first stumbled upon each other. She has been filling him with her heat and light. And now, even as she folds herself into his embrace, she knows that this is the last time because he has brought the boy's mask that he made for her to conceal herself when she begins her journey away from this place to escape whoever is looking for her. Across the room are the shears she will use to cut her hair as soon as they have finished and caught their breath. Maybe she will ask him to cut her hair for her so she will have one more thing to keep and to remember him by when the time they have shared is lost and gone.

She rises above him, pushing against him with her hands on his shoulders, drawing a kind of music from deep inside both of them that sounds to her like a cello repeating a solemn melody that echoes softly against the walls of the room before it seeps out into the night, pouring itself across the dunes and pastures, under stars shimmering with light, on its way to the sea where it causes fishermen to pause, lift their heads up, and listen.

Sam carries a chair outside next to the pump house. There he cuts her hair short enough so she can stuff it under the wool flat cap that he found for her at the castle. The transformation is stunning to him even before he fits the mask on. He holds a small mirror in his hand while they both stare at her reflection.

"Who is this boy?" she wants to know. "He looks too young to be one of your soldiers."

"Someone I knew at home. He was a few years older. He was famous. He rode a bicycle in the Olympics in Athens."

"You made it from memory?"

"I wanted to be like him when I was very little. He was from the next town, but he often rode on his bicycle across our fields. He always wore white. My mother would put me at the window so we could watch him. She would count out the time out loud. He got faster and faster as he trained. He rode like the wind."

"What was his name?"

"Frederick Keeping."

She playfully gives Sam her hand to shake. "Say hello to Frederick Keeping," she tells him.

They climb up into the lighthouse in the first light of morning. The Irish Sea is as still and calm as a millpond. The small parade of fishing boats moves about like pieces on a game board. She has made him promise not to ask her where she will go when she leaves him because she is afraid this will only weaken her resolve. But he can't seem to help himself. He can feel her disappearing. "You can live in the castle," he tells her. "You'll be safe there."

She moves closer to him, laying her head against his chest. "Just hold me," she says. She could try to tell him something that would make sense to him, so he would understand why she is leaving him, why she has to get her life back into her own hands. But her only concern is that he doesn't believe he has something to do with it; she doesn't want him to live on believing that he was not enough, that he lost her because he wasn't strong enough or beautiful enough to contain her. She doesn't want to leave him crippled in that way. Because that is what she has believed about herself for much of the last year. When Brian didn't come for her, she blamed herself at first. She had somehow proved unworthy of him and so he cast her away. For the longest time this feeling persisted and it was enough to paralyse her. There were months of paralysis when she felt worthless because she felt unworthy of being loved. Until she decided that none of us is worthy of being loved. Being loved is a *gift* that someone bestows upon us.

"You know what you mean to me," she says. Her lips brush against his canvas shirt. In the fabric, she can smell the scent of the alcohol he uses to clean his brushes. She waits for his response and she will examine it carefully to see if he can tell that she is saying goodbye now. She wants to say goodbye without saying it. Saying it would cause her to break into pieces.

When Sam tells her that they are having goose for tomorrow's dinner and he wants her to come, it tells her everything. He doesn't know, and maybe it's better this way because how would she explain her decision if he asked her to? How would she explain to anyone the feeling she has deep inside her that she must pull herself away from him in order to preserve herself? It makes little sense even to her. It is just a feeling that rides through her steadily and then sometimes picks up velocity on a surge of restlessness, and makes her want to scream.

"I have something to give you," she tells him. "Wait here."

She places the boy's mask he has made for her in his hand before she climbs down the iron stairs of the lighthouse and crosses the garden to the house, thinking that she might have told him how she has this feeling that something waits for her out in the wide world. Something that will require her to be on her own, unattached to anyone.

She is climbing the stairs to her room to get the wedding dress that she has wrapped in brown paper and white string that the baker's wife gave her. There is a sound outside the front door and it makes her wonder why Sam has followed her when she asked him to wait for her in the lighthouse. And then comes a loud, impatient knock on the door that stops her heart and freezes her on the stairs. Whoever is outside the front door coughs suddenly and while he is coughing, another person speaks. So, it is two of them. And she knows at once that it must be the two British soldiers in sheep's clothing.

She has the package in her arms and she could easily make it down the back stairs and out the door, but she wants to get a closer look first at these two people she will soon be trying to outrun. It means she must risk walking the length of the hallway to the front window that looks down to where they are standing outside the door.

It seems to take forever to reach the window, moving so slowly, one foot barely touching the floor before she lifts it and takes another step. It takes long enough for her to consider that the baker's wife was wrong and that these men who have come for her are bringing word from Brian. *Perhaps one of them is Brian!*

But, of course, they are strangers. Looking down from the window, her face concealed behind the curtain, there is a bulkiness to both of them. They seem too big for their sheep's clothing. They have none of the grace about them that Brian had. None of Sam's fineness. One of them takes off his fedora and pulls what is left of his black hair from above one side of his head across his pathetic bald skull. The other one spits his chewing tobacco on the ground. A brown strand of drool hangs from his lip.

She makes her way out from the back of the house and kneels down below the lighthouse glass with Sam until they have gone. "You have to leave here," he tells her.

"I know, Sam."

"Stay right here. Don't go back into the house. I'll bring you some money so you can travel. Just give me an hour."

She nods her assent, but she doesn't need any more money;

she has saved enough from the money Brian gave her. So then, they part company on a lie.

She hands him the package. "Take this," she says. "Keep it for me, please." He looks at her and something passes between them. Some understanding, she thinks.

She watches him make his way, running across the dunes, down to the shore. It takes all her strength to keep from following him.

BOOK IV

holiness

Almost as soon as Lily leaves his life, Sam misses her and begins to dwell on how he might have let her down or disappointed her. When he walks back to her place and stands in front of the empty house, he hears the burning horse shrieking in agony again, he sees the madness settling in the animal's bulging eyes. He sees a man's toe, the nail perfectly clipped, on the blade of his shovel. He smells the foul air that gushed from the dying German's bowels.

He should have done something for her. He should have gone with her. He should have led her somewhere she would be safe. That's what Ned would have done. But is there any such thing as a safe place now? Maybe here in the castle. Did he offer to bring her here? He can't seem to remember. But surely she could have hidden here behind the mask he made for her. He could have kept her safe here if he had been someone else, someone who wasn't too broken to be trustworthy.

To endure his loneliness after Lily leaves and the guilt he feels for how he might have let her down or disappointed her, Sam begins each day disappearing into the photograph of Ned with Katie and Charlotte. Some mornings they look like strangers to him, and other mornings he gazes at their faces, wondering if he might have seen them somewhere as they passed through his life. Other mornings he feels like he knows them better than he knows himself. And there is no way he can explain this.

With three new soldiers at the castle, his days are full, his work is never-ending, and for this he is eminently grateful. But no matter how completely the work engages him, there is a space in his mind that is inhabited by the three people in the photograph, and if they are strangers to him or not, it seems that they all want something from him. They want him to *do something.* Something he cannot name or even guess at. But in the early mornings before there is enough light in his room to see their faces, he believes that he will find the answer. In time, he will know what it is that he is meant to do for them. In time, he will walk into the clearing with them, and he will understand. For now, the clearing seems very far off. For now he is having some difficulty with simple things like knowing which of the three new soldiers he is talking with because they all look the same when they are sitting in front of him in the temporary, unpainted plaster masks he has made for them. There is Wilkinson, who wants to go back to work in his father's barbershop in Chester. He lost part of his jaw and when he talks, he whistles. In addition to losing one arm, Brookes, who worked as a coal miner on the coast of Scotland, has no forehead left, though the rest of his face is perfectly intact. And Brigham, who dreams of living in Paris and being a fashion designer, had his lips and his nose burned off. Every time Sam turns around, one of them is waiting for him. They wait outside the door to his room. They wait in his workshop. They are identical in their blank plaster masks and, until they begin to speak, Sam is often confused in their presence, unsure who he is talking with, whose life is in his hands. At the end of each day, they leave their masks on his bench so he can work on them late into the night, or in the mornings before anyone awakes. Shaping the tin to precisely follow the contours of the plaster mask is tedious work, done with a set of tiny bronze hammers that he must strike as delicately as the hammers strike the strings of a piano. Painting is the easy part for him. But this shaping requires such concentration and repetition that Sam has memorised the individual topography of each face. Even when he is by himself he is never alone. Their faces animate his imagination.

This morning as he passes through the dining room, he sees one of the new soldiers standing at a window, looking out at the rain. He turns slightly and Sam sees his empty sleeve. *Brookes*, he thinks. The coal miner. "You must be hungry," Sam says to him. He doesn't move. "I'll be in the kitchen if you want something to eat," he says.

Sam has just begun to walk away when the soldier calls to him. "I don't want to eat. I need to go home."

Sam waits a moment, then says, "I'm just going to make some tea. Are you sure you wouldn't like some?"

The man shuffles behind him into the kitchen. Outside the window, another man with an identical blank plaster mask is clipping the hedges. It occurs to Sam that no one on earth is living as strange an existence as he is.

Soon after Sam begins work on the copper masks, Oliver decides that dinners should be formal affairs. The soldiers wear their masks that are all in different stages of completion. They are all having great difficulty eating. They keep smearing mashed potatoes and gravy on their faces. He wipes off one man's mask with his linen napkin. Sam attends to another's.

Finally, he establishes a new rule. For a while, until they get the hang of it, they can take their masks off to eat. But they must turn their chair away from the table. Oliver reminds them that all their efforts will be rewarded when one day after they've returned home and they are able to take their dear sweethearts out for dinner and no one will notice them at all. Unless they stare at them long enough to see that their expressions are not changing.

Sometimes Sam looks down the length of the table to Oliver sitting at the far end, and he sees himself sitting there instead. He wonders if this will ever come to an end. If he might spend his whole life here until he has turned into an old man like him.

When dinner is over, they all do the clean-up together in the kitchen and Oliver encourages them to talk about the lives awaiting them at home. One of them was raised by a woman he calls 'Nana', who taught him how to bake pies. How to roll out the crust so that it is thin and delicate. He wants to bake a peach pie with her when he returns home, but the war will have to end first so that they have the butter they need. "You can never use too much butter," he claims.

Brookes vows to return to the coal mine even though his five pals from the same mine who went to war with him are all dead now. He will descend below the ground each day at work and this will make him feel close to his friends again. Not only the memory of working the mine with them, but the fact that what remains of them is also underground. "We will be together again in spirit," he says.

The other soldier describes the barbershop down to its finest detail. The way sunlight falls onto the blue tiled floor. The scent of the shaving soap. There is an indelible quality to the details and they arrange themselves into a picture in Sam's mind, a picture so vivid that it seems quite possible to him that he has been there before. And he believes it must be the same for Oliver.

* * *

Out on the turret one evening after they have read the new names of the newly killed and missing soldiers, Oliver asks them to talk about the girls at home who are waiting for them. At first they speak haltingly, as if they are trying to learn a new language. But with time, it becomes easier and the girls come to life. One of them has promised Brookes that she will be wearing the pale yellow dress he bought for her before he left for the war. He describes how it gathers at her waist. It is almost too heartbreaking to listen to. And it makes Oliver think of Katie. This girl whom he has never met is almost constantly on his mind. Katie on her own in the world. Katie who will be looked at by other men now. *What has she told her daughter?* he wonders. What words did she claim to explain to the child that she would never see her daddy again? One of the words might have been *heaven*. Perhaps she has told her that her daddy is waiting for her in heaven with the other daddies who died in the war, who were torn apart by machine-gun fire, or who suffocated with mud stuffed in their mouths and throats. Or perhaps the child is still too young to be told anything about her father. Perhaps there is still time for Katie to decide how to tell her.

One evening up in the turret, Oliver tells the new soldiers that there are two churches in town for them if they are so disposed. "As for me," he exclaims, "this turret is my church. And here we will mark the passing of those soldiers who have lost everything. We'll read their names aloud beneath the stars and clouds. There's a holiness to that, don't you think?"

He looks at each soldier and at Sam. And he can tell that they are all trying to believe him.

* * *

Life for Sam has assumed an unhurried quality and a logic that is reassuring. There are no intrusions. Even when Brookes interrupts his work one afternoon to ask him to please remember *not* to paint him smiling on his mask, this request seems only to be part of the natural order of things.

Even today. Another day of rain. Mid-afternoon, Sam is on his way up to his workshop when Brigham stops him. He is in high spirits. He wants Sam to do him a favour. "I've had a look at a photograph of Wilkinson's girl," he says with great enthusiasm. "And I've decided that I want you to give me *his* mask when you've finished it. If you cover for me and let me get a head start on him, I figure I'll have time to give her a quick shag before he gets home to murder me."

For some reason, Sam doesn't laugh, though he knows this is a joke.

"Only kidding, old chap," Brigham says. "No offence intended." He extends his hand. Finally, Sam shakes it.

Later, as he works at his bench, Sam smiles to himself about this, and realises that he must try harder to recover his sense of humour. But he can't really remember if he ever had a sense of humour. Yes, of course he had. He had laughed with Daisy from time to time. He remembered the time she had sat on his lap and made him draw with his arms reaching around her to the sketch pad. At the time, they had both giggled like children. And Ned had always made him laugh. It was easy for him to laugh when he was with Ned. They were always engaged in some kind of antic that Ned had cooked up. Around the age of thirteen, whenever they were bored, they would assault the golf course in town where the toffs played. They would hide in the trees and scamper out onto the fairway to steal the golfers' balls before they could get to them. Like stealing eggs from a henhouse. Sam always wanted to grab the balls and just run away; that was enough for him. But Ned insisted they hide behind the treeline so they could be entertained by the golfers' befuddlement when they couldn't find their balls.

Now as Sam walks across the room and opens the window to bring in some of the clear, warm air of this summer afternoon, he wonders when was the last time he had laughed. When Lily spoke to him about shelling peas, he must have laughed along with her.

Considering this as he turns away from the window, he hears someone speaking whose voice he cannot recognise. Then he sees him. The young boy drowning in his father's postman's coat. Tommy Falcon. He is down below speaking with the three soldiers, and even before Sam has any reason to be certain the boy is speaking about him, he is *certain*. Sam can hear him plainly. And he can feel the deliberate rolling pressure of panic rising inside his chest again and throbbing against his ribs so that they feel like they might crack like eggshells.

"My father wrote to us about one man who got his best friend killed because he wouldn't leave the trench. His friend had to go back for him and a shell exploded and killed him when he was trying to pull the coward into the fight. My father told us that they need to shoot all cowards on the spot from now on so they don't infect the rest of the men."

He is relating this with great eagerness and a trace of hostility.

And then Sam runs for the stairs. He doesn't stop until he is in his room, leaning over the sink and staring at the scars across his wrists while his hands shake. And he can hear the distant booming of artillery as he leans close to Ned in a long line of men about to climb up out of the trench into a blizzard of machine-gun fire. He can see his own face frozen in fear. Ned grabs him by the shoulders and tells him not to look back. "When the whistle blows, it's every man for himself. I can't help you here, Sam." Then there is the shrieking whistle and suddenly Sam watches Ned's face contort in fear. A fear that matches his own. And to see Ned's resolve disappear so completely terrifies him.

What brings Sam back from that memory is the sound of another voice in the courtyard below his window. A voice that had to belong to this world, this world he lives in now, and not the world of the war. Because it is a child's voice, high-pitched and full of excitement.

Sam walks slowly across the floor, to the window. Each step takes him nearer to where his refuge from the world ends.

For a moment, he stands there looking down at Katie and the child and wondering how this can be. And then he drops quietly to his knees. He is conscious of something then as he hides his face below the window. It is a feeling that everything he has ever been sure of is slipping away from him.

falling

Oliver hesitates outside the door to Sam's room before he knocks and opens it and stands in the threshold with a plate of food. "It turns out that Brookes was once a chef. He's made us curried lamb and rice. First-rate."

Sam is sitting on the floor in one corner of the room, his head bowed in his hands. Oliver walks to the bedside table and sets the plate down there. When he turns, he sees Sam looking up at him with a bewildered expression. "I've settled them in a rooming house in town," he relates, anxiously. "I imagine they'll sleep. It was a long journey. I spent time in Dorset years ago. It felt like the end of the earth."

Sam says nothing. He just keeps looking at him. It is as if he were mute.

Oliver is in something of a hurry to get it all out in front of them. "You've seen those notices in the newspaper," he says. "That's how they found you."

The word *they* sounds odd to Sam. As if the child who has no memory of him has been looking for him. *Strangers who have met before*, he thinks. *Friends who have never met. I have returned to a place I've never been to. All my life I've been returning here. It was inevitable. It is my destiny. And Katie's too. Like wheels set rolling on an iron rail.*

* * *

"You'll want to know why I responded to her notice," Oliver says. "You'll want to know why I told her how to find you. But first, you must believe that I never… never in a million years did I believe she would come here. I only wanted to inform her that you had survived the war and were well. And now I realise that I could have done that without telling her that you were here. I suppose that is what I should have done. You've got to get up off the floor, son. Please. Here, let me help you."

It surprises Oliver when Sam lets him help him to a chair. He leads him to it like a child that has fallen out of bed in the night. *Perhaps this happened to him in hospital as well*, Oliver thinks. His body is limp. It is as if all his bones have been broken. It makes him feel even worse for what he has done. "I see now that I broke some trust between us," he starts again. "I remember speaking with you when you first arrived, and telling you that trust was the most important thing for you to heal. So, I've made a mistake, and I hope you will forgive me for this, Sam. When you grow old, you make a lot of mistakes."

Sam bows his head for a moment and mutters something under his breath. Then finally, he speaks. "Why are they here?"

That is the question. They look at each other.

"They came a long way to try to help you recover from whatever happened to you…

from what you went through in the war. And perhaps more than that. Perhaps Katie was searching for you because if she found you, she would find a small piece of what she lost. Her husband. Your best friend. Does that make sense?"

"I can't do anything for them. You should have known that."

"Maybe she just needed to see you. Alive."

"Am I alive?"

"Of course you are. Look at the work you've done here, Sam."

"It's just my work."

"It's a great deal more than that. It's your soul. You put your soul into your work. And the soul is what war attempts to destroy. In your case, war failed entirely."

Sam looks to the window, at the trees bending slightly in the wind. The room is filled with the scent of the sea. "I can't see her," he says.

"I thought you might need them, Sam. She's your best friend's wife."

"Widow," Sam says.

He stands up from the chair then and begins pacing the floor.

To Oliver, he looks like he might break into pieces, and he feels responsible for this. He has done the wrong thing. And now he has said the wrong things.

"We all fall, Sam," he says. "No matter how strong we are, we all fall in the end. Sometimes we get back on our feet by helping someone who needs us. She's lost her husband. She's lost the father of her child. Maybe you can console them. Just give them a little hope."

Sam doesn't say anything in response. But he stops pacing and this seems to give Oliver permission to say more. "I'll leave you alone," he says. "Eat your supper. We all need to eat. Even in times like this." He is almost out the door when he stops and says, "She's a lovely little girl, chattering away with the soldiers."

* * *

Sam does eat the supper that Brookes has prepared for him. Despite himself, he eats. One bite of food at a time. He watches his hand lifting the fork. He watches the fork moving towards his mouth. It is as if someone else is feeding him. He thinks of Oliver climbing back down the stairs, going into his room, knocking himself out in his gold chair. He knows that he has to see Katie. It is like going over the top when the whistle blows. *There are things one has to do if one is alive.*

He looks at the empty plate. Stop eating and you will no longer be alive. Just stop. Render yourself so weak that your eyes close and it's done. He wonders how long it would take, and then remembers wondering this before.

Night has fallen. He stands at his window watching clouds blow across the sky. The tide is up and he can hear waves turning onto the sand like some giant thing breathing. Then he hears the train whistle sweeping across the dunes and he remembers watching the trains roll across the countryside beyond the farm. He was very small, working in the field when his father caught him leaning on his rake, watching the train. "Imagine where that train might take you in this world," his father had said to him. It was a small thing, but Sam has never watched another train without thinking about this. Where he might go in the world. His talent for rendering things in a sketchbook had already been recognised. To him it was nothing that made him feel exceptional. But there were his teachers, and his own parents, who had assured him that he had a gift and that his gift would take him somewhere if he worked hard enough.

It has brought him here, to this window, to this night, to this place. And it feels like his gift has betrayed him. A part of him wants to go downstairs and wake Oliver and scream at him. *What the hell do you know about me? And what gives you the right to intrude upon my life the way you have? Just who are you anyway? What gives old men the right to lord it over young people? You don't even have a wife or children. What can you possibly know about anything that matters?*

And what does matter to me? Sam wonders. This is the most difficult question he can ask himself. Why should his life matter in any way in a world where millions have been slaughtered in the last few years? Millions just like him, sacrificed for nothing. Vanished, despite whatever talents they possessed, whatever made someone believe they might be exceptional and that they might make their mark on the world.

He closes his eyes and tries to keep from thinking about anything, but this is impossible. He knows what matters to him. There is only one thing now. He must protect Ned at all costs. Ned, who is no longer here to protect himself.

apple tree

In the morning, Katie is waiting for him, alone. The woman who runs the boarding house has a small daughter of her own matching Charlotte's age and is watching over them while they play together.

What neither Sam nor Katie knows as they hold each other in those first moments together is that they are already lashing out at each other in some way. It is what we do. When we are in pain, we lash out at the people who love us best because we think they should be able to *end our pain*, and they cannot.

She finds Sam just beyond the courtyard where he is hanging a homemade swing from one branch of an apple tree. It had been Oliver's idea. A swing for the child. "All children love to swing, I think," he'd said to Sam as they worked on it together after feeding the three soldiers their porridge and toast.

Her hair has the scent of pears. Against his cheek, it feels like velvet. When she speaks his name, he closes his eyes, drinking in all these sensations, and reminding himself through a mounting dizziness in his mind of what matters. Ned. Ned is all that matters. Ned, who is no longer here, but should have been the one in her embrace.

She speaks first and Sam is surprised by how calm she seems in contrast to the turmoil that fills him. "I'm so grateful that Mr Blackburn reached out to me so we could come here and be with you. It feels good to hold you. To see you. My God, Sam, you're alive. You look well. Does it feel good to be holding me?"

This is not easy for Sam to answer. In fact, it stuns him so that he can't speak.

Katie goes on as if his silence is perfectly normal. "In you, I've always recognised a kindred spirit. A fellow soul. You know this. You've always known this, just as I have."

He isn't aware that he has bowed his head until he feels her hand on his chin, gently lifting his face to her.

"Sam?"

"Yes."

"What can I say to you?"

"I don't know," he tells her. "I'm not sure."

He sees that he is upsetting her and he apologises.

"No," she says, shaking her head slowly. "That's all right. I know it must be difficult for you to see me."

"Ned," he says, despite himself.

She looks into his eyes for a moment with a curious expression. He hears the train whistle again in the distance and longs to be on the train going somewhere, anywhere. "I loved you both," she says. "From the start, I loved you both. But in that strange silence when you were both gone and your letters stopped coming for months, it was *you* I spoke with constantly. It was you I pretended was just beside me. My friend."

Now Sam looks into her eyes for the first time. He is trying to decide what he sees. In addition to her calmness, he sees something else that he can't comprehend.

In the silence between them, she takes something from her pocket. It is a piece of paper that looks like it has been folded and unfolded many times. Sam thinks it might be something he drew for her years ago.

"This is the notice I was sent, Sam," she says. "This is all I have left of Ned. Just a piece of paper telling me of his death in a place in France I'd never heard of. A handful of words, Sam. But now that we're together, you can tell me what happened.

When you're ready. I know you have your own grief. I know you loved him too."

Protect Ned, he thinks.

Then she notices the swing and when she touches it, she says, "You've made this for Charlotte. How sweet and thoughtful of you, Sam. She was such a stoic little traveller all the way. She never complained once on our long journey here. She's speaking in sentences now, Sam. It's a wonder to me. For months after she was born she screamed bloody murder, but she's so contented now, and we've become such fine friends."

His silence is a problem; he knows that. But he can't manage to say anything. She takes him in her arms again. She is laughing faintly when she asks, "Why didn't you jump to me?"

This only confuses him more. He wonders what she could possibly mean.

"You remember," she says. "From the cliffs."

He is surprised to hear his own voice. "I wanted to," he says.

She holds him at arm's length. "I wanted it to be you," she says.

Her smile is so generous that it confuses him even more. For all the time he has known her since they were very young, she has always seemed to withhold something and to protect her private thoughts. Now she seems to be standing out in the open. Completely visible for the first time.

"It's not too late. Tell me that it's not too late," she says.

How strange to hear these words, when he has been thinking their exact opposite. "Ned's gone," he says. "It's much too late."

Her expression changes abruptly. He can tell that he has disappointed her. "Why?" she asks.

"*Why?*" he says.

"Why must it be too late? I loved you both equally. You must know that. It's just that Ned was so bold. He gave me no choice. He carried me away from you. If I had married you, I would still have my husband. Charlotte would still have her father."

This sounds deranged to him. And he realises in an instant the full extent to which she is suffering.

She looks away for a moment, gathering her strength for what she tells him next.

"I haven't told her," she says. "I haven't told her that her father is never coming back to her."

Sam is shocked to hear this. And Katie sees his shock.

"What, Sam? Have I done the wrong thing? Do you think I should have told her?"

His hands have begun to tremble. He takes hold of one of the ropes on the swing to steady himself.

"I don't know what's right or wrong," he says.

She doesn't seem to hear this. "I was hoping," she tells him, "that if I came here, you might help me tell her. If we can do this together, perhaps we can find the right things to say."

He is momentarily drawn to her eyes, wondering why he doesn't remember how vivid the blue is. It is a depthless blue that he often tried to define and to paint, but never quite succeeded in rendering.

"Anyway," she says as she draws herself away from him. "Why didn't you write to me after Ned was killed? Why didn't you tell me that you were here?"

Now he sees something familiar. Her toughness and that stern quality in the way that she presents herself to the world. She has always driven a hard bargain with people. He acknowledges once again that she would have made a far better soldier than he was. And he realises that she has been trying to accommodate him until now. Trying hard to be gentle with him as she often had in their past.

"I didn't know what to do," Sam manages to say. "I haven't known what to do since Ned…" His voice trails away.

She takes a step away from him. "Well, I'm here now. Charlotte and I are here. We came a long way to see you. And we're not going to stay in some boarding house. I have been kept in the dark for more than two and a half years, ever since you and Ned left for this absurd war. I'm not going to remain in the dark any longer. There are plenty of empty rooms here for us. We're going to stay here and you can help me. The way Ned would want you to."

Sam knows then that this is going to be very difficult, and that the hardest part will be what he keeps from her. He doesn't finish that thought. The dizziness in his mind expands suddenly and he feels himself falling through her piercing blue stare that has transfixed him. He sees himself lying face down in the mud, moments after the world turned in on itself with the explosion. He inhabits that moment when he found himself lying in the mud. *How can I be breathing when I'm dead?* he had wondered. *How can I be moving my fingers in the mud?* The only sound was a howling silence in his head. He felt time rushing past him though he had no idea how much of it had passed when his eyes were open and he saw Ned lying still and lifeless just beyond the reach of his arm.

Katie's voice brings him back. She is thanking him again for making the swing for Charlotte. She sounds like a stranger being courteous. *It's the least that I can do for you*, he thinks. *It's the only thing I can do for you.*

kite

Before dawn, Sam is at his workbench, painting the thin scar on the left side of the forehead on Wilkinson's mask. The scar that has marked him since the summer morning when he was seven years old and went over the handlebars of his bicycle trying to get out of the way of a neighbourhood dog. Sam can barely see the scar in the photograph he is working from. And he cannot stop thinking that in some ways, the war was easy. You didn't have to know who you were. And there was nothing to hide except the one thing everyone tried to hide. Fear. There was no shame or guilt like there is to hide now. And the things that terrified you were real. Bullets whizzing past your head. And the cloud of suffocating gas that melted around you. And the exploding shells that filled the air with searing metal shards. Now what terrifies Sam is that Katie is going to tell him that she is glad he didn't die with Ned. Because that comes very close to what he must hide. That comes very close to the anger he feels at the centre of his body, the anger that makes his hands shake. He cannot let anyone know why he is so angry. He must do everything he possibly can to keep anyone from knowing that he is angry at Ned. He must hide that, and the question behind his anger. The question that no one except Ned can answer.

When Oliver comes to summon him to breakfast, Sam declines and is unable to look at him. He knows that he has hurt the man's feelings and when the guilt overcomes him so that he can no longer concentrate on his work, he puts his brush down and wanders into the dining room, where he is surprised to find Katie and Charlotte sitting at the long table along with Wilkinson, Brookes and Brigham. The child is entertaining them all by singing 'Ring a Ring o' Roses', but she stops the moment Sam takes his place at the table. And when she turns towards him, it takes his breath away to see how much she looks like Ned. The only time Sam had seen her before was when she was newborn. Somehow across the time since then she has become a person in her own right. Katie whispers something to her and she immediately climbs down from her chair and walks to Sam, and stands before him, presenting herself with perfect posture and self-assurance.

"Your name is Sam," she exclaims happily.

He manages to look at her, but can't speak.

Brookes raises his cup of tea in a toast. "Here's to Sam. Our artist."

The others raise their cups and Oliver passes the child a glass of orange juice so she can join in.

"My daddy's friend," Charlotte tells them.

"He's our friend too," Brookes says to her.

"He's our saviour," says Brigham.

"He's the very best of friends," Oliver says.

There is a marvellous scent coming from the top of Charlotte's head unlike any Sam has ever encountered before. He breathes it in deeply and it seems to fill his lungs with lightness. In a playful, high-pitched voice, she tells him that the sea makes noises and that she wants to go to the sea with her mummy. "Seashells," she exclaims.

When he manages to smile at last, Katie looks on with deep satisfaction.

"Go to the beach," Brookes exclaims. "Take the day off and leave the painting to me. I'll make these two look like something the cat's dragged in."

Apparently, Wilkinson has been too self-conscious to eat

in the child's presence. As soon as Charlotte begins singing again, he quietly turns away from the table, tips his plaster mask up onto the top of his head and quickly eats his porridge.

Katie reaches across the table and takes hold of Sam's hand. When he looks up at her, she is smiling with deep satisfaction. To Oliver, she appears in that moment to have everything she wants and has waited so long for.

Brookes leans toward both of them. "When I look at this wee child," he says solemnly, "it reminds me why we fought this war. The sight of your little girl, ma'am, makes it all seem worthwhile."

"That's very sweet of you," Katie tells him. She glances at Charlotte, then looks back at Brookes. "I wasn't sure that I had the right to come here," she says. "I don't want to intrude."

Brookes understands. "It's not an intrusion at all," he tells her. "It's a blessing. Isn't that right, Sam?"

The panic that Sam is trying so hard to conceal begins to roll through him again like seasickness. He can taste the mustard gas, and feel the mud beneath his fingernails. "Excuse me," he says as he gets to his feet. When he is halfway across the room, making his way from all of them, the child calls to him. "Goodbye, Sam." He hears this and it seems to take all his strength to keep his legs from buckling beneath him.

He rallies for them that afternoon when they all work together in the shop making a kite for Charlotte. It had been Katie's idea. Sam cuts the narrow strips of balsa wood and notches them to fit together while Katie and the others work on the fabric, sewing little pockets in the corners to accommodate the frame.

Later, Sam stays behind and stands at the windows watching them fly the kite in the garden. The soldiers take turns riding Charlotte on their shoulders while Katie and Oliver talk. *About what?* he wonders. *Almost certainly about me.*

* * *

Sam is right about this, of course; they are talking about him. Together they are trying to figure out what is wrong with him. Katie is asking Oliver why he didn't seem glad to see her, and he, in turn, is telling her that he can't explain this.

She tells him about the day at the cliffs at Durdle Door before the war and how she had asked Sam why he hadn't jumped. She didn't believe it was fear that prevented him from jumping to her.

* * *

Katie was right, though she could not know the real reason that Sam had stayed on the clifftop that day, that he had decided long before that he could never have her and that she deserved Ned. And more than that, he had decided that the only way he could keep both of them in his life was if she gave herself to Ned. Without her to rein him in, he would eventually lose Ned to the wild currents of the world that were so irresistible to him. He would go searching for something that matched the power she had over him and Sam would never see him again. He would be nothing more to Ned than a childhood chum who turned up from time to time in the mosaic of his boyhood memories. Without Katie, there would be no one holding the end of the string, and the kite would fly off and Sam would watch it disappear.

bones

Long after the soldiers drop off their masks for the night, Katie comes into the workshop. He hears her walking towards him, but he doesn't turn to look at her. Soon she is standing beside him as he paints the faintest trace of red into one cheek of Brigham's mask.

She tells him that Charlotte is sound asleep, and he can hear the relief in her voice. "Which one is this?" she asks.

He must try to be more accommodating, he thinks. "Brigham," he replies.

"He's told you, I'm sure, that he plans to live in Paris? He wants to design clothing."

Sam thinks that he might have nodded his head to her, but he can't be certain. Then he watches her reach down and touch the photograph of Brigham taken before the war that he is using to paint the mask. "It's so unfair," she says. "And Ned couldn't wait to go. Do you remember, Sam?"

He knows that he remembers this. But she is getting too close to him again and he tries to distract her. "The left side of his face is completely intact," he says. "Brigham wanted me to make him a partial mask at first. I tried and failed. I could never get... where his face and the mask met, I couldn't..."

He stops there and gives up.

"I read that they allowed friends to bury their friends," Katie says. "Did you bury Ned?"

The dead burying the dead, they used to call it. He shakes his head.

"No one ever told me where he was buried," she says.

He shakes his head again.

She looks straight at him as if she doesn't believe him. There is something slightly inimical in her expression.

She continues to talk to him and question him at the same time. "We argued, you know? We argued a great deal about the war. He always spoke about it as if it were *his* war. I mean, he seemed to think that the whole affair had been orchestrated for him to prove just how brave he was. I always thought that you were braver. I know he possessed physical courage. The way he used to charge at things; his bones meant nothing at all to him. But deep inside, to be an artist, you have to be made of steel, I think. You have to feel all of the world's pain and suffering more deeply than the rest of us. That takes more courage than most of us have."

As soon as her voice stops, he can hear these words inside his head: *She knows. She knows what I am hiding from her.*

And just before his hands begin to shake, he lets the paintbrush fall onto the bench and puts his hands in his pockets.

This alerts her to something; he can tell by the way she narrows her eyes. "What is it?" she asks him.

"Nothing."

"You must be tired from all this work."

"Yes. Yes, I suppose I am."

"I can see that. I can see that you're exhausted." Then she touches his face tenderly the way a mother would. "And your girl must be absolutely splendid. Oliver told me about her. Her name is Daisy? Such a lovely name, I think."

"She's not my girl," he tells her. "She's no one's girl."

"That's the way to be then, isn't it? To be a woman who belongs to herself. And not to a man. It's a man's world and men have made a royal mess of it. But tell me about her, won't you?"

"We knew each other when I was at art school, that's all," he says.

"That's not all," she says, smiling demurely. "You were lovers. And I suppose that would mean that she was your first love."

When he doesn't confirm or deny this, she teases him. "Come on, Sam. No secrets between such old friends as we are. Such old souls. She was your first, as Ned was mine. Though I imagine I didn't occupy quite the same place on his list. I was quite a way down, I'm certain."

"He loved you," Sam says. Then he takes the photograph of the three of them from the drawer on the bench. "He always had this with him."

In the boyish way she has of moving, she pulls herself up so she is sitting on the bench and takes the picture in her hand. She stares at it, kicking her feet gently as if she is riding on the swing he built. Then she begins to talk again of her last night with Ned. "I wouldn't say goodbye to him properly," she said. She looks away for a few seconds. Then she turns quickly and faces Sam directly. "Do you find me appalling? Did Ned tell you? Boys always talk about these things as if they matter more than anything else."

Sam shakes his head.

"It's sad, though, isn't it? The war was already taking its toll before he even got to France. I knew very well just what was expected of me, Sam. I knew what Ned expected. I left our bed and walked outside. The stars overhead seemed especially bright. Do you ever get tired of doing what's expected of you? Can you imagine how tired we'll be if we live to grow old and we've spent our lives doing what is expected of us?"

She reaches for one of the masks and lifts it to her face. He sees a small imperfection in the nose he has made for Wilkinson. "Of course I felt guilty. For leaving him so unsatisfied," she confesses.

She speaks through the mask, affecting the voice of a man. "Would thou leave me so unsatisfied?"

Then without the mask. "What satisfaction would thou have tonight?"

Then with the mask. "The exchange of thy love's faithful vow for mine."

Then without the mask. "I gave thee mine before thou did request it. But I would it were to withdraw it."

Then with the mask. "Why would thou withdraw it? For what purpose, love?"

Then without the mask. "But to be frank, to give it thee again."

She sets the mask down and puts her arms around Sam, drawing him close. Then she whispers, "And yet I wish but for the thing I have. My bounty is as boundless as the sea. My love is deep. The more I give to thee, the more I have, for both are infinite."

He gently pulls away from her, hoping that she will let go of him and not be offended. But she holds on even more tightly. "You used to say my *Romeo and Juliet* was glorious," she reminds him sadly. "I guess I'm a terrible actress. I can't persuade you to be my Romeo?"

"It's not your fault, Katie," he tells her.

"There," she exclaims. "You said my name. Say it again. The name you've said ten thousand times since we were children. Please."

"Katie."

"It's not so terribly difficult, is it?"

"No."

"Whatever's happened to you, Sam – whatever this war has done to you, I know who you are still. And I'm not so much unlike your Daisy, you know. Oliver told me what she's doing for the soldier. I could take that poor man into my arms… into my bed… into myself. To make him believe that he was still beautiful, still enough of a man to be loved by a girl, despite his wounds. Despite what made him grotesque to the rest of the world. I could stay here, you know? Yes. I could make each of these men believe in their beauty again. I have that power within me. I could do it because it's so…" she searches for the word, "inestimable. And so completely unacceptable."

He hears her sternness again. He doesn't doubt her at all.

"And as for being glorious," she goes on, "that was always your domain. Ned and I both knew it. He and I were the plain ones, but we knew that you had a greatness in you. We both predicted your greatness. And look at you. Look what you're doing now for these soldiers. There isn't another person in the entire British Empire who is doing what you're doing."

"It's really not so much," he says.

"A drop in the bucket is what you feel, I suppose. But that's just you, Sam. That's just your modesty. Your humility. You don't see it, but your humility only makes your greatness shine that much brighter."

Now she lets go of him and jumps to the floor. "Anyway, it's lovely here, isn't it, Sam?" she says. "Charlotte and I took a long walk today. It's the kind of place where you could begin a new life, I think."

She looks at him with concern.

"We can't pretend, Katie," he says. But he realises that she isn't really listening to him.

"The thing about little children is that they only live in the present. There is no past. No future. Just the moment that they are standing in. And if you don't inhabit that moment with them, then it's gone and you've missed it, and you'll never get it back."

He watches her walk across the room in silence. She begins to speak, but then pauses when the train whistle sounds in the distance, waiting until it stops. "The whole time you and Ned were gone, I lived for the future. For when you would both return. I don't remember a single moment that I spent with Charlotte in her world. I've missed almost all of these last years. That's a long time. That's more than two years with my daughter that I've lost and that I will never get back. I don't want to lose this time that we have now. From the moment

I learned that Ned had been killed, I began praying that you would survive. And that you would come back to us."

She bows her head for a moment before turning to face him. "These people we lose; they've never gone completely. They reside in us. Ned will always be in both of us."

He thinks of what Daisy has written to him, about how when we make love, we are making love to everyone we ever made love to before and lost. It makes Sam wonder if all women feel the same about these things. If only men believed that the women they make love to *belong to them* and to no one else. If men need to believe this and women do not.

"I know a woman who lost her husband in the first month of the war," she goes on. "Three months later, she remarried. She had a baby. 'Life is for the living,' she told me."

She looks into his eyes.

"The world is on fire," he says slowly.

"The world may be on fire, Sam, but not our world. Not now. We're here together. You and I. And Charlotte. And you know it's what Ned would have wanted."

She walks back to him. She takes his hand and places it over her heart. "What do you want me to do?" she asks him.

"I don't know," he tells her. "Nothing."

"Well, maybe it's better if we don't know. Maybe we should both let go of everything we believe we know and just hold on to nothing. That would be a good place to start, don't you think?"

This sounds right to him. In this particular moment, she is beginning to convince him that there might be a way for them to move forward through the world. Maybe he could just let go of everything that is tearing him apart inside. He looks at her and begins to compose her face when she is old. The narrow lines at the corners of her mouth. The light in her eyes grown dull. Her dark hair turned silver. *How terribly strange to be old*, he thinks. But, in truth, he already feels like he is there. His life and his future are behind him. But then, another story comes into his mind: the two of them are living on the farm where he grew up. They drink their tea in the first light of each morning. They wait for Charlotte to come and visit them. They have told her about the old castle on the Irish Sea where they began their new life in the third year of the war. The Great War. The war to end all wars. The war that had taken her father from her life.

For a few moments, the story seems possible to Sam. It seems real.

bicycle

The child is small enough to fit in the wicker basket fixed to the handlebars of the bicycle, when Sam and Oliver cut two holes in the bottom for her legs to pass through. And with Katie riding side-saddle on the crossbar, and Sam on the seat, the three of them roll along the shore road and into the town centre. It occurs to him that to the people on the streets who watch them pass, they must appear to be just a normal family on an outing together on a lovely August morning. Except, of course, that normal families with husbands or brothers Sam's age, healthy enough to pedal three people on a bicycle, no longer exist, and that is why everyone they pass is looking at them with a certain envy, and perhaps even bitterness.

"Aren't we glorious?" Katie calls to her daughter.

"Yes, Mummy," she cries back. Then she tries to say the word – *glorious* – as best she can manage.

"It means we're blessed, my love."

Maybe we are, Sam thinks. *Maybe we are blessed.* He allows himself to consider this for a moment as the idea expands inside his mind. *This is my new life. I have a beautiful wife who I love deeply and a child who I will one day know well. We live by the sea. And nothing else matters. There never was England or France. There never was a war where men were torn apart.*

It is a pleasant fiction, but it collapses because of Ned. Because of the metal shard, shaped like the twisted handle of a spoon, that tore the opening in Ned's heart and came to rest against one of his ribs. And because of the tuft of grass the size of a penny, that held one small piece of the faded shell of a robin's egg.

Sam knows that he is only here with them for a little while. He is only here with them because he has a duty of care.

In the town centre, they stop where a delivery cart has pulled to the side of the street so Charlotte can talk to the horses. Sam holds her in his arms and is trying to follow her animated discussion as she chatters away.

It is Katie who sees it first. In the square, one of the soldiers is being taunted by two teenage girls. They watch for a while and then Sam starts to pass the child to Katie, but she insists on intervening. "Let me go," she says.

From where Sam stands, he can make out Katie's rising voice as she scolds the girls and sends them away. He can see the soldier bow his head. It is Wilkinson, he decides.

He puts Charlotte back in the wicker basket and has just started pushing the bicycle towards the square when Katie meets them halfway. "It's all right now," she says.

"Is it Wilkinson?" Sam asks.

"Yes. I'd like to walk him back," she says. "Will you be all right with Charlotte?"

He has never been responsible for a child before and his immediate reaction is fear that borders on terror. But he doesn't oppose her idea. He has never found it easy to oppose any of her ideas.

What surprises him is how quickly his fear subsides and how thoroughly he is absorbed into the child's world. In no time, he is aware of himself settling into her rhythm that lifts him away from everything that has ever frightened him. It is like he is being set free, and rather than take the shortest route back to the castle, he pedals them to the beach where they walk hand in hand for a while and then lie beside each other, on their backs, looking for the shapes of animals in the clouds sailing above them.

"That looks like a zebra to me," Sam says, pointing to the sky.

"I don't see his stripes?" she says.

"Oh, well, maybe because he's so far away."

"How far?"

"So far. So, so far."

"I see an elephant."

"Where? Show me, please."

"Over there," she says, pointing.

"Ah, yes, I see him. What a beautiful elephant."

"Am I your friend, Sammy?"

No one but his mother has ever called him 'Sammy'. "Yes, you are, Charlotte."

"And you're my friend?"

"Yes, I am."

"Do you live in the castle?"

"Yes."

"I thought so."

"You're a very clever little girl, you know that?"

"Are you grown-up, Sammy?"

This makes him smile. He turns his head and looks at her, feeling enveloped by her radiant beauty and her completely honest curiosity. *What have I ever done to deserve this?* he asks himself.

Somehow she has found a way to connect him to his own innocence, an innocence that he had completely forgotten. He finds himself amazed again by how easily he has adapted to her world and by how comfortable he feels there. This is the first time since he'd left for the war that he doesn't feel like he is only *temporary*. It is a transcendent feeling. An awakening. And he knows that this is what Oliver had first spoken to him about. The way of feeling that means you are alive.

"No," he says, "I'm not grown-up yet. But when I am grown-up, I want to be a zookeeper."

"A shoe keeper?"

"Yes. A shoe keeper indeed."

"What is a shoe keeper?"

"He's the person who finds everyone's shoes when they get lost. Or when their feet grow bigger, he finds them shoes to fit."

"Oh," she says. And he sees that she believes him completely. He could tell her anything and she would believe him. He could lie to her about what had happened to her father in the war. It would be just another one of Lansdale's lies about love. Purposeful and benevolent.

He looks at her little hands, pudgy, with a row of dimples behind the knuckles. They look like starfish. He knows that she will never remember this time they are sharing and she will have no memory of the lie he is going to tell her.

"We should go back now," he says to her.

"To see the soldiers?"

"Yes."

"They have white faces. They're pretty."

"I'm glad you like them."

"My daddy is a soldier. Mummy told me."

"Your mummy is right."

"Does he have a white face too?"

"No, I don't think he does."

"Will you paint my daddy's face, Sammy?"

Suddenly he can barely speak. "No, sweetheart," he says. "I think we'd better be going now."

She sings all the way back and is delighted at dinner when Oliver passes around straws for the soldiers' first practice session and gives her one of her own.

Brookes says to her, "I hear you had a bicycle ride today. I've known my girl, Kelly, since we were four years old. Just about your age."

"I'm two and a half," she says, looking up from her drink.

"Two and a half, is it? Well, you're very grown-up for your age. I could have sworn you were four. I taught Kelly how to ride a bicycle."

He takes a small photograph of her from his pocket and shows it to everyone.

Wilkinson asks to hold it. As he looks at it he says, "I trust she returned the favour by teaching you how to ride her."

He laughs at his own joke as silence falls over the room. The only sound is Charlotte blowing bubbles in her cup with her straw.

"We've been saving that," Brookes says with a tense formality, "until I get home and we're married. Her uncle is a vicar. He's going to perform the ceremony."

"You were saving it?" Wilkinson goes on. "Well, now what are you going to do?"

"That's enough, soldier," Oliver says.

"Why?" Wilkinson asks.

"Because I said – it is enough."

Wilkinson pushes his chair away from the table and stands up with great ceremony. He begins to walk away as the silence intensifies. He stops for a last word. "I have a suggestion. I think we should invite the girls I met in town today to come take a look at our faces and tell us if they would ever take a single one of us for a ride in their beds."

That night in his room, Brookes struggles to write a letter to his girl. His tears keep falling onto the paper, smearing the ink. He finally gives up and goes downstairs and shoots balls in the billiards room for a while. In the darkness, he cannot see the balls, but it steadies him to listen for the clacking sound they make when they strike one another, and by the time Sam comes into the room, he has stopped crying. "It's Brookes," he calls to Sam. "Couldn't sleep. You're still working?"

Sam thinks of trying to tell him something to make him feel better about what Wilkinson said at dinner. Instead he tries to pretend it never happened. *Better that way*, he thinks. "The game is hard enough in the daylight," he says. "You prefer to play it in the dark?"

"I never really cared about the shelling," Brookes says softly. "It wasn't personal the way a bullet was. I guess that's the answer, isn't it?"

Sam has no idea what he means. "The answer?" he says.

"Not to take any of this personal, is what I mean. There's no plan for any of the things that happen to us. I enlisted two days after war was declared. I thought it might last a few months. I was afraid I wouldn't get there in time. It would all be over and I would never be able to make up for what happened to my brother when we were kids. There was ice on the pond behind our school and he fell through. I could have gone in after him, but I was too scared."

Sam is grateful for the darkness in the room so that Brookes is thinking of this. To see how Sam might judge him for this.

"I had my chance in France. The war gave me my chance for – what is the word? Atonement? A man in my unit was stuck in mud in no man's land when a German flare landed on him. He was face down in the mud and the flare landed in the centre of his back. It was burning a hole right through him. He was screaming in agony. I climbed out of the trench and crawled to him and turned him over in the mud. But that's why we wanted to go, isn't it? To find out if we were capable of bravery? If we had courage?"

Nothing could be further from the truth for Sam. But he says yes, just hoping to bring the conversation to a close.

"If Kelly doesn't want me any more," Brookes goes on, "then I'm just going to tell myself that it's nothing personal. It's just that she's decided to look for another bloke to give her the happiness she deserves."

There is great resignation in his voice, and when he stops, Sam is grateful that it is over. He is just about to say goodnight when Brookes speaks again. "What will anyone remember about all this? What do you think?" he asks. "A hundred years from now, will they think that we were all just mad? Men were mad for their countries? But why should a man care about a country? What is a country compared to a girl who holds you in her arms? Or a swim in the sea? Or the chance to sit and smoke out under the stars? Or food? Or that lovely wee child looking up at you? Those are the real things, aren't they, Sam?"

daddy

They lie talking in Katie's bed, in the small room that Oliver has given them below the turret with the stamped tin ceiling and the old piano pushed up against the north wall.

"Are you sad, Mummy?"

"Mummy's not sad. Mummy has you."

"Daddy's a soldier."

"That's true, my love."

"Is Sammy?"

"No. Sammy is an artist."

"I like him, Mummy."

"Yes, I like him too. Just hold me now."

* * *

Oliver has called Sam into his room to ask him to bear down on Wilkinson's mask. "We need to send him along as quickly as we can," he said. "One bad apple, as they say. Anyway, may I say this to you? Even if you hold it against me for telling them you were here, I've noticed that your spirits are brighter since they arrived. And that was my hope. I don't know if what I did was right or wrong? War changes what is right and what is wrong. The right thing to do would be to run as far from war as you could possibly run. But we don't run. We stay. We stay for each other. We're still fighting the war here, Sam."

He makes his way to his gold chair. He feels terribly old and wonders if Sam can tell. Maybe he can see the strain he is under and he feels sorry for him and doesn't want to add to his troubles.

"I only need two more days on his mask," he says.

"Thank you. Why don't you sit down and talk with an old man? I would greatly appreciate your company."

Sam looks at him, then starts to turn away, but stops. "I don't know what you want me to say to you. I don't know what anyone wants me to say."

Oliver understands and nods. "Was it always that way for you? Did other people always make you uncomfortable?"

"I don't think so."

"At the Academy?"

Sam shakes his head.

"So it was the war then."

Sam nods. "Sometimes I hear shells exploding," he says. "Will it always be like this? If I live to be an old man, will I hear shells exploding whenever I'm reminded of the war?"

"It won't always be this way," Oliver tells him. How miserable, he thinks, for this young man to be tied to something like a dog chained to a stake.

"I suppose you'll be encouraging them to return to Dorset soon?" he says.

"I haven't thought about it, to be honest."

Oliver smiles at him. "You are impeccably honest. That much is certain." He waits, then asks, "Have you always been so honest?"

Sam looks at him. "Why do you always want to talk this way?"

"What way?"

"About things like honesty and feelings. Don't you ever just want to talk about the weather, or... I don't know... Would you like a bowl of soup? Ordinary things."

This makes Oliver laugh heartily. "I suppose you're right," he says. "I take things far too seriously. I've always been one of those people who prefers to get to the heart of the matter. Peel away the paint, you know, see what state the wood is in. I may have inherited this trait from my father, who disdained small talk."

He walks to the windows behind his desk and looks out briefly. "It's beautiful here, isn't it? Peaceful. But that won't last. Not after the Easter Uprising, as they are calling it. I knew after we executed those fifteen Irish rebels by firing squad that it was only the beginning. There will be war in this place in time. The Irish people won't be denied their independence. And who can blame them? We all want to be free, don't we?"

Free. Oliver hears Sam say the word under his breath. It is probably a word without meaning to him now. Sam listens politely as he goes on.

"It's the young people who need to be free. Nothing matters more when you're young. There's not much point to being free when you're too old and crippled to enjoy it. Though I suppose freedom is as much a state of mind as it is action." He turns toward Sam. "Would you agree?" he asks.

It occurs to Sam that the only time he has felt free in the last two years is when he no longer cared if he was alive. "How long will they stay?" he manages to ask then.

"I don't know, Sam. I guess if they make you uncomfortable and you don't want to tell them to leave, I'll tell them myself. But I think you should give them some time."

He seems to be thinking this over. Then he finds himself talking about how he had felt sitting on the beach with Charlotte. "I was in her world. And I felt something."

"That's good," Oliver says eagerly.

He says this so quickly that it must feel like an intrusion and it annoys Sam. "Why is it *so good*?" he asks.

"I'm sorry. I should have let you finish."

"I felt her innocence, that's all I mean," he says. "And for a little while, I felt what it was like before the war."

Oliver is very pleased to hear him say this. When Sam is going out of the door, he thinks of one last thing and calls to him. "You can miss it, you know?"

"What?"

"I missed my chance for a real life. A woman to share the years with. Children. I was too scared. I saw too much when I was young like you are. The destruction. The brutality. So, I put my head down and built a little world for myself where I felt safe. It was too late when I realised that there was no room in that world for anyone else." He sits down in his chair then. "I'm sorry," he says. "Go on. You have better things to do than listen to me."

Sam lingers for a moment and Oliver feels him drifting away.

"What is it, Sam?" he asks.

"I was thinking about the rain," Sam says.

Oliver is confused and looks out the window at the clear sky.

"In France," he says. "It had been raining for days and all my focus was on fixing a small piece of canvas on the back of my helmet to divert the rainwater from running down my neck."

He turns quickly and walks out of the room. And Oliver is suddenly filled with fear.

plaster

The next day, Sam works until night on Wilkinson's mask, then makes his way upstairs. The corridor is dark as he walks to his room. He sits down on his bed. He lies down and waits for sleep to come.

Some time passes before he gets up and walks to their room. He finds their door open slightly and when he looks in, he sees Katie sitting on the bed staring at Charlotte, who appears to be sleeping.

He calls softly to her. "Are you all right?"

Katie smiles at him, then nods her head. He listens to her voice whispering to him to come in. He steps inside the room.

"People think that you have a baby and suddenly you are a family," she says. "But actually, it takes time. We were barely getting started when the war came."

"It isn't fair," Sam says to her.

She smiles at him again. She gestures with her hand for him to sit beside her on the bed, and he obliges her.

"We only had a few nights together as a family. But it was at night when Ned would read to us," she says. "That's when we were closest. In those hours, I felt like we were going to be a family. I miss that the most, Sam."

She leans toward Charlotte and sees something that makes her raise her hand to her lips as her eyes widen. "Look at her, Sam," she whispers. "That expression, do you see it? Can you see Ned there? You can, can't you? Just after she was born, when we first brought her home from the hospital, I would stare at her, and to me she looked like someone who had taken a long journey to reach us. When she would wake and look around, sometimes she seemed to be thinking – *Oh my, starting all over again so soon.* As if she had lived before."

Sam can feel himself breaking into pieces again and he wishes that she would stop. But she carries on.

"Wouldn't it be wonderful if there were other worlds, Sam? If we live on and on. If this world isn't the end."

He wants to give her something and to make her stop. He takes her hand. "There are," he tells her.

* * *

For a while, Sam disappears so deeply into his work that he feels connected to the world only in isolated moments. One moment he looks out the window and sees Brookes teaching Katie how to split firewood. Each time the head of the axe comes down, Sam hears a shell exploding. One moment passing through the billiards room, where he sees Oliver playing all three soldiers at the same time in three separate games of chess.

Another moment at dusk, Sam sees Brigham standing out in the rain, hiding behind a hedge, and staring at Katie, who stands across the courtyard. She is standing with her head tipped back, letting the rain wash over her face.

She looks so lonely to Sam. So impossibly lonely. While he watches, Brigham takes off his jacket and hurries through the rain. He covers her with great tenderness. And she never moves. The two of them just stand there in a strange familiarity.

It is late that night when Sam goes into his shop and begins cutting strips of gauze that he soaks in plaster. He uses a mirror and carefully lays the strips over his face and does not move until the plaster has set.

time

Charlotte runs around the courtyard kicking a ball with Brookes and Brigham while Oliver walks with Katie through the poppy field in front of the castle.

"Let me take the blame for whatever comes of this," he says to her.

"I came here on my own," she says.

"Yes, but it was my idea."

"When you think of all the terrible things that people are doing to each other right now, is what we've done really so awful?" she asks.

"Of course not."

"He's not the same person."

"I'm certain he is. If you give him time. War does things to a man."

"Man?" she says with surprise. "He's a boy, that's all. And so was Ned. And I was just a girl."

She looks up at the sky and Oliver watches her expression change. "Sometimes when I hold Charlotte, I do it for myself. So she can comfort me. And I don't think that's fair at all. I should be the one comforting her. But that's how it is now, isn't it? Everything is out of balance."

"Quite right," he says.

"Sam told me that the world is on fire. I tried to make him

see that we could still find a place where we can be safe. But I know he doesn't believe that."

She turns away for a moment and is silent. Oliver sees the waves in her dark hair catch the sunlight. He almost reaches out to place his hand on her just to comfort her in some way, and to assure her that she is not alone in her desolation. In some way, he knows that he is responsible for her, and for all her misery, because he is one of the numberless men who had believed in the nobility of war.

"My father has a friend who tends the gardens at Cambridge," she says. "He told us that when the war was announced, all the boys went running to sign up. Some of them just dropped their books where they were standing and went rushing off to their death. Or worse. These men here have it much worse. Death. I took my vows – 'till death do us part'. I didn't know then that there are many kinds of death. The death of the spirit. The death of hope. The death of one's belief in oneself."

"We must try to keep our faith," Oliver tells her, and the words sound far too empty for either of them to believe.

"Faith?" she says. "Faith in what?"

"In your child."

"I brought her into this world, Mr Blackburn. How can I ever be forgiven for that?"

"We do our best," he says. Another perfectly useless thing to say – he knows this.

"Ned couldn't wait to get into the war," she says. "But it was different for Sam. He only went to be with Ned. And I made him promise to bring my husband back. *Husband.* That word is still unfamiliar to me. In some ways, I despise the word."

Oliver has bowed his head, trying to turn away from her and conceal his shame, but suddenly he is aware that she is waiting for him to look at her. When he does, she seems to be looking through him.

"I don't know what happened to Ned," she says. "I asked

Sam to tell me. Do I have that right? Don't I have a right to know?"

"Yes."

"Can you tell me? Has Sam told you what happened?"

Oliver shakes his head slowly.

"You've asked him?"

"Yes."

"Well?"

"He's unable to talk about that."

"Why?"

"If you give him time," he says.

"Time? What good can time possibly do? And please don't tell me that time heals."

He rushes to affirm precisely that. "I've seen it," he says. "I've seen that we heal ourselves over time."

"How? By forgetting? Don't ask me to forget. I don't want any of us to ever forget what this war has done to us. Or it will happen again. Can't you see them?"

He wasn't following her. "Who?"

"Those boys, dropping their books and running to sign up for the war. A whole generation of lost boys. A whole generation… was there ever another generation that deceived itself so eagerly?"

Yes, he says to himself. *And it will not be the last.*

She goes on. "And of the entire generation, do you want to know who was the most stupid of all?" She turns her head slowly from side to side. "I feel sorry for poor Charlotte, to have a mother so stupid," she says.

That night, Oliver leads the procession into the turret where they read the names from the newspaper while Charlotte holds the torch.

Sam is not with them. He works in his shop, painting Ned's face on the new plaster mould. He has the photograph on the bench as a guide, but he really doesn't need it. He can paint Ned's face from memory. He can paint it with his eyes closed.

And with his eyes closed, he is suddenly standing at the

edge of the cliffs looking down at Ned as he swims towards Katie. He watches her draw him in to her naked body. And then his eyes open.

He feels something cold turning through his chest again. It only lasts a moment and then he returns to his work.

Three days later, he walks through town wearing Ned's mask. His intention is to gauge the way people look at him. Their expressions and movements. He buys a newspaper and the man behind the counter who takes his money seems to barely notice him. It is the same in the bakery. And the library where he sits, pretending to read Charles Dickens' *Pictures From Italy*. He thinks that he should have talked with Katie first. Or perhaps he should have asked Oliver's advice. Instead he followed his own instincts. He knew what he wanted to do for the child. And for her father.

Early the next morning he wakes Katie in her bed where she is sleeping with Charlotte. He asks her to come to his room.

She stands in the threshold as he walks into the room and opens a drawer on his bureau. He takes the mask of Ned from the drawer and holds it in front of him for Katie to see. She is immediately overcome. Her knees buckle and when she begins to sway, he steps close enough to her so she can lean against him. She seems mystified as she raises her hand.

Sam watches her hand touch the mask before she quickly withdraws it. "I'll only wear it with your permission," he says to her. "I thought that I might read to Charlotte tonight."

mice

First Sam wants to create a book he can read to Charlotte. As he sits at his workbench, he hears the train whistle again, and before long he is painting a series of pictures about two mice who have somehow made their way onto a train travelling from London's Victoria Station to Dorset. On the final page, the two mice sit on the headrest of an upholstered seat and watch out the window while two boys jump from the cliffs into the sea.

He is very nervous when he takes his place on the bed beside Charlotte. As soon as she realises that her daddy has come to be with her, she throws her arms around him.

"Of course I came to see you," Sam says. "I've been very busy, working. I'm sorry it took me so long. I hope you'll forgive me."

"Will you stay when I wake up?"

"No, love. But I will be here at night to read to you. And I have a special book that I brought with me."

She reaches up and touches his face. "Does it hurt, Daddy?" she asks. "No. Not any more. If you're brave, things heal very quickly."

"Read to me now, please."

She settles herself against him and puts her thumb in her mouth.

* * *

While Sam begins the story, Katie opens the cupboard and changes into her nightgown behind the door. She stands there for some time, listening to Sam reading. His voice has a restful cadence to it that calms her. She never could have imagined this moment. Never in a million years. And yet it bears a certain familiarity. She had always believed that life was less about fate than accommodation. Fate, she believed, was for the poets. Let them use it to explain what remains a mystery. But as she watches Sam and her daughter, she begins to wonder if perhaps the poets were right. For surely it has to have been something less plain than accommodation, something more like fate that has carried her here to bear witness to this.

She walks to the bedside. Sam looks up at her. Their eyes meet, and then he looks away. The whole time they were growing up he was always preoccupied the way all artists are. The way all people are who are born to bring truth and beauty into the world. He couldn't simply *see* something. He had to study and examine what he was seeing and this required him to step back and hold the world at a distance while he turned it through light and shadow, walking its boundaries, pressing himself up against its borders to define the meaning. She sees something else in him, something she had never seen in Ned when he was with Charlotte. It is a completeness. She can tell that he has surrendered to the child. Ned had always been in too much of a hurry to surrender.

She sits on the bed and listens to his story. Soon Charlotte is asleep. She always takes one deep breath before she drops off, as if she were going underwater.

"Thank you, Sam," Katie says.

"I should go," he says.

She watches him take off the mask. She touches his cheek. "Just let me hold you," she says. "Maybe we'll fall asleep and when we wake up, everything will be better." She feels him settle against her. She lays her wrist on his chest and feels his heart beating. "The last night, after we argued, I slept with her. In the morning, we left the house and went for a long walk. Ned was gone when we returned. We found him at the station. But it was all very hurried. We never had the chance to say goodbye to him properly."

She realises then that Sam is already asleep. She is exhausted, but she can't drop off. The first light of morning is in the sky when she wakes him with a kiss. *Maybe this is love*, she thinks as she moves against him. Maybe this is real. Maybe this is as real as the shepherd boy was.

"I want to make you smile," she whispers. She sits up and pulls her nightgown over her head. She watches his eyes as she takes his hands and places them on her breasts. She hears the breath rush from his lungs.

And when it is over, his eyes close again. He does not see her looking down at the scars on his wrists. She leans closer to make sure. And she is suddenly filled with a bitter anger. She takes hold of his hands and lifts them from the bed. "Why would you ever do such a thing?" she says.

He is caught. He can't move.

"People are struggling to live," she says. "To just stay alive."

She moves to the side so he can get up from the bed. "Why wouldn't you have wanted to come home to us? To help us through our grief? You wanted to leave us to fend for ourselves? How could you do that to anyone you cared about?"

He hears this as he leaves the room like a thief who has trespassed. Like someone who has no right to be in their presence.

* * *

Katie bursts into Oliver's room a few minutes later and startles him in his chair. She says the first thing that comes into her mind.

"Do you know why little children cry so often? It's because they don't have the illusions we have as adults to persuade us

249

that we're safe and secure in the world. A child watches her mother walk out of the room, or her father board a train, and she bursts into tears because she knows that they might never return. Without our illusions, children understand that we are all just barely holding our lives together."

Oliver looks at her for a moment. "In that regard then," he says, "soldiers who have been through war are like children. Stripped of their illusions."

"What has Sam been through?" she asks him.

"War," he tells her.

"Why would he try to kill himself?"

"Because he survived, I suppose."

"How did he survive? Ned was so much stronger."

"Strength has almost nothing to do with it. It's only chance – that's all it is. You don't survive because you did something right."

"Did you know cowards that survived?"

Oliver sees her anger. Before he can try to answer her question, she turns away and leaves him. He has no intention of trying to fall back to sleep. When he goes into the kitchen to make some tea, he is surprised to find Sam there standing at the slate sink. He has opened the window and in the silence just before dawn, they can hear a train clattering through the countryside. *Maybe she is right and time doesn't heal*, Oliver thinks to himself as he watches Sam standing there with his shoulders pitched forward. But time is an anaesthesia – he knows this from experience. Time can dull the pain.

His hand is shaking when he reaches for the boiling kettle. He keeps pouring the water as it spills over the rim of the cup. Sam stands just a few steps away, running his fingers across the scars on his wrists.

"It's her grief, that's all, Sam," he tells him. "She needs someone to blame."

"What have you told her?"

"You know what I told her. I told her that you were here to help these men."

250

"I don't mean that," Sam says, cutting him off sharply.

Oliver looks deeply into his eyes and says very calmly that he has not told her anything. "She needs time, Sam," he says.

He can tell that Sam feels like he is at the edge of the abyss. "I can't breathe," he says. Oliver reaches for his shoulder, but he turns away just as Katie had.

shoes

Katie is pushing Charlotte on the swing when Sam approaches her. He has been trying to summon the strength to talk to her and to find the words that will satisfy her. He has not found those words, but the moment he is standing beside her, the words find him.

"I hope someday to be able to tell you," he says. "To tell you what happened to Ned." When she doesn't turn and look at him, he says, "To your husband."

"Someday?" she says derisively.

He sees the anger rise up in her. "When I can remember it clearly," he says. He is not trying to defend himself. He is telling her the truth.

"I can't play this game with you, Sam," she tells him.

Just then, Charlotte calls to her. Katie glances at her with a blank expression as if she is wondering who this child belongs to.

How does this happen? Sam wonders. *How do people who love each other become enemies?*

"This man will take you to the sea," Katie says to the child. Then she turns and walks back towards the castle.

* * *

On the beach, the child is up on Sam's shoulders again as they walk. He feels her leaning forward, looking down over his head. "My daddy has paint on his shoes too," she says.

This paralyses him so he can barely keep walking.

"Do you have my daddy's shoes?" he hears her asking him.

"No," he says. "These are my shoes."

"Is he far away again?"

"Do you think your daddy would leave without saying goodbye?"

"No," she tells him.

"You're right. He would never do that." He stops then and swings her down from his shoulders so he can look into her eyes.

"Your daddy would never leave without saying goodbye," he tells her.

"Did you talk to him?"

"Yes," he says. "Your daddy and I are friends. He's my very best friend. I know him very well. And I know how very much he loves you. So you have to promise me something, Charlotte."

"What?"

"You have to promise me that you will always remember how much your daddy loves you. Every day when you first wake up in the morning, you have to say, 'My daddy loves me more than anything in the world.' Will you remember to do that?"

"Yes."

"Good girl. You're such a good girl."

* * *

Katie is in the kitchen with Brookes and Brigham preparing lunch when the postman's son arrives with the day's mail. He has something on his mind. He glances around the room as if he has lost something here and has come to reclaim it.

"Do you happen to know if the artist is still here?" he asks.

"He's taken my daughter to the sea," Katie says.

"Well, I hope he's gone for good," he says.

Her eyes widen. "Why would you say that?"

"My da is back from France. He's told me the story."

"What story?"

"He's the coward, ma'am. He's the one who got his friend killed. My da wants to strangle the blighter."

* * *

Oliver hears of this from Brookes and intercepts Sam and Charlotte on their way back from the beach. "Wait here," he says. "I'll take her to her mother."

"I can take her myself," Sam says.

"Just wait here," he says again emphatically.

Sam has never seen him this upset before. Oliver can tell that he knows something bad has happened and he immediately suspects that he is to blame, though he has no idea what he might have done wrong. "Just wait here, please," he tells him.

When he returns, he has Wilkinson with him, wearing his finished mask and carrying his duffel bag. "This man has a train to catch," he says to Sam. "Come along with us."

Wilkinson walks two paces ahead of them all the way to the station as if they are strangers to him. Then he gets on board without saying goodbye or thank you.

"Good riddance," Oliver says, gazing at the train. Then he turns to Sam. "You did a marvellous job. It looks real," he says.

"It's not real," Sam says. "It's an illusion. None of this is real. We're all just pretending."

"That's called living, Sam."

"Pretending. Feeling. It's all living to you? Are you going to tell me what's happened?"

He waits until they are in the pub to tell him. Sam takes the news stoically. He says nothing in response. "What are the odds that someone from your unit would be in this place?" Oliver says, as if he were speaking to himself.

"It doesn't matter," Sam says. "I'm not going to run away from him."

"Of course you're not," he says. "You're not someone who runs away, are you?"

They look at each other in silence.

"If you say so," Sam says.

"I do," Oliver tells him. And in that moment, he knows that he is getting close.

"Well, at least I've given her what she wants," he says.

"What does that mean? What does she want from you?"

"You told me yourself – she wants someone to blame. So, what happens now?"

Oliver suddenly feels like he has to be very careful. "If you want me to tell them to leave, I will. But the little girl. You know these children… They're the light, Sam. If we do anything to extinguish that light, there's only darkness. Without her father—"

Sam interrupts. "I'm not her father. Ned was her father and he's dead."

He says this more sternly, perhaps more sternly than he'd intended, and Oliver just bows his head against the sting of his words.

"I don't want to talk about *this*!" Sam shouts, turning on him. "Why did you bring me here?"

"I didn't bring you here – the army sent you here. And I'm sorry," he tells him.

"You're sorry? What good does it do for you to be sorry? You know what I'm sorry about? I'm sorry I ever came here and met you. Can't you see? Can't you see anything?"

"See what, Sam?"

Sam closes his eyes and Oliver wonders if he is going to say anything more. He wishes that Sam was still a little boy and he and his father were going about their chores at the farm. Oliver pictures the two of them on a winter morning, walking to the barn with their breath freezing white in the air.

When Sam speaks again, his voice is calm. "He practically lived in my house when we were boys. We slept in the same room. I'd wake up in the morning and he'd be staring out the window. He was always waiting for something to happen. He was too restless to sleep. And after she gave herself to him, it was worse. And we both loved Katie. We both did from the start. But he was the one she wanted."

He stops and looks away for a moment. A picture settles in his mind of when he was a small boy, raking leaves with his father. Then he bows his head before going on. "Can't you see she's always going to hate me? I'm never going to forgive... she's never going to—"

He stops suddenly. He looks deeply into Oliver's eyes in silence. The old man knows that he has found his way to something. It is like a door has swung open to another room. Some time passes while he looks away and when he turns to him again, Oliver can tell that he is close to something.

"What is it, son?" he asks.

"I don't know," he says softly.

"Yes, you do. What is it?"

"I think I just realised who has to be forgiven," he says.

He stands up and walks calmly to the window.

"I wanted her to choose me," he says. His voice is soft now and Oliver thinks he feels safe, perhaps for the first time since before the war. "But I could never compete with Ned. He was someone... I wish you could have known him."

"So do I," Oliver tells him. "He was a very lucky fellow."

"Lucky? Why do you say that?"

"He was lucky to have you as his friend."

"I let him down."

"That's all part of it, Sam. That goes with the territory."

"We were close. Closer than brothers, I think."

"Are you going to be able to forgive her?" Oliver asks him. "For not choosing you."

He is suddenly almost too exhausted to speak. "I want to try," he says.

"Good. That's good." Oliver steps closer to him and places a hand on his shoulder. "That's good, Sam, but that's only part of it. There's someone else you'll have to forgive."

Sam is waiting for him to elaborate. But he has already decided that he will say no more.

"Who?" he asks.

"You're the only one who can answer that question."

"No. Tell me. *Who?*"

"I can't tell you, Sam. I can't answer that for you. I'm sorry."

"Don't tell me that I have to forgive myself because that's just so much nonsense," Sam calls as Oliver begins to walk away. "Do you hear me? Did you hear what I just said?"

Even before no more than a few feet separate them, Oliver senses that Sam feels incredibly alone in a way he had never been before, and then after a few more steps, he feels the same way. He is lost in a silent exhaustion that suddenly envelopes both of them. It is as if he has led them into a dark field where a storm is raging, a storm without sound, and they have lost each other somewhere in the storm and are left to find their own way.

taxi

Oliver is with Katie in the kitchen preparing a meal while Charlotte contents herself, playing with some pots and pans and a wooden mixing spoon.

"It's been a long time since I baked a cake. I might get it wrong," Katie says.

"As long as it's sweet, that's all that matters." Oliver gives her an extra cup of sugar that he has been saving.

Katie takes the sugar and carefully pours some of it into her mixing bowl, one spoonful at a time at first, until finally she grows exasperated and dumps the entire cup in. "What has he said to you?" she asks.

He gives her a distant look, intending to convey to her in no uncertain terms that she is trespassing and that he is not going to reveal anything.

"I suppose you're going to tell me that it's private," she says.

He says nothing.

"Things are always so private between men, aren't they? Women tell each other everything, but for men, privacy matters. Why does it matter so much?"

Oliver shakes his head and tells her that he doesn't know.

She surprises him when she says that she does. "It's fear," she says. "Men have this thing about hiding their fears from each other. They think their fears make them look weak. So they keep them hidden behind their private rule. They like to keep things hidden."

He is aware that anger is mounting in her and his first impulse is to avoid a confrontation.

"Maybe we shouldn't talk," he says. "Maybe we should just bake this cake together."

She dismisses this by telling him that it is something her own father would say. "I suppose Sam thinks I've tricked him by coming here with my plan. And then finding out his deep dark secret."

"The cake will be most appreciated," he tells her, thinking this might end the conversation. But she picks up immediately where she had left off.

"I'm the one who was tricked," she tells him.

"Someday all of this will be far behind you, and you will find happiness," Oliver says to her, as if he is reciting a line someone else has written.

"I don't even know what it is any more. You tell me – what is happiness?"

"Contentment, I suppose."

"Contentment? Contentment after all that has happened?"

"You must—"

She interrupts him. "I don't mean just what has happened to us. I mean to the world. The whole world. Men start their wars and tear the world apart, killing each other. And then they end up in places like this trying to fix what they've broken. And women are left minding the children and preparing for the men to return, preserving the world they left behind so it looks precisely as it did, so they can pretend that nothing's changed, when in fact, everything has changed. It's a charade. This place is a charade as well. Who gives me a mask to hide behind? I can tell you in all honesty that I would change places with any of the men here. Any one of them who thinks the worst thing in the world is to have to persuade a woman to make love to them. As if that is the only thing that accounts for a life."

He tries to look away from her, but he can't.

She goes on. "And you tell me that one day I will be happy again? What gives you the right to say such a thing? To speculate on such a thing? A thing that doesn't even exist."

"It's not fair," he finally says.

"No, it isn't fair. It isn't fair at all."

Early the next morning, Oliver finds Sam in his room. "I've called a taxi for them," he says, a little breathless from climbing the stairs as fast as he could. "They're leaving us. I thought you would want to know."

The taxi is already rolling away when Sam reaches the street. He can see them through the rear window. He runs until he catches up with them and he sees Katie ask the driver to stop. He walks around to Charlotte's window. He is wearing Ned's mask and when he opens the door and kneels down, the child throws her arms around him. "Daddy, can you come with us?"

"I can't come with you," Sam tells her. "I have so much work to do."

She looks down at his feet. "You have Sammy's shoes on."

"Yes, I do," he says.

"You won't be my daddy any more, will you?"

He shakes his head. "No," he says. "But I'll always be your friend." He looks into her eyes. "Do you know that, Charlotte?" he asks.

She nods her head as if she believes him.

He kisses her goodbye and closes the door. He has begun to walk away when Katie gets out of the taxi and calls to him.

They hold each other for a moment. She lays her head on his shoulder. Their eyes do not meet before she lets go of him. Perhaps this means that there is something she is keeping from him, something she decided to tell him when she got out of the taxi, but then decided not to.

He watches her get back in the car. And then he runs back to the castle and up to the turret where he watches them drive away until they stop at a crossroads, turn left, and disappear.

forgiveness

When the doorbell rings, they are all seated at the long table in the dining room – Sam, Brookes, Brigham, Oliver and the new soldier, Wintersteen, who is just nineteen years old and who, in addition to his horribly mutilated face, has been blinded.

"I didn't know we had a doorbell," Oliver exclaims with surprise. "Mr Brookes, will you please see what kind of mannerless oaf has interrupted our dinner?"

When Brookes returns, he is accompanied by Lansdale.

"The prodigal son has returned," Oliver says happily as a round of applause goes up.

Lansdale is full of life. "He does return, sir. Indeed he does. And I'm here to report that all is well in the world beyond the castle walls."

"Well, that is music to my ears, son," he says. "And if you'll excuse me for a moment, I have been saving the appropriate elixir for just this occasion."

They all have a grand time drinking Oliver's single malt whiskey, and when it is very late, Lansdale drinks the last of his with his straw while he watches Sam working on a mask in his shop.

"Michelangelo at work," he says.

"I'll be finished with this by morning, and then Brookes can go home."

"Where is that again?"

"He says he's going back into the coal mines in Scotland. Not too far from Edinburgh."

"He's a far better man than I. I don't think I could hold up to that kind of work for more than a day. But at least he'll be going home. Thanks to you, Sam. And I know you must be curious about how I fared with my new face. It was magnificent. Just magnificent. I never had one person stare at me, or one child point at me. I felt like I was invisible. I never imagined how wonderful it could be to feel invisible. And I saw the future there in the streets of London. I saw more automobiles than horses! Everything I saw filled me with such hope for the future. Once this war has burned itself out, there are going to be bright days for our beloved country."

He talks on and on and though Sam wants to interrupt him to ask about Daisy, he doesn't want to do or say anything to knock him off his stride.

Finally, Lansdale says, "I'll be home soon with Amy. I'll leave in the morning. I think all the beds are filled at this swanky hotel. I'll pass out on a sofa."

"No, you won't do that," Sam tells him. "Take my bed. The sheets are clean and there's an extra blanket. I'm going to be up most of the night."

"I couldn't be so selfish," Lansdale says.

"Yes, you can. It's like sleeping on rocks anyway."

"All right then, Sam. See you in the morning. My head will be clear then and I'll tell you all about Daisy. What a marvellous girl she is. You were blessed to have such a girl."

He looks into Sam's eyes when he says this. They shake hands then. And something seems to give way in Lansdale. His shoulders slump and he sighs deeply. And for a moment, he holds Sam's hand and seems unable to let go. Then he catches himself and pulls himself to attention and gives a sharp salute. "Right then, sir," he exclaims. "If you're in the kitchen before me, put the kettle on."

Sam watches him walk away. A picture comes into his mind of Daisy walking arm and arm with him in the streets of London.

Just after dawn, Sam is waiting for the kettle to come to the boil when he hears a strange sound. He looks out the window and sees nothing. But the sound unnerves him so that when he reaches for the kettle, he burns the palm of his hand. He runs water over it and as he looks down at the scar on his wrist, a sick feeling passes through him, and he suddenly runs outside as fast as he can.

There is Lansdale hanging from a rope from Sam's window.

Sam runs to him. He can only reach his shoes. He tries to lift him and place Lansdale's shoes on his shoulder to slacken the rope. But it is no use.

He runs inside and up the front stairs to his room. He yells for help as he pulls on the rope, trying to haul Lansdale up. He stumbles and falls to the floor. The whole time he is pulling on the rope, he is falling back into a nightmare. He hears a whistle shriek. He sees his own face grimace in terror as he climbs up out of the trench, following the two soldiers in front of him into a hail of machine-gun fire. Men fall around him, some of them silently, some of them screaming in agony. That is when he begins looking for Ned. And calling his name. He drops to his knees. He turns and runs back to the trench. When he looks down, he sees Ned sitting in the trench shaking with fear. Paralysed. Sam climbs down beside him. He wraps his arms around him and pulls Ned to his feet. Then there is a deafening explosion.

It is still ringing in his head when he looks down from the window and watches Brookes, up on a stepladder, cutting the rope. He and Brigham and Oliver bring Lansdale's body gently to the ground.

After the burial, Oliver finds Sam on the floor in his room. "He was doing so well. He was strong!" Sam yells at him.

Slowly, the old man walks across the room. He kneels down in front of him and almost reaches out to touch him. "No, Sam," he says.

"He was strong!" Sam yells once more.

"No!" he shouts. "He wasn't strong. His strength was gone." Now he takes hold of Sam's shoulders. "Look at me," he says. And he waits for their eyes to meet before he goes on in a low, measured voice. "He wasn't strong, Sam. *He just had courage.* He was a soldier and he was being brave for us, poor chap. That's what he was doing. He was being brave for as long as he could. But he wasn't strong. The war took all his strength."

That night, Sam sits in Oliver's gold chair, looking up at him. He has told him everything that he has been hiding. When he tells him that it was Ned who had been too frightened to leave the trench, he says that for as long as he lives, he will never tell another person.

"It never made sense to me that you were a coward," Oliver tells him. "I knew you were the opposite of that. You took the blame to protect him. You were willing to face a firing squad."

Sam can't speak. He slips gently back into his nightmare. "Why didn't you come with me?" he says.

Oliver can see that he is talking to Ned and so he answers for him. "Because I wasn't as strong as you, Sam," he says. "I just wasn't as strong as you."

"Goddamn you! How could you let me go over without you!"

"I was too scared."

"Well, goddamn you then!"

Tears stream down Sam's face. When Oliver puts his hand on his arm, the fear and the anger drain from him instantly. He looks up suddenly.

"Can you forgive him?" Oliver asks. "Can you forgive him for not being as strong as you?"

At first he doesn't move. But then he nods slowly. "I couldn't tell her," he says softly.

"Katie?"

"I couldn't tell her. I didn't want her to know." He pauses for a moment before he says, "God, I loved him so much."

mountain

There is a beautiful moment the evening they celebrate Brookes, who is leaving for home the next morning. The blind soldier, an Irish fusilier, climbs up onto the billiards table and sings a marvellous ballad in Brookes' honour.

In the morning, Sam stands beside him waiting for the train. "If it weren't for you, I would not be going home," he says.

"No, it wasn't me."

"It was. It was you. Your work," Brookes says forcefully.

Sam smiles at him.

"And look at me. You'll be wrinkled, and I'll still be young." They share a laugh. Brookes looks up at the mountain range.

"Do you know what I should like very much? I would like to come back here someday and climb to the top. It must be a beautiful view from there."

They both look up at the mountain for a moment. Then Brookes says, "Why don't I take a later train, and we'll have a go at it?"

Sam nods and they both run from the station.

They begin climbing slowly, but in time they are running again with all the strength they have in them. And as they run, they both can feel some power returning to them. Just the power of being so young. And free. And with that sense of freedom, they feel very much alive.

They race the final fifty yards and Brookes reaches the

peak just a few paces ahead of Sam. They stand there looking down at a beautiful scene. The sea glistens in the morning light as if diamonds have been scattered across its surface. From this height, the world seems ordered in a reassuring way. The streets are laid out in a logical pattern. The trees reach proudly toward the empty blue sky. The matching rooftops and chimney pots of the houses stand like modest monuments to the families that live beneath them.

"Look at us," Brookes says to him. "Many of us didn't make it, but we both have. And the world belongs to us now. We can make it whatever we choose." He pauses and then asks Sam if he believes this.

"I want to believe it," Sam says.

"You must, Sam. And I want you to know that I'm going to live. I'm not going to give up. So I need to have some way to write to you as time goes on. I want to tell you when I've got married. I want to send you pictures so you can see the good that you've done. Where will you go after this is… when your work is finished here?"

"I'm not sure," Sam says. And then a look of sheer surprise settles in his eyes.

"What is it?" Brookes asks him.

"It's the first time since I left for the war that I've considered the rest of my life. I'd forgotten what it feels like to have a future."

Brookes smiles understandingly. "When you leave here, will you keep in touch with Oliver, so I'll have a way to reach you?"

"Of course."

"Good," Brookes says as he looks out at the sea again. "At home, one of my closest friends is Jewish. He tried to teach me Hebrew, but I was quite hopeless. But there's a saying in the Talmud. 'Whoever saves a life, it is considered as if he saved an entire world.' You must never forget that. Will you promise me you'll remember that?"

266

A few days later, Sam and Oliver are stacking firewood. "Fairly soon we're going to have a lot of people here, Sam. More artists. More wounded soldiers."

"It will have to end."

"Why?"

"Because everything ends, Oliver."

"You're right."

"How many more artists?"

"Two sculptors. Two painters. I've ordered extra beds."

"That's good. How many more soldiers?"

Oliver shakes his head. He has no idea really. "I remember telling you when you first got here that if it worked, this place would become a factory."

"Has it worked?"

"Yes, it has. It has worked. But I've written to the powers that be and asked them to relieve you."

"Relieve me?"

"Yes. I think it's time for you to return to art school. Not right now. But in the autumn. So you have time to prepare yourself."

Sam says that he will think about it.

"Of course, you will always be missed here," Oliver assures him. "And the work you've done here will always hold a place of importance."

"Thank you."

"Are you hungry?" he asks him.

"Hungry? Yes. Yes, I'm hungry."

"I'm starving. Let's go and eat."

That night, Sam puts Brigham's finished mask on him. Then he holds a mirror up for him to have a look. Ten days later, the blind soldier, Wintersteen, makes his way home.

It is the last day of August when Sam and Oliver say goodbye, embracing each other briefly in front of the castle before Sam walks to the station with his duffel bag. He passes the benches that the two of them had painted and it seems to him as if years have passed since then.

The train pulls to a stop. Sam walks toward a door that has just swung open. He is about to climb on board when a soldier, his face wrapped like a mummy, climbs off and walks past him.

Sam watches him for a moment. As the man looks around, trying to get his bearings, Sam thinks of the difficulties ahead of this soldier, and all that he will have to overcome if he is ever going to make it home. It makes him realise that he is not ready to leave, and that a part of him will never leave. He hurries after the man. When he catches up, they shake hands, and Sam walks beside him to the castle.

BOOK V

beginning

Another year passes for Sam. Then summer draws on to its end with a succession of warm and peaceful days, and were it not for the new soldiers arriving every week, and the work that goes on hour after hour, Sam and Oliver might believe there is no longer a war being fought. Joining him in the workshop are five other artists with whom he shares a mutual trust that renews him. When each day ends, they sit around a small open fire in the courtyard under the stars, talking and sharing their stories and speculating about how many more soldiers will find their way to the castle. On the walls of the workshop hang the plaster moulds that have been used to make the finished tin masks. Thanks to a brilliant sculptor from Montrose, Scotland, by the name of Neil Ryan, who arrived at the castle with a set of homemade golf clubs that he found time to use every day, giving lessons to the soldiers no matter how poor the weather, many of the masks are only partial and cover just the scarred or missing portion of the soldier's face. Ryan has perfected a way to treat the edge of the mask so that it joins the man's skin seamlessly and renders nearly invisible what he calls the 'demarcation line'. By then the masks have become far more intricate than the ones Sam first built. The initial step is still to cast the patient's face in plaster of Paris, ensuring a perfect fit for the eventual prosthesis; then the mould is chalked and a clay with paste used instead of cumbersome wire, giving a positive model of the 'healed' wound. Once the missing features have been sculpted, a final cast is taken and electroplated to produce a copper mask just one thirty-second of an inch thick. This is coated in silver and then painted cream-coloured, spirit enamel providing a good base for flesh-matching Caucasian skin. The correct glow of skin is captured with varnish that is dulled to match the patient's complexion. Sometimes hair is used for eyebrows and lashes instead of just painting them on the mask. One sculptor from Dublin perfects eyelashes, made from metallic foil which he cuts into delicate strips, colours, curls and solders in place. These masks are a perfect union of art and artifice and they are so far superior to the first ones created at the castle that soldiers from those early days are invited back for upgrades.

Those men who return always make Sam think of Lansdale and wonder if a more lifelike mask might have saved him. It will always worry Sam that he has not done enough for these soldiers. He accepts that he will always be haunted this way; it is who he is.

By late August of 1918, 236 soldiers who have lived there as a family for a while are memorialised by the plaster moulds of their faces mounted on the workshop walls, each with the name of a man engraved inside. Sam and Oliver both think of them as a gallery of ghosts.

One of those soldiers, a jeweller's son from Derby, had stood up one night around the fire, raised his glass of sherry, and declared that the place should forever be known as *the Tin Nose Shop*.

"I believe that name will last," Oliver says to Sam as they walk to the train together the day Sam is leaving. "Clever, wouldn't you say?"

"Very clever," Sam says.

Oliver looks up at the Mourne mountains. "Doesn't it seem almost like another lifetime when you and I went searching for Lansdale up there in the forest?"

"It was another lifetime."

"Two years and five months. My Lord. When you're as old as I am, great heaps of time just seem to vanish."

"It didn't vanish. You made fine use of it," Sam assures him. "You held the place together. I don't know another person who could have done that. You never gave up on any of us."

"I thought of it as God's work," Oliver says. "A ministry, I suppose. But I kept that bit to myself. I never wanted to push God on any of them. Still I prayed constantly for each soldier. I prayed for you as well."

Sam asks him what he prayed for.

"That God would place his hand on you," he answers. "And give you strength. There is that passage from Isaiah I've always been quite fond of: 'But they that wait upon the Lord shall renew their strength. They shall mount up with wings as eagles. They shall run, and not be weary. They shall walk and not faint.'"

A flock of young boys goes racing past them, kicking a football up the street. They both stop to watch for a few moments. "All that energy," Oliver remarks. "We're both thinking the same thing, Sam, aren't we? We're wondering if they will grow up and have to go to war."

"You know me well," Sam tells him.

"We won't speak any more of that," Oliver says. "You have a train to catch."

Oliver begins walking, but Sam stops him, placing a hand on his shoulder. "Wait," he says. "Just another minute." He doesn't want to turn away from the boys. Their hair blowing in the breeze. Their arms and legs flying in all directions at once. The sound of their feet on the cobblestones. It is such a pleasant scene that captures for him so much that is beautiful about life. He feels as if he could watch them for hours. Of all that he has seen since he arrived here, Oliver knows that this is what he wants to remember the place by and to one day paint.

"With wings as eagles," he hears him say.

At the station, they watch the train pull in. "In forty-eight hours, you'll be back at the Academy where you belong," Oliver says.

"I don't really want to leave," Sam tells him.

"I know. But you have to. We've got good people here to take your place. You deserve to be back at art school. Develop your prodigious talent. The one thing that I really believe deeply is that all of us have a duty to reach our full potential. That's the only way the world gets better."

A wet brown leaf has blown from down the tracks and comes to rest on one of Oliver's shoes. Sam sees the effort it is taking for him to bend over and brush the leaf away, so he does it for him. While he leans down, the old man places his hand on his head. He just wants to touch him one last time. Immediately, a calmness falls over him. Then he speaks these words. These last words after all that they have come through. "If I had ever had a son," he begins, and then he pauses, and waits for his voice to steady itself before he starts again. "If I'd ever had a son, I would have wanted him to be like you, Sam."

academy

We carry stories with us through our lives only to discover when we look back that some of these stories carried us.

Sam takes Oliver's words with him back to the Academy, a place he had loved so completely and then had made himself forget entirely for so long that he is shocked to discover it exactly as he had found it when he arrived the first time.

This time he arrives in the dead of night. The city of London is silent. But when he enters the grand courtyard, his footsteps echo off the broad stone buildings as if announcing the arrival of a distinguished visitor. There is an Indian porter who shows him to the top floor room that has been set aside for him. It is just a room until the moment when the porter sweeps aside the heavy draperies on an arched window that look out across the lights of London. Sam knows at once that this is where he will set up his studio and disappear again into his work if the engine of his imagination will permit it.

That first night he spends sitting on the floor in front of the window waiting for something he cannot be sure of. When dawn rises, he stands up and surveys the city from its distant buildings to the ones nearest him. Then he knows that he is looking for signs of the war. And when he finds none, it amazes him. Of course, he had known there was no fighting here, but it still seems so improbable to him that the wholesale destruction and slaughter he had witnessed has not reached every corner of the earth. Not a single shell or machine-gun burst has even been heard by the inhabitants of this city. This means there are a million people surrounding him who have no real idea what war is. Now he is among those people, and he begins to wonder what he would answer should one of them ask him to describe the war. In the castle, surrounded by soldiers, such a thing had been unnecessary, of course. But it is different now. It leaves him short of breath and a little dazed to consider that from this day forward, he is going to have to learn how to live in a world that has been untouched and undamaged by the war. He is going to have to learn a new normal way of acting and relating in a normal world. This unnerves him, but he vows to himself to give it his best. To put his *best foot forward*, as his mother used to say.

He figures out quite quickly that the best chance he has of learning to act normal is by not simply observing the normal people going about their normal lives, but by joining them. And so he sets upon doing normal activities. He joins a group of art students who play badminton every Wednesday evening. He dashes about the court like the other players and laughs and jokes along with them. They don't need to know that inside his head he keeps repeating one line Oliver had recited to him in order to steady his nerves – *They shall mount up with wings like eagles.*

Going out for fish and chips is normal and he does this twice a day to try to put on some weight so that his trousers will stop sliding annoyingly down his hips. He will not permit himself to bring the fish and chips back to his room to eat alone. Instead he eats them in the shop surrounded by other patrons whose voices make them seem so full of life. And he comes to look forward to the hours he spends sitting inside the Lion's Head pub, listening to the conversations around him even though those conversations often centre on the war.

He returns from the pub one evening in late September to find a uniformed soldier standing at his door with his big square shoulders drawn back, almost as if he has been ordered to attention. It sends a chill through Sam that the soldier must have picked up on because he immediately begins smiling and striding towards him with his hand extended to shake. "Sorry to startle you, old chap," he says with a strong baritone voice. "Sassoon is my name. I've heard about your talent. I've come to commission you. Might we talk?"

He has a great deal to tell Sam, and he is in a great hurry. "So glad I caught you," he says while Sam is unlocking the door. "My train leaves in two hours. Back to the office."

"The office?"

"France, old chap. Still a few odds and ends to finish up over there. So I'm told anyway."

Standing in front of the arched window with the shimmering city spread out before them, he reacts the same way Sam had when he first stood there. They talk about this for some time, both of them marvelling that the people who have been in charge of the Great War have managed to contain the carnage to just a few thousand square miles of France and Belgium.

"If we'd been armies on the move instead of dug into the mud, it would have been a different story," Sassoon says. "But let's not talk about that now. Here's what I've come for."

He takes a photograph from his tunic pocket and hands it to Sam.

"Just another bloke," he says as Sam takes in the face. Dark eyes peering at you. Dark hair parted in the middle. The short moustache. The dimpled chin. Mostly it is the expression that leaves an impression. A look of calm rage.

"I'd like to commission you to paint that face for the cover of a book. A book of poems," Sassoon explains. "I secured a publisher for his book just this morning. Gave the chap my personal assurance that it would become a classic. Truth is, it won't sell worth a damn. War poems. Far too honest, I'm afraid. The stuff people won't want to read. Here. Brace yourself," he says as he draws his shoulders back and begins reciting.

Bent double, like old beggars under sacks,
Knock-kneed, coughing like hags, we cursed through sludge,
Till on the haunting flares we turned our backs,
And towards our distant rest began to trudge.
Men marched asleep. Many had lost their boots,
But limped on, blood-shod. All went lame; all blind;
Drunk with fatigue; deaf even to the hoots
Of gas-shells dropping softly behind.

Gas! GAS! Quick, boys!—An ecstasy of fumbling
Fitting the clumsy helmets just in time,
But someone still was yelling out and stumbling
And flound'ring like a man in fire or lime.—
Dim through the misty panes and thick green light,
As under a green sea, I saw him drowning.

In all my dreams before my helpless sight,
He plunges at me, guttering, choking, drowning.

If in some smothering dreams, you too could pace
Behind the wagon that we flung him in,
And watch the white eyes writhing in his face,
His hanging face, like a devil's sick of sin,
If you could hear, at every jolt, the blood
Come gargling from the froth-corrupted lungs,
Obscene as cancer,
Bitter as the cud
Of vile, incurable sores on innocent tongues,—
My friend, you would not tell with such high zest
To children ardent for some desperate glory,
The old Lie: Dulce et decorum est
Pro patria mori.

Sam can barely breathe when he has finished. "Do you know your Latin?" Sassoon asks. "*Dulce et decorum est pro patria mori*." When Sam doesn't speak, he supplies the translation: "It is sweet and fitting to die for one's country."

Sam can hear someone shouting *GAS! GAS!* inside his mind. It takes all his willpower to ask a simple question. "What is his name?"

"Wilfred Edward Salter Owen," he answers. "Met him ten months ago. Truth is, we were in the looney bin together. A touch of shell shock. The army had us boarded up in the Highlands of Scotland. About as far from the war as—"

He stops there and drifts off on his own thoughts. Sam feels a need to draw him back. "Where is he now?" he asks. "Owen, I mean."

Sassoon recovers immediately. "Back in it," he says. "I hope to run into him in the next week so I can give him the good news. About finding a publisher for his book, I mean. And about you painting his portrait for the cover." He looks off at the distant lights of the city for another moment. "In the interest of full disclosure, I need to tell you that when Wilfred and I met up in Scotland, he had been reading my poems and was full of praise. And then when he told me that he was writing poetry too, I dreaded having to read it. It is one of those things… well, I suppose it's the same for you as an artist. When someone else asks you to judge his work, you're always in a quandary over how honest you should be. It's a bit of a sticky wicket. So I was reluctant, especially, as I've said, after all the praise he had heaped upon my work. He had not been writing about the war and the first poems I read were only mediocre. I told him to bear down as hard as he could on what he'd seen and heard and been through in the trenches."

He looks away again before he finishes.

"His *war poems*, as I call them, are nothing short of pure genius. A towering achievement. I'm quite certain they will last forever. And speaking of genius, one of the deans here at the Academy told me what you've been up to in Northern Ireland. Bloody marvellous. Making masks. Ingenious idea.

Even if you say no to the commission, I'm honoured just to have met you, Sam Burke."

He thrusts his hand out again for him to shake.

"I'd be honoured to do it," Sam tells him.

Sassoon is delighted. He produces several notes from inside a leather-bound journal and presses the money into Sam's palm. "I'm afraid that I can't pay you what you're worth," he says.

"That's far too much," Sam objects.

"Trust me, Mr Burke," he says, "it isn't nearly enough."

It is not long after Sam's meeting with Sassoon when he learns that they have closed down operations at the castle and the Tin Nose Shop, minus Oliver, is being reconstituted at Queen Mary's Hospital in Sidcup, Kent, where there are better facilities to treat the wounded soldiers and to construct their masks. He reads that the government estimate there might be as many as 5,000 soldiers in need of them. *A factory*, Sam thinks when he learns this. Just as Oliver had predicted.

Three times Sam takes a bus across the city to the hospital with the intention of having a look around and maybe saying hello to some of the people working there. Each time he walks from the street and up the fifteen granite steps to the front entrance but then cannot go inside. He might never have learned an extraordinary part of his own story if he were not met on his last visit by Neil Ryan, who calls out his name just as Sam is walking back to the street. They shake hands vigorously. It surprises Sam to see him with hedge clippers under his arm. "I would have expected a golf club," he remarks. "Have you given up the game for gardening?"

"It's a lot less maddening, I'll confess," he relates pleasantly. "No, I'm just trying to be useful. Here, have a look." He holds out his right hand. The fingers tremble uncontrollably. "It just started one morning up at the castle," he says. "And then never stopped. I'm only good for rough work now. But they've placed me in charge of job training. We're teaching the soldiers to build toys, glaze windows, even run cinema projectors. Work they can do in solitude. It's amazing how eager they are to learn. They want the chance to earn a living. And these hedges get me outside, to clear my head when it gets to be too much."

He relates all this joyfully, which puzzles Sam. "You mean the suffering?" he asks.

"Exactly. One of the doctors told me that the tremor came on as a result of seeing too much of that. Too much desolation. He called it a 'psychological sympathy wound'. Interesting, isn't it? But you know, Sam, I never served like these fellows did, and like you did. I wasn't a soldier like you were, and so I'm rather proud of my wound. It makes me feel like I've done my part. Does that make sense?"

Sam is thinking about that question and how he might answer it when Neil goes on to ask him if he remembered the conversation they'd had at the castle one night. "We were trying to decide if the purpose of the masks was to mercifully allow a soldier to shield his disfigurement, or to allow the government to hide what happens when it sends its boys to war. You were the one who brought it up."

Sam tells him that he does remember.

"Well, I've reached my own peace about that," Ryan says. "I suspect the latter has driven the establishment. But I choose to believe that there's a humanitarian impulse behind it as well."

"I hope you're right," Sam says.

Then Neil looks at him a moment longer. "I wonder if I should tell you something else."

"Well, now you'll have to, I suppose."

"Yes, I suppose."

He tells him that Katie returned to the castle. "Not long after you left," he says. "Oliver told us that she didn't want you to know. She was there with her little girl and the presence of that child was a great help to soldiers who had little children waiting for them at home. And her mother… Katie. She was remarkable really, Sam. She poured her heart into the soldiers who were having the most difficulty, the ones who just couldn't imagine being with their wives or girlfriends again. She would have tea with the men. Take walks. Dance. She told me once that she tried to make them believe they were worthy of being loved by the people who had loved them best before the war. I thought of her as an angel. A real angel to those soldiers. I'll always think of her that way."

snow

The artists run around the courtyard like children one morning in early November when they awake to find that a storm has blanketed the cobblestones in brilliant white snow. Sam is making a snowman with two sculptors when Daisy first sees him. They have been writing to each other for several months after she first sent him a letter in the early spring to inform him that Lansdale had never met her in London. She is working as a stenographer in Oxford, and planned only a short visit to the city. But in those first moments when she sees Sam again, she knows with a deep certainty that she will never leave him.

From that night when she shares his room and his bed, the passage of time is never quite the same again for Sam. For so long he has felt that time is moving past him like smoke or fog riding the wind. Now he suddenly feels himself moving through time with purposeful strides.

A week later, the armistice that brings the war to its end comes on the eleventh hour of the eleventh day of the eleventh month. All the bells in England are ringing and in the streets of London, a raucous party is just commencing when Sam and Daisy walk together through Mayfair to the publishing house on Grafton Street to deliver the portrait of the poet. It is there, inside the plate-glass windows, that an elderly man who appears to be stone deaf even with the megaphone he holds to his ear to help him hear informs them sadly that Wilfred

Owen had been killed one week earlier. "I've only now just received word that his family was notified by telegram this morning," the man tells them.

The two of them slowly make their way back to the Academy, holding on to each other, both of them dazed and silent as they walk through the crowded streets. They seem to be barely moving. The war is over, but the sorrow is still mounting. And because of this, they feel as if they are walking against a current, something as powerful as the tide, that is pulling them in the opposite direction of the happy people surrounding them. Maybe they are the only sad people in a city swarming with revellers.

They are married a few blocks from the Royal Academy on a Thursday morning, with Daisy wearing the dress that Lily passed on to Sam in brown wrapping paper tied with white baker's string. It is just a few weeks after the war ends in November when the city's celebration is over and it is common to see soldiers in uniform, many of them with a stunned look in their eyes, up and down the streets and in the pubs and the train stations. There is a weary dignity about these men and often when Daisy catches Sam watching them as if he has seen someone he recognises, she imagines that he has caught an unexpected glimpse of himself, and the soldiers he had known at the castle.

The war never really leaves Sam in the two years he spends completing his studies at the Academy, and Daisy has come to believe that their life together will always be defined and haunted in some way by what Sam has experienced in France and at the Tin Nose Shop. She grows accustomed to how he drifts away from time to time, to the far-off look in his eyes that sometimes makes her feel like a stranger, and to his nightmares that wake them both from their sleep.

But then that changes quite suddenly when a letter from Brookes arrives in one morning's post with a picture of him standing beside his wife, holding their newborn baby son. Oliver had forwarded the letter to Sam.

That is in late winter. As soon as summer arrives, Oliver comes to visit them in London. One afternoon they take a train to Dorset. Oliver stays on the beach with Daisy while Sam climbs the cliffs at Durdle Door. He has Ned's mask with him and when he reaches the spot where his friend had jumped that sunstruck afternoon before the war began, Sam pauses for a moment before he sails the mask out into the sea. Oliver watches it settle gently on the rolling swells before it disappears. When he has climbed down, Daisy takes him into her arms. They both have a faint sense of the future now, and how they will go on from here to embrace all the joys and sorrows of a shared life, with the understanding that even though all we have in common are the ways that we can be broken, the world can surprise us at any moment with its beauty.

cover photo

The photograph of the soldier on the cover is that of Nathan Neville Levene, a Lieutenant in the Kings Irish Liverpool Regiment. He was the great-great uncle of my editor, Cari Rosen.

Lieutenant Levene was killed on the 8th of August, 1916 while leading his men over the top on the Somme. He was in his mid-twenties when he died and though he has no marked grave, his name is inscribed on the memorial at Thiepval. His brother, Leon (1889 - 1971), served as a surgeon in the Royal Army Medical Corps at the rank of Captain. It is very likely that some of the soldiers who served with Lieutenant Levene and his brother, and who survived the war, suffered facial wounds, and made their way to the Tin Nose Shop.

acknowledgments

I carried this book alone for many years, or perhaps it carried me, until I was blessed with a brilliant editor, Cari Rosen, who shaped it with compassion and a clear vision, and a remarkable filmmaker in Belfast, Northern Ireland, named Jon Beer, who collaborated with me on a film adaptation of this story.

I am in their debt, as I am to a new generation of soldiers who found their way to the Caddie School For Soldiers in Elie, Scotland where they inspired me with their courage, and their humble nobility. Like the soldiers at the tin nose shop, these soldiers suffered in their wars and have done their best to rise above the darkness that haunts them, and to carry on with a measure of dignity they are entitled to. Those soldiers turned my life, as did Paul Bresnick, who believed in me, and the people of Omagh, County Tyrone in Northern Ireland, wounded by the bombing there, who remain in my memory at the point of origin of this novel.

DJS
caddieschoolforsoldiers.com